MURDER COMES TO TOWN

Detective Salvatore was a trim, dark-haired man, dressed in a plain blue suit and a black overcoat. He had his wallet out as he came up the stairs and held his badge out for me to see. "May I come in?"

Thaddeous stood, obviously not sure what the proper etiquette was for a visit from the Boston Police.

"Is there a problem?" I asked.

"Mrs. Fleming, are you aware that a deceased individual was found behind your building this afternoon?"

"One of the neighbors told me when we came in a little while ago."

"We found your name and address on a piece of paper in his pocket. Could you step outside a minute and see if you recognize him?"

"Of course," I said.

At the very end of the alley was a white van with blue letters that said "Chief Medical Examiner." Next to it was a stretcher with a shiny black body bag on it, obviously filled. A number of police officers were milling around, measuring and taking photos, but they took no notice of Thaddeous and me.

Salvatore leaned down and unzipped the top of the bag, as if it were a sleeping bag, and pulled it down just far enough for me to see the face.

"Recognize this man?"

I could tell right away, but I took a couple of deep breaths before answering to make sure my voice was under control. "Yes. I do. It's Philip Dennis."

Books by Toni L.P. Keiner

DOWN HOME MURDER
DEAD RINGER
TROUBLE LOOKING FOR A PLACE TO HAPPEN
COUNTRY COMES TO TOWN

Published by Kensington Books

To Robin Perry Schnabel:

My dearest sister, fare thee well:
The elements be kind to thee, and make thy
spirits all of comfort! Fare thee well.

Antony and Cleopatra, Act III, Scene 2

Acknowledgments

I want to thank:

- Stephen P. Kelner, Jr., for story conferences, edits, and holding the baby so I could work
- Magdalene Ward Kelner, for taking so many naps and occasionally sleeping through the night
- Elizabeth Shaw, for proofreading and finding words that missing
- Dr. Rich, on GEnie, for able research assistance
- The raccoons, for all their help

Chapter 1

The doorbell rang while I was in the middle of writing to my husband, Richard. He had left for England only the night before, but overseas mail is slow and I told myself that I wanted him to get a letter right away so he wouldn't be lonely. Of course, the real reason I was writing was because it would make *me* feel less lonely.

I pushed the intercom button. "Who is it?"

"Laura? Is that you?"

The voice sounded familiar, but I couldn't quite place it. "Yes, this is Laura."

"It's Philip. Can I come in?"

I hesitated, more out of shock than anything else. I hadn't seen Philip Dennis for at least three years, and I really wouldn't have minded if it had stretched to four or five.

"Laura?"

I pushed the buzzer so he could come in, then wondered if I should have. Philip had a knack for making me question every action.

I opened the door to my apartment, and watched as Philip came up the stairs to the second floor. He looked almost the same as he had the last time I had seen him. Maybe his hair was a bit thinner, I thought meanly, but that was the same ratty blue jean jacket. When he saw me watching him, he grinned that grin I used to find so attractive. I hadn't known what "insouciant" meant until I'd met Philip.

As soon as he got to the landing, he said, "You look great! Better than ever."

"Thanks," I said, though I knew I didn't look all that great. I hadn't intended to go out that evening, so I was wearing my most faded jeans and a stretched-out red sweater. With anybody else, I'd have thought they were being polite. With Philip, I was suspicious. "This is a surprise."

"Aren't you going to let me in?"

I stepped back to let him in the door and closed it behind him.

"What a great place!" he said, looking at everything—the furniture, the pictures on the wall, even Richard's sword, hanging above the couch. Philip pulled off his jacket and sat down, instinctively picking Richard's favorite chair. I tried not to wince.

I sat down on the couch, a safe distance away. "I didn't realize you knew my address."

"I got it from Jessie. So how's Rich?"

Nobody ever calls Richard by anything but his full name. "Richard's fine. How's Colleen?"

He shrugged his shoulders, always his favorite way to change the subject. I wondered if he could read me as easily as I could read him. Probably not. I hadn't been nearly as important to him as he had been to me.

"So what brings you out this way?" I asked. Snow was predicted for that night, and though he had been born in Massachusetts, Philip never had been fond of winter weather.

"Actually," he said, "I need a favor."

"What's that?" I said, half expecting him to ask me for a loan.

"Do you think I can crash here for a while? I know Rich is out of town, so you could use a man around. I'll sleep on the couch, of course."

That got me mad, and I wasn't sure what I was madder about: that he would ask such a thing after all this time, the idea that I needed a man around the house, or his thinking that I would consider letting him sleep anywhere but on the couch. "I don't think so, Philip," was all I trusted myself to say.

"Look, Laura, I really need someplace to crash."

"What happened to your house?"

"Colleen's been a real bitch lately, and today I'd had it, so I decided to split."

In other words, she had thrown him out. "Why don't you sleep at the office?"

"I can't. Vinnie and Inez are on the warpath. They want to fire me as it is, so I don't dare sleep there."

"You're kidding." Philip had cofounded Statistical Software, Inc., right out of college, and he was the author of Stat-Sys, their mainstay software package. Though Vinnie and Inez were officially in charge, I couldn't imagine them actually firing Philip. In fact, I would have thought that he'd have set up the company so they couldn't.

Philip looked disgusted. "Vinnie got the bright idea that we should sell stock and let a bunch of ignoramus investors run the company. Now he and Inez want me to be Mr. Corporate, and you know that's not me."

"Not hardly," I said. In fact, I had always suspected that Philip had founded his own company so he wouldn't have to get a suit to wear to interviews. "But there must be some-body from SSI who can put you up."

"You'd think so, wouldn't you? As much as I've done for them, and now they're ganging up against me. They're a bunch of losers anyway." He did his best to look forlorn. "You're all I've got."

A few years back, I'd probably have fallen for it, but not now. "No, Philip."

"Come on, Laura, it'll be like old times. I'll eat whatever you've got handy, and I don't make much of a mess."

I translated that to mean that he'd allow me to cook and clean for him. "No."

"It won't be for long. A few weeks, a month or two at most."

"No."

"All I've got to do is to rattle a few cages at SSI and they'll get off my back. Once I've got my job settled, I'll be able to convince Colleen to let me go back home. They need me, all of them. How long can it take for them to realize that?"

"I'm sorry, Philip. No."

"Look, I know it's going to be awkward, after all we've been to one another, but I swear that I won't come between you and Rich."

As if he could! I was getting tired of being polite. "Forget it, Philip. You're not staying."

"Why not?"

"Because it's my house and I said so. I'm not going to argue with you." Paw, the grandfather who raised me, had taught me that it's never a good idea to get into a pissing con-test with a skunk.

"At least let me sleep here tonight. You know it's supposed to snow. And I left the car with Colleen."

"Then you'd better get moving and find someplace to stay." It sounded callous, but I knew that once I let him into my home, I'd never get him out again without the help of the police. And he had to have enough money to get a hotel room, if not with cash, then with a credit card. He just preferred mooching. And his next plea made me so mad I wished I had said something meaner.

"What about that Southern hospitality y'all used to tell me about, like in Byerly, North Carolina?" he said, in a Southern accent so patently false that it hurt my ears. Though we had dated for two and a half years, he never had bothered to figure out that "y'all" is plural.

"Since you used to refer to Byerly as the armpit of the universe, I don't think you should be invoking its name now."

"I was kidding."

"Well, I'm not kidding. You cannot stay here. Not a month, not a week, not a night. In fact, I want you to leave now."

"But Laura . . ."

I went to the door, opened it, and held it open.

For a minute he just sat there as if daring me to throw him out. But I guess he could tell that I would if I had to, because he finally got up.

"Jesus, Laura, what a bitch you've turned into."

I didn't answer, just kept holding the door.

"This is your revenge for my breaking up with you, isn't it? I can't believe you'd be small enough to hold that against me." With the word "small," he stretched to his full height, which was nearly a foot taller than me. "I guess you can take the girl out of the country, but you can't take the country out of the girl."

"That may be," I said, "but I sure can take the asshole out of my apartment." I shut the door firmly behind him, and loudly rattled the locks to make sure he knew that he couldn't get back in.

Chapter 2

I didn't have a chance to brood about Philip because the phone rang right after I heard him stomp down the stairs. "Hello?"

"Laurie Anne?"

"Vasti? What's up?" My cousin rarely spends money on long-distance charges from North Carolina to Boston, and it wasn't even weekend rates yet.

"I wanted to make sure that he got there all right. Mama was watching the Weather Channel and she said that y'all were having a snowstorm up there."

"Richard left last night, and the storm hasn't started yet, so everything's fine," I said, touched by her concern. I should have known better.

"Richard? I'm talking about Thaddeous."

"What about Thaddeous?"

"Did he not make it in?"

"In where? What are you talking about?"

"Aunt Nora said he was leaving first thing Saturday morning, and even with changing planes in Charlotte, I thought for sure he'd be there by now."

"It's Friday, Vasti."

"Oh dear!" she said unconvincingly. "I've gone and spoiled the surprise."

"What surprise?"

"I'd better not say another word. 'Bye, now!"

"Vasti!" It was too late. She had already hung up. I thought I knew what was going on by then, but I called Aunt Nora, Thaddeous's mother, to make sure.

"Hello?"

"Aunt Nora? This is Laura."

"Why, Laurie Anne! This is such a surprise," she said, in a theatrical voice that would have told me that something was up even if I hadn't already known it.

"Aunt Nora, is Thaddeous coming up here?"

There was a short silence. "How did you find out?"

"How do you think?"

"Vasti?"

"She just called."

"I knew I shouldn't have told her, but it slipped out. And Thaddeous wanted it to be a surprise."

Looking at the mess in my living room, and remembering that the kitchen was even worse, I was pretty sure that it was Thaddeous who would have been surprised. "How was he planning on getting to my apartment?"

"He figured he could take the subway, like you do." As I was trying to imagine my cousin making his way to my place on the subway all by his lonesome, Aunt Nora added, "He figured he could stop and ask somebody for directions if he needed to."

"It'll probably be better if I meet him at the airport," I said, trying to be diplomatic. Knowing how much Aunt Nora likes surprises, even vicarious ones, I said, "Tell you what, don't tell him I know, and I'll surprise *him* instead."

"That's a good idea." She paused. "Then you don't mind him coming?"

"Mind? I've been wanting him to come visit for I don't know how long." I would have preferred more notice, but that was neither here nor there.

"That's good. He hasn't taken any time off from the mill in a coon's age, and he's got so much vacation stored up that they were going to take it away from him. Besides, I thought maybe you could use the company with Richard being gone."

I knew which of those reasons was the real one, of course. Though Aunt Nora tries to be a nineties woman, she just hates the idea of my being in a big city without my family around. But she meant well, and I really was looking forward to seeing Thaddeous. I got his flight information, and before I hung up, warned her, "Now don't let him talk to Vasti before he leaves."

So much for my plans to mope about Richard, pig out on sour cream-and-onion potato chips, and watch the snow come down. I looked out the window. No snow yet, but I could tell from the gray glow in the sky that it was coming. Then I went into the kitchen and sighed. I knew Thaddeous wouldn't expect my place to be as clean as his mama's, but he wasn't going to be expecting dirty dishes on every available surface, either.

I was pushing up the sleeves of my sweater to start washing up when I thought about something else and opened the refrigerator. It wasn't empty, but I didn't have enough food to feed my cousin even one meal. Thaddeous is a big fellow with an appetite to match. That meant I was going to have to go out to the store. Normally, that wouldn't have been a big deal, but since it was right before a storm, the stores would be filled with people buying enough milk and bread to last in case this storm turned out to be as bad as the legendary Blizzard of 1978.

I wasn't happy about it, but there was nothing else I could

do. So I pulled on my coat, grabbed my pocketbook, and left. I did check to make sure that Philip wasn't hanging around when I left the building, but the coast was clear. I just wish it had been that empty in the grocery store.

By the time I got to the airport the next day, I had finished my shopping, washed all the dishes and most of the laundry, mopped the kitchen and bathroom, vacuumed and dusted the living room and bedroom, and neatly stacked everything I couldn't actually put away. I didn't think Thaddeous would write home about my housekeeping, but he wouldn't decide to stay at a hotel, either.

Boston's Logan Airport maintains what they call "sterile concourses," meaning that I couldn't go down to the gate to meet Thaddeous as he came in. Instead, I waited at the end of the concourse, hoping to catch sight of my cousin before he headed for the baggage claim.

I needn't have worried about missing him. Thaddeous towers over most crowds, unless the Boston Celtics are around, and I spotted him long before he got to me.

"Thaddeous!" I yelled. "Over here!"

He peered over heads until he saw my wildly flailing arms and grinned. "What in the Sam Hill are you doing here?"

"I live here. What's your excuse?"

By now he had made his way to me and nearly lifted me off my feet in a great big hug I did my best to return.

"Just thought you might like some company for a few days," he said.

"A few days? If you try to get back on that airplane in less than a week, I'm going to knock a knot on your noggin. And two weeks would be better than one!"

"How did you find out I was coming?" Then, before I could

say anything, he answered his own question. "Never mind. I knew Mama shouldn't have told Vasti."

I saw we were blocking traffic, so I said, "Come on, we'll go get your luggage."

I've flown in and out of Logan enough that it took me no time to find the right baggage carousel, meaning that we had that much longer to wait for his suitcase to arrive.

It was while we were waiting that Thaddeous leaned over and whispered, "Am I dressed all right?"

"You look fine," I said. He was dressed in blue jeans, a flannel shirt, and his winter jacket, and carrying his Walters Mill ball cap. His mama must have reminded him to take it off inside. "Why?"

"I just wasn't sure what I should wear up here. I didn't want to embarrass you by looking like country come to town."

"Thaddeous, I'm so glad to see you that you could be wearing a lime green polyester suit and I wouldn't mind. Besides, this is Boston. You can get away with wearing anything here."

"Is that right? Then I should have brought my Stetson, like I wanted to."

Actually, it was just as well that he hadn't. The only men I see wearing cowboy hats in Boston are tourists, gay, or both.

Thaddeous's suitcase showed up then, and after he grabbed it, I said, "I thought we'd take a cab into town."

"What about that subway you keep telling me about?"

"There'll be time for that later. This way you'll get to see a little bit of the city on our ride in."

Fortunately the cabbie knew my neighborhood, so I didn't have to spend the whole trip directing him. Instead, I could show off for Thaddeous. "That building with the clock is the Custom House Building," I said. "Just wait until you see it lit up at night. And that's Faneuil Hall and Quincy Market. It's just filled with funky shops and places to eat. The Aquarium is right by there, and I know you'll like that."

"I thought y'all had snow last night," he said, "but it looks like everything's open."

"We did get about six inches, but Boston doesn't close down every time it snows, like Byerly does. They get the streets cleared pretty quick, so about the only real difference snow makes is messing up the sidewalks and making it even harder to find a place to park." I pointed to a snowbank blocking two car lengths along the curb of a side street. "See what I mean? Makes me glad I don't have a car."

"I'm right surprised that there's so much traffic," Thaddeous said. "I thought I'd miss it coming in on the weekend."

"This isn't much traffic, Thaddeous. Wait until you live through rush hour." I kept on pointing things out for him until I decided he was overloaded. Then I leaned back and watched him. Seeing his face made me remember how I had felt when I first came up North to go to college. Until then, the biggest city I had ever seen was Charlotte, and Boston had seemed magical to me. I envied Thaddeous, seeing it all for the first time.

When we got to my street, the end was blocked with police cars, so I paid off the cab there and we walked the half-block that remained.

My upstairs neighbor, a man I knew just enough to speak to, was standing on the steps of my building.

"Hi, John," I said. "This is my cousin, Thaddeous Crawford, from North Carolina." The two men shook hands. "What's going on?"

"The police found a body in the alley behind the building," he said.

"Are you serious?"

He nodded. "Some bum froze to death back there." A car pulled up and honked its horn. "There's my ride. See you later."

Thaddeous looked at me, but all I could say was, "Welcome to Boston."

Chapter 3

It wasn't exactly the introduction to my adopted city that I would have wanted for Thaddeous, but as I told him while we went inside and up the stairs to my apartment, such things did happen. "There are shelters," I said, in defense of Boston, "but some homeless people don't like them."

"It even happens in Byerly, sometimes," Thaddeous said.

"I suppose it does," I said, though I didn't much like the idea of that side of modern life affecting my hometown. "Anyway, this is a very safe neighborhood." I might have been more convincing if I hadn't had to unlock two locks and a deadbolt to get in my front door.

"Take your coat off, and I'll give you a tour." Not that it would take long, I thought, as I took his coat and put it on the brass rack by the door. Housing costs are atrocious in Boston, especially in the Back Bay, where Richard and I live.

"This is the living room. And the guest bedroom. The couch folds out, but it's pretty comfortable."

"I'm sure it'll be fine." He turned around to see the whole room, like Philip had, but while I hadn't liked Philip looking at my things, I was glad to show them to Thaddeous. He was the first of the Burnette family to come up North to visit.

"Those are the old Burnette property lines," he said, looking more closely at a map I have framed on the wall.

"Sure are." The map might not be antique, but it is darned old. The Burnette family had once owned a good chunk of land in Byerly but had lost most of it during the Depression. Paw had left the map to me in his will as a reminder of where I come from, something he was always concerned that I'd forget. That's what happens when you're the only one from the family to move up North. Despite Paw's concerns, or maybe partially because of them, I had grown closer to my family over the past few years.

Then Thaddeous looked at Richard's sword. "Don't tell me you keep that up there to defend yourself."

"Well, gun laws are pretty strict up here," I said, but I couldn't keep a straight face. "It's just decoration. Richard played Hamlet in college, and that's the sword he used."

"I'd like to have seen that."

"It was something," I said. My husband has a friendlier face than is traditional for the melancholy Dane, but he had carried it off with aplomb. As much as he quoted Shakespeare, speaking in iambic pentameter came naturally to him. And his frequently unruly hair was quite appropriate for those scenes where Hamlet is acting insane.

I went into the kitchen, just off the living room. "The kitchen," I said, unnecessarily. It was small, just enough room for the usual appliances and a table for two. I took a minute to show Thaddeous where I keep important stuff like glasses and silverware, then said, "I've got Coke in the refrigerator, and I made some iced tea this morning." Unlike most Northern restaurants, I serve iced tea all year round.

"In this weather, I'm surprised you're not drinking coffee or hot chocolate."

"You call this cold?" I said airily. "For up here, this is a fine spring day."

"Uh huh," he said, which told me that he didn't believe a word of it.

Continuing the tour, I pointed out the bathroom and then showed him the bedroom. It was good-sized, unusually so for a Boston apartment. One wall was lined with bookcases, all of which were filled.

"You still read a lot?" Thaddeous asked.

"You bet," I said, "but some of these are Richard's." The room held a double bed, a dresser, a chest of drawers, and a tiny desk with my laptop computer on it.

"That's it," I said. "Kind of tiny, compared to places in Byerly."

"It looks plenty big enough to me," Thaddeous said. "And living right here in the middle of the city must be all kinds of exciting. It's just the kind of place I'd imagined you and Richard living in."

That sounded like a compliment to me. "Thank you."

Thaddeous sat down on the couch, and I got us both something to drink before joining him and asking, "So what's going on back home?"

His answer took a while, because we had to go through every aunt, uncle, and cousin. Though Aunt Nora and I exchanged letters fairly often, there was always news I missed. Thaddeous's parents, my Aunt Nora and Uncle Buddy, were both doing well, and Aunt Nora had recently talked Uncle Buddy into taking square-dance lessons. I found this hard to believe until Thaddeous reminded me that this was a way for Uncle Buddy to take Aunt Nora out without having to talk much. Thaddeous's older brother, Augustus, was still in Germany with the Army, but he had recently taken a trip to

France. His younger brother, Willis, was likely to be promoted to night shift supervisor within the month.

Aunt Daphine had added a new hair stylist at her beauty parlor, and her daughter, Vasti, and son-in-law, Arthur, were reportedly trying for a baby. Thaddeous looked at me meaningfully when he said that, probably because I'm a couple of years older than Vasti, but I didn't say a word about Richard's and my plans in that direction, and he moved on.

Aunt Nellie and Uncle Ruben had finally given up trying to sell water filters door-to-door, but they were looking into the idea of starting a video rental place in Byerly. For most people, this could be a good idea, but with Aunt Nellie and Uncle Ruben, it was probably a recipe for disaster. Their three daughters—triplets Idelle, Odelle, and Carlelle—had been trying to talk them out of it, but Thaddeous didn't give a whole lot for their chances.

Aunt Edna was still seeing her beau, Caleb, and the family was expecting a proposal any time now. The fly in the ointment was Edna's son, Linwood, who wasn't ready to let any man replace his late daddy.

Aunt Ruby Lee and Uncle Roger, newlyweds for the second time, were certainly acting the part. She'd started accompanying him to most of the performances of Roger's Ramblers, his country music band, and was starting to learn how to manage the group. It looked like their three children, or rather their daughter and Aunt Ruby Lee's two sons from previous marriages, were going to form their own band. Thaddeous had brought a cassette of some of their practice sessions, and he pulled it out so we could listen to it.

While it played, Thaddeous asked me how Richard and I had been doing, but that didn't take nearly so long to tell.

Thaddeous already knew that Richard had gone to England to teach a class for Boston College students in Stratford-upon-Avon and to see as many Shakespeare productions as he could squeeze into a month. It was a wonderful opportunity for him, and though I wasn't crazy about him being away from home that long, I wasn't about to ask him to miss it. As for me, work had kept me pretty busy for the past few months, but the project I was on was finally winding down. "So your timing for coming up is perfect," I said.

"Then you think you'll have time to show me around a little?"

"Absolutely! I'll be finished up with my project by the first part of this week. Speaking of showing you around, are you hungry?"

"I am, at that. They fed me on the plane, but it wasn't hardly enough food to bother with."

"I thought we could go out for an early dinner."

"We don't have to go out. Whatever you've got here would be fine."

"Oh, no, this is your vacation. Let's celebrate." I didn't want to admit that Richard and I almost never cook. Our kitchen, like so many in Boston, is so tiny that it's a pain to fix anything in it. And the apartment itself is so small that the smell of anything we do cook lingers for days. "What are you in the mood for? I know good places for American, Italian, Mexican, Tex-Mex, Chinese, Thai—even Argentinean, if you're feeling adventurous."

With all those choices, it took us forever to decide, and the doorbell rang just as we had picked a place.

"Lord, I hope that's not Philip again," I said.

"Who's Philip?" Thaddeous asked.

"I'll tell you later," I said, and pressed the intercom button. "Hello?"

"This is Detective Salvatore of the Boston Police. May I have a word with you?"

"Certainly," I said, and rang him in. Thaddeous looked curious, but no more than I was. I opened the door and waited.

Detective Salvatore was a trim, dark-haired man, dressed in a plain blue suit and a black overcoat. He had his wallet out as he came up the stairs and held his badge out for me to see. "May I come in?"

"Please do."

Thaddeous stood, obviously not sure what the proper etiquette was for a visit from the Boston Police.

"Is there a problem?" I asked.

"I've just got some questions I need to ask. Now, you're Laura Fleming."

"Yes, sir." The "sir" was automatic, brought on by my mother's training.

"Would you be Mr. Fleming?" he said to Thaddeous.

"No, sir. I'm Thaddeous Crawford, Laura's cousin."

"My husband is out of the country," I said, a little relieved. If he had come to tell me that Richard was in trouble, he'd have known that already.

"Mrs. Fleming, are you aware that a deceased individual was found behind your building this afternoon?"

"Yes. One of the neighbors told me when we came in a little while ago."

"We found your name and address on a piece of paper in his pocket."

I stared at him. "You're kidding."

"No, ma'am, I'm not."

I thought of something, or rather, somebody. "Do you know who it is?"

"There's been no formal identification, but there was ID found on the body."

I didn't want to ask, but I had to. "Is it Philip Dennis?"

"Then you know this man?"

"Yes, I do. He was here last night."

Salvatore looked more alert all of a sudden. Thaddeous, on the other hand, lost every bit of expression. I realized how that must have sounded. My husband was out of town, and here I was, admitting that I had had a man in my apartment.

I quickly added, "Philip Dennis is an old friend of mine. I hadn't seen him in ages, but he showed up here last night and told me that he didn't have anyplace to go. He wanted to stay here for a while, but I told him he couldn't, and he left."

"And what time would that have been?" Salvatore asked.

"Around six, six-thirty."

"Before the snow?"

"Yes, sir. I went out for groceries after that, and it wasn't snowing when I left."

Salvatore relaxed a bit. "He must have died sometime after he left here. There was snow on the body, but not as much as there would have been if he had been out there all night. Could you step outside a minute and see if you recognize him?"

"Of course," I said.

"I'll come with y'all, if it's all the same," Thaddeous said.

"No problem," Salvatore said, and I was glad of that. I had seen dead bodies before, but it wasn't something I enjoyed.

Thaddeous and I put on our coats and followed Salvatore outside. A pair of uniformed police officers allowed the three of us to go down the narrow alley beside my apartment building to get to the wider alley in back, lined with dumpsters from the block's apartment buildings. Ribbons of yellow tape kept people back from an area near the end of the alley.

At the very end of the alley was a white van with blue letters that said "Chief Medical Examiner." Next to it was a stretcher with a shiny black body bag on it, obviously filled. A number of police officers were milling around, measuring and taking photos, but they took no notice of Thaddeous and me.

"Is it all right if we take a look?" Salvatore asked a woman who was holding on to the stretcher.

"Help yourself," she said. "The doctor's done with him for now."

Salvatore leaned down and unzipped the top of the bag, as if it were a sleeping bag, and pulled it down just far enough for me to see the face.

"Is this the man you were talking about?"

I could tell right away, but I took a couple of deep breaths before answering to make sure my voice was under control. "Yes, sir. That's Philip."

Chapter 4

Philip didn't look bad, exactly. First off, there wasn't much expression on his face, for which I was grateful. There was what looked like a bruise on his forehead, and his coloring was funny, I guess from being out in the cold. Or maybe just from being dead. Like Salvatore said, there was some snow encrusted on his hair and eyelashes. He didn't look bad, but somehow he looked very sad.

"Did Mr. Dennis have that mark on his forehead when you saw him?" Salvatore asked.

"No, sir."

"Had he been drinking?"

"I don't think so. I know I didn't smell it." It was hard for me to remember that he had been in my apartment less than twenty-four hours before, annoying but very alive.

Thaddeous put his arm around me. "I think she's seen enough."

Salvatore nodded and zipped Philip back up again. Then he called over to one of the other police officers. "We've got our ID." A young officer came over immediately with a pad and pen. "Mrs. Fleming, would you know who Mr. Dennis's next of kin would be?"

"His wife, I guess. Colleen Dennis."

"Address and phone number?"

I shook my head. "I know they have a house in Cambridge, but I'm not sure where."

Salvatore nodded at the uniformed officer, and he scurried away. "I know this must be upsetting for you, but I'm going to have to ask some more questions."

"I understand."

"Could we go back inside?" Thaddeous asked.

"That would be fine."

The three of us made our way back up the alley, Thaddeous keeping his arm around me and staying right next to me, even though there really wasn't enough room for us to walk two abreast. There was a small crowd gathered out front, murmuring rumors, and they looked at us curiously. We went back up to the apartment without speaking, and when Thaddeous and I took off our coats, Salvatore did the same, and we all sat down.

"I'd like to get a little background information, if I may," Salvatore said, and pulled out a notepad and pen.

I dutifully answered questions about my age and occupation, and the same about Richard. He even took down information about Thaddeous.

"You say you two are cousins?"

"Yes, sir," Thaddeous said. "First cousins. Our mamas were sisters, but Laura's mama passed away a good while back."

"Do you live around here, Mr. Crawford?"

"No, sir. I live in Byerly, North Carolina. We were both raised there."

"Now, I can hear Mr. Crawford's accent, but Mrs. Fleming, you don't seem to have much of one."

"It comes and goes," I admitted. "I've been up here a while. I went to school in Cambridge."

"Harvard or MIT?"

"MIT. That's where I met Philip."

"Did you two keep in touch?"

"No, we didn't. I hadn't seen Philip in years."

"And how many years would that have been?"

"Three, I think. A friend of ours had a party, and we ran into one another then." I hadn't much enjoyed the party, mostly because of Philip. Despite the rest of us trying to change the subject, he had made snide remarks about Shakespeare's "real" identity the whole time, trying to annoy Richard.

"But he had your address."

"He said Jessie gave it to him. Jessie Boyd. She's a mutual friend who works at the same company as Philip."

"And what is that company?"

"Statistical Software, Inc., in Cambridge."

"Were you and Mr. Dennis close friends?"

"We used to be. I dated Philip for a couple of years when we were in college."

"I take it that you and he parted on good terms?"

I shook my head. "Not at all. I broke up with him and started dating Richard a little while after."

"Richard would be your husband?"

"Right. Philip didn't think I was serious about breaking up. When I finally got the message across that I meant it, he was pretty mad."

"Yet he still asked you for a place to stay?"

"His wife had thrown him out and most of the other people he was close to were at SSI, and he said they were ganging up on him. Besides which, Philip was a master at deciding what things *should* be like, and then believing they really *were* like that. There was no reason for him to think I'd let him stay, but he thought it anyway." I paused. "I sound awful, don't I? Here he is dead, and I'm making fun of him."

"You're answering the detective's questions like you're supposed to," Thaddeous said firmly.

"Your cousin is right, ma'am. I just want to get a full picture of the man."

"How did he die?" I asked. "My neighbor said he froze to death."

"The autopsy won't be completed for a while, but the results of the preliminary exam are consistent with that."

"Then he didn't kill himself?"

"It doesn't look that way. Did he say something that implied he was considering suicide?"

"No, I was just afraid that . . . that I had driven him to it. If I had just let him stay . . ."

"Mrs. Fleming," Salvatore said, "I've investigated many deaths, and each time, somebody has an 'if-only,' but nobody has ever found a way to change what's already happened."

"He didn't have no business staying here anyway, what with Richard gone," Thaddeous said.

Salvatore nodded, which I appreciated, but I wasn't convinced.

"Now, when did your husband leave?" Salvatore asked.

"Thursday evening," I said. "A six o'clock flight."

"The airline?"

"Virgin Atlantic."

"And Mr. Crawford didn't get here until today?"

"I got in at around two," Thaddeous said. "I was on USAir, if you need to check."

Only when Thaddeous added that last part did I realize

what Salvatore was up to. Presumably, they'd be able to figure out when Philip had died and he wanted to know where we were when that happened. Of course, Richard had already been gone by then, and Thaddeous hadn't arrived yet, so both of them were in the clear, but I was without an alibi. So I wasn't altogether surprised at Salvatore's next question.

"Now, when did you say Mr. Dennis left here?"

"Somewhere between six and six-thirty."

"And that's when you went to the grocery store?"

"Not right away. My cousin Vasti called, and after I got off the phone with her, I called Aunt Nora."

"My mama," Thaddeous explained.

"Vasti told me that Thaddeous was coming, and after I checked with Aunt Nora, I looked in the cabinets to see what I needed from the store."

He dutifully wrote all this down. "How long did these calls and looking in the cabinet take?"

"Maybe half an hour. I wasn't paying close attention, but I know I was hurrying to get out and back before the snow started."

"Then what?"

"I went to the store and came back."

"How long did that take?"

"Probably an hour and a half. The store was packed with people getting stuff before the storm."

"That put you back here at . . . ?"

I was tempted to tell him to add it up himself, but I reminded myself that he was just doing his job. "Somewhere between eight and eight-thirty."

"What did you do for the rest of the evening?"

"Cleaned up, mostly. Getting ready for Thaddeous."

"There wasn't no need for that, Laurie Anne," Thaddeous said. "I'm not company, I'm family."

"I had to clean up anyway," I said, which was true enough. I just hadn't planned to do it then.

Salvatore asked, "Did you have any other visitors?"

"Not a one."

"Phone calls?"

I shook my head.

"You don't think Laurie Anne hurt that boy, do you? Because you're crazy if you think that."

Salvatore said, "Laurie Anne?"

"That's what my family calls me." Given a choice, I go by Laura, but I didn't want to say so in front of Thaddeous and hurt his feelings.

"Mr. Crawford, I don't think anything right now. It looks like Mr. Dennis was drinking, passed out, and froze to death."

"What about that bruise on his forehead?" I asked. "Could he have been mugged?"

"Doubtful," Salvatore said. "He still had his wallet and was wearing his gold class ring from MIT. If a mugger had been interrupted, he might have left those things, but then the person who interrupted him would probably have called us. Chances are he hit his head when he passed out. Probably never even felt any pain."

"That's good," I said.

He asked us a few more questions, nothing big, then closed his pad and stood.

"Are you going to need us to go down to the station to sign a statement?" I asked.

"You sound like you've done this before," he said.

"The police chief back home is a good friend of mine," was

all I said. If Salvatore even remotely suspected me, the last thing I wanted to do was tell him I had been involved in other murders, even in solving them.

"Well, I don't think it'll be necessary. If I need to talk to you again, I'll be in touch. Here's my card, in case you think of anything else I should know. Mr. Crawford, I hope the rest of your visit will be more pleasant. I'm sure Mrs. Fleming will tell you that this is not an everyday occurrence. Not in this neighborhood, anyway."

"If it was, you can bet I'd pack her up and take her home with me," Thaddeous said.

Since he was family, I waited until Detective Salvatore left before turning on him and saying, "Pack me up and take me home? You and what army?"

He looked right ashamed of himself. "I knew as soon as I said it that it was a mistake. I didn't mean anything by it, Laurie Anne. Mama was the one who was worried about you being by yourself, not me. I told her you'd be all right, but I didn't argue with her too hard because I was just as glad for the chance to get out of town for a few days."

"Is anything wrong at work?"

He shook his head.

"Woman problems?"

He nodded.

"Oh dear, I'm sorry," I said. Thaddeous had the worst luck with women of any man I'd ever met. I don't understand why, exactly. He was nice-looking and so good-natured that he'd give you the shirt right off his back if he thought you needed it. He just couldn't find the right woman. To change the subject, I said, "I know I promised you an early dinner, but can you hold out for a few more minutes? I want to call somebody to tell her about Philip."

"Not a problem," he said.

I offered him a snack, but when he turned it down, I got out my address book, to look up Jessie's phone number. Jessie had been a good friend in college, and we had kept in touch fairly regularly since then. She was among the crew that Philip had recruited to form SSI.

"Jessie? This is Laura."

"Hi, Laura. I guess you made it through the storm."

"Jessie, I've got some bad news. It's about Philip."

"Damn it, Laura, did he come over there? I'm sorry about that. He asked if I knew your address, and when I gave it to him, I mentioned that Richard was going out of the country. I should have known better."

"Don't worry about it. He did come over, but I didn't let him stay. That's not why I'm calling."

"Oh?"

"Jessie, the police were just here. They found Philip in an alley with my name and address in his pocket."

"He slept in an alley? I had no idea he was that bad off." She sighed. "Tell me where they've taken him, and I'll go bail him out. I guess I can take the money out of petty cash."

"He's dead, Jessie. He froze to death out there." There was no response. I couldn't even hear her breathing. "Jessie? Are you there?"

"Jesus, Laura. Are they sure it's him?"

"I saw him."

"Jesus."

"I gave the police Colleen's name, but I didn't know the address. I did give them the number at SSI, so they'll probably be calling over there."

"I'll check the machine for messages," she said, suddenly businesslike. "Who was it you talked to?"

I gave her Salvatore's name, and the phone number from his card. "Philip said that he and Colleen had broken up and that Vinnie and Inez were trying to chase him out of SSI. What's going on?"

She sighed. "It's a long story, Laura. Things have been pretty bad at the office: Vinnie and Inez fighting, Murray and Dee and Dom complaining, and Philip . . ."

"Being Philip," I finished for her.

"Exactly. But I don't want to talk about that now. You said Philip was in an alley?"

"Behind my apartment, as a matter of fact."

"He died behind your apartment?"

"Yes." Knowing that was an awful feeling, too.

"You sent him away in the snow?"

"It wasn't snowing when he left here," I said defensively. "There was plenty of time for him to find a hotel before it started." She didn't say anything, and I added, "What was I supposed to do? Keep him?"

"No, of course not. Don't mind me. I'm just trying to take this all in. I know this must be awful for you. Did he look terrible?"

"Not too bad," I said.

"And you're all by yourself now?"

"Actually, my cousin Thaddeous is visiting."

"So you wouldn't have had space for Philip anyway," she said, as if to soothe me.

Since I hadn't known that Thaddeous was coming when I'd turned Philip down, it wasn't all that soothing, but it was nice of her to say. "If Colleen and he have split up, who's going to be taking care of the arrangements?"

"His family, I guess. I'm going to have to talk to some people. Listen, thanks for calling. I'll be in touch as soon as I know more."

"You know my number if there's anything I can do." I hung up, put on the best fake smile I could manage, and said, "Well, let's go get something to eat."

Thaddeous didn't move. "Are you all right?"

"I'm fine."

"This fellow Philip meant a lot to you, didn't he?"

"He used to. My first love."

"I thought that freckle-faced boy in Byerly was your first love."

"Steven Jones? Thaddeous, I was in the second grade—that doesn't count. No, Philip was my first serious boyfriend. At one point I thought I wanted to spend my life with him."

"How come I never heard anything about him?"

"I guess I didn't talk about him much." In fact, I had told Paw all about Philip right after we'd started dating, but Paw hadn't been one to gossip. Besides, even though Paw never actually said anything against Philip, I could tell he didn't think Philip was the right one for me. Since Philip never called or wrote me during Christmas and summer vacations, it had been easy to keep him separate from my life in Byerly.

"So what happened? Did Richard steal you away from him?"

I grinned at the idea of Richard and Philip fighting over me, but that wasn't how it had happened. "I think I knew it wasn't going to work with Philip long before I met Richard—I just didn't want to admit it. You know when you fall in love with somebody, and you daydream what your life together would be like?"

"I've done that a time or two."

"Well, I just couldn't picture me being with Philip other than right there and then, in college. I couldn't imagine taking him home to meet Paw, or what kind of house we'd have, or raising children with him, or anything. Once I realized that, I started to realize that he really didn't treat me very well. He put me down a lot, and made fun of my being from the South."

"Doesn't sound like he deserved you."

"He didn't." I hesitated, then added, "He slept around on me, too."

"Son of a bitch!"

I nodded. It was a long time since I had thought about Philip's betrayal and how upset I had been when I'd found out, and I was almost smug that it didn't hurt much anymore. Still, I was sorry he was dead, and I said so.

"Of course you are. Anybody would be. You remember how I was when Melanie died, and we didn't even date, not really."

Thaddeous had carried a torch for Melanie Wilson for years, and he'd been devastated when she was murdered. In fact, he looked downright glum thinking about her now.

"Enough of that," I said briskly, as I reached for my coat. "We're going out so I can show you what I like about this city."

Chapter 5

It took us a little while to get ready because I had to make sure Thaddeous was ready for Boston weather. He had a good coat and his Walters Mill cap, but he didn't have a scarf and his gloves weren't even lined.

"The trick to surviving the winters up here," I told him, "is to dress properly."

"You sound like Mama."

"I'll take that as a compliment," I said. Aunt Nora could be a mother hen, but she was usually right. Richard and I have a drawer of spare equipment, so I went through it until I found a scarf that didn't clash with his coat and a pair of leather gloves.

"How do you keep up with all this mess?" he wanted to know.

"We don't—I lose two or three gloves every winter. Why do you think I have a drawer of spares?"

Once I had him outfitted, we headed for the subway. Though we could have walked to where we were going, I knew he'd enjoy the trip underground. So I guided him through buying tokens, passing through the turnstile, and using the graffiti-decorated map of the transit system. "Everybody just calls it the T," I told him, as we waited for a train, and he nodded as seriously as if I were teaching him a new language. Which I was, in a way.

Once we got sat down, I automatically started studying the ads on the walls of the train, the way I always do when I don't have a book to read.

A minute later, Thaddeous nudged me. "You're not thinking about Philip, are you?"

"No. Why?"

"You were looking pretty sad."

I looked across at my reflection in the window on the other side of the train and realized what he was seeing. "That's my subway face."

"Come again?"

"My subway face. I don't know what it is, but everybody looks like this when they're on the subway. See?" He glanced around at the other riders, and sure enough, they all had the same blank expression as I did. "I guess it's a privacy thing. Or maybe it's for safety, so you don't give the nuts a chance to talk to you."

"All right," Thaddeous said doubtfully.

After that I watched him, and though I could tell he was trying his best, his face just couldn't help but look interested in what was going on, watching the people who got on and off at each station. I spoiled my own subway face with a grin, remembering when I had acted the same way. Then I frowned a little, thinking about the time Philip had laughed at me for looking like a tourist. I don't think he'd meant to hurt my feelings, or at least, I hadn't thought so at the time, but that's when I'd first adopted that expression of studied disinterest.

We got to our stop, and I decided that I was going to leave

my subway face and any thoughts of Philip behind us. I was going to show Thaddeous a good time, and if that meant we looked like country come to town, then so be it.

It was dark when we emerged from the subway, but the city lights were more than enough to see Boston by. I had purposely brought us up right into the middle of town, next to the Boston Public Library and in sight of Trinity Church, the view that gets onto the most postcards. All the while I was watching Thaddeous's face, and his grin made me darned pleased with myself.

Of course, the people behind us kept going, and I had to grab my cousin by the arm to pull him out of the way before he got run over. Thaddeous, used to driving everywhere, was amazed by the number of people out walking at night, even though it was in the thirties and there was snow on the ground.

Our first stop was Division 16, an old police station that's been converted into a restaurant. Before we ordered, I said, "By the way, they probably don't have iced tea."

"Why not?" he asked.

"Most places only serve it between Memorial Day and Labor Day. I found one place that did have it in September when I first got up here, but I nearly choked because I didn't realize that they don't sweeten it. And I thought I was going to die when I found out that they had charged me for refills."

"Well," Thaddeous said kindly, "they just don't know any better."

After dinner, we walked down Boylston Street to the edge of the Public Garden, then went over a block to walk back up Newbury Street. Some of the best stores in Boston are on those two streets, everything from expensive department stores like Lord & Taylor to funky shops like the one that only sells gargoyles.

It was half past ten when we got back to the apartment and well toward midnight by the time I rounded up sheets and a pillow for Thaddeous, unfolded the couch, and fixed his bed. I made sure to put on lots of blankets.

Once he was situated, I went into the bedroom and stared at the telephone. I wanted to call Richard and tell him about Philip, but it was nearly five in the morning in England. I'd have woken him for an emergency, but this wasn't exactly an emergency. So reluctantly I turned out the light and crawled into bed, trying hard not to think about the spot where Philip's body had been found, just a few feet from where I was lying.

The next day Thaddeous and I got up early and stayed busy the whole day. It was wonderful weather for Boston in February. It was cold, of course, but the sky was clear and a color that Thaddeous claimed was Carolina blue in honor of his visit. We took the subway to Park Street, then climbed up to the Boston Common.

The sidewalks were covered in gray slush from people trampling over the snow, but all Thaddeous had eyes for was the brilliant white covering the Common. There were some footprints crossing between the trees, but most of the snow was untouched and the trees were frosted with white. We just stood there a minute, looking at the snow. I knew it wasn't the first time he had ever seen snow, but those six inches were likely the deepest he had seen.

"It looks like something out of a magazine," he said. Then he noticed the people walking down sidewalks and vendors selling papers and hot pretzels. "They're not paying it one bit of attention."

"You get used to snow after a while."

"I don't think I ever could." He was so delighted that he didn't even notice it when I moved a few feet away and stooped to get a handful of snow and mold it into a ball. Not until I pelted him with it, that is.

"Hey!" I took off running across the snow-covered grass, but he quickly returned fire.

After we were both white with snow and laughing so hard we couldn't run anymore, we called a truce and tried to knock the worst of the snow off before it could melt through our clothes. Then I treated us both to hot pretzels with mustard.

"This is good," he said, taking his first bite. "I've seen them in movies, but I never had one before."

I nodded in agreement, my mouth full.

"It still seems funny to me that nobody else is playing in the snow."

"As I said, you get used to it. I don't know when I last played in the snow."

"Really?"

"Really." Though I couldn't remember the last time I'd played in the snow, I could remember my first time in Boston. The snow had started falling while I was in class, and by the time I'd come out, the ground was already covered by two inches of white stuff. I was looking at it, just as delighted as Thaddeous had been, when a snowball hit me squarely in the face. Philip, of course. He found a battered old sled, and we went sledding all afternoon. I wasn't dressed for it, and I was sopping wet by the time we gave up, but it was so much fun I just didn't care.

So much for avoiding thoughts of Philip. This time I caught myself blinking away tears. I guess it's only natural that when a relationship ends badly, you only think about the bad memories, not the good ones. But there had been good times with Philip. It bothered me that it had taken his death to make me remember them again.

Thaddeous and I spent the day on the Freedom Trail, a walking tour that includes most of Boston's historic sights: the State House, the Old Granary Burial Ground, the site of the Boston Massacre, Faneuil Hall, the statue of Paul Revere that shows up on so many postcards, and the Old North Church Revere used as a message post. The trail is usually easy to follow because it's marked with a red line painted across the streets and sidewalks, but since the line was covered with snow, we had to rely on a guidebook.

We grabbed lunch and dinner along the way, but by the time we decided we were ready to head back to my place, I was hungry again. I said, "Are you up for ice cream?"

"In this weather?"

"Folks up here eat ice cream no matter how cold it is. In fact, I was told once that I wouldn't be a true Bostonian until I had gone out in a snowstorm to get ice cream."

"Laurie Anne, with that accent, nobody's going to think you're a Bostonian."

"Hey, I'm bilingual." In fact, my Southern accent had gotten thicker since Thaddeous had arrived. Usually I keep it toned down in Boston, but Detective Salvatore wouldn't have any problem picking it up now.

We were walking back to the subway station when Thaddeous said, "Now, explain to me why it is that Northerners will eat ice cream all year long, but not drink iced tea."

"The same reason Southerners drink iced tea all year long, but don't eat ice cream."

When we made it back to my apartment, there was a message from Jessie on my machine telling me that Philip's wake was scheduled for the next night.

Chapter 6

Once again it was late for me to call Richard, but I really needed to talk to him. It seemed like a month since he had left, instead of just a few days. So I left Thaddeous in front of the TV and went to my bedroom to dial the number of the hotel where Richard was staying.

As it turned out, he was still awake. "Laura, I was just thinking about you. Longingly, I might add."

"Glad to hear it. How was the trip to Stratford? Any problems with jet lag?"

"The trip was fine, but now I remember why they call it the red-eye. And I haven't been having problems with jet lag because I've been having so much fun that I don't want to sleep anyway." Then he quickly added, "Of course, I miss you terribly. I keep turning around to tell you something, and it throws me that you're not there."

"That's sweet," I said, "but it's okay to have a good time without me there. Just don't go quoting the Bard to some pretty Englishwoman."

"Are there Englishwomen? I hadn't noticed," he said innocently. "How are things in Boston?"

"I've got company. Thaddeous is here." I explained how Aunt Nora had maneuvered it.

"That's great," Richard said. "I'd rather you had someone there with you. Have you two been hitting the hot spots?"

"Some," I said.

There was a pause. "Is something wrong?"

I should have known that he'd be able to tell. "Well, I've got some weird news. You remember Philip Dennis, don't you?"

"Oh, yes. The Oxfordian." An Oxfordian is somebody who claims that the Earl of Oxford actually wrote Shakespeare's plays. Stratfordians, like Richard, realize that the true author was indeed William Shakespeare of Stratford.

I explained the whole story, from Philip's visit to how I'd been asked to identify his body the next day.

"Oh, Laura, I'm so sorry I'm not there with you. Are you all right?"

"I'm fine."

"Are you sure?"

"I think I'm sure."

"But you feel guilty."

"How can you tell?"

"Because I'd feel guilty if something like that happened to me. What would you say if I were you?"

I thought about it for a minute. "I'd say that there was no reason for you to feel guilty. That you couldn't have known that Philip was going to die, and that you had nothing to do with it."

"That's right."

"Would you believe it if you were me?"

He chuckled. "Maybe not at first. But it's true."

"I know. I just feel so bad about him."

"Why wouldn't you feel bad? You were close once."

"I know, but face it, Philip treated me like garbage. I don't think he had any more feeling for me than I've got for . . . for Prince Charles."

"Philip's feelings—or lack of them—aren't the point. Yours are."

"But why do I still have feelings for him? Am I stupid?"

"No!" Richard said, sounding exasperated. "Listen to me, Laura. You loved him, didn't you?"

"I thought I did. But that was before I'd met you."

"I don't mind it that you loved another man before me."

"Okay," I conceded. "I loved him."

"And you're not the kind of person who can just shut off your feelings. With some people, love turns into hate, but you're not that kind of person, either. Of course you feel something toward Philip. So even though your head knows that Philip's death is not your fault in any way, your heart doesn't know it yet."

"How long will it take for my heart to catch up?"

"Not long. I promise."

The big thing taken care of, we talked for a while about less urgent matters, like Richard's plans for his time in England and how we already missed each another. Eventually I looked at the clock, realized how long we'd been talking, and told him goodbye.

Chapter 7

I would have liked to have taken the next day off to run around with Thaddeous some more, but I had work that needed doing. Besides which, my feet needed the rest. I left him with a guidebook, the spare set of door keys, a pocketful of subway tokens, and directions to my office in Cambridge. The plan was for him to meet me later so we could go to Philip's wake together.

I spent the day finishing up the last details of the project I had told Thaddeous about, so time went by quickly. It was about five-thirty when Michelle, my company's receptionist and a friend, called me.

"Laura, there's somebody here looking for Laurie Anne," she said, and I could tell she was smiling.

I sighed. There was a reason I had never told Michelle or anybody else at work what my family called me. "I'll be right there."

Thaddeous was standing by the front desk. "Hi, Thaddeous. Did you have a good day?"

"I sure did. That Aquarium is something else. You know that big tank with the sharks in it? They have divers who go in there to feed the fish. They've got more guts than I do."

I turned to Michelle, who clearly wanted to know who

Thaddeous was. "Michelle, this is my cousin, Thaddeous Crawford. He came up to keep me company while Richard is gone. Thaddeous, this is Michelle Nucci."

"Pleased to meet you," Thaddeous said.

"My pleasure. So you're one of Laura's cousins from Byerly. Laura's told me *all* about her family. Are you one of the country singers?"

"No, that would be my cousins Clifford and Earl."

"Then you must be the one who went into the Army."

"No, that's my brother Augustus."

"I can tell that you're not the quiet one."

"That's my little brother, Willis."

"You're not the one who makes Yankee jokes, are you?"

"No, that's Linwood."

She grinned. "Then you must be the handsome one."

Poor Thaddeous turned bright red and didn't have a word to say.

"Would you like to see where I work?" I said, giving him an escape.

I took him back to my desk, showed him a little of what I was working on, then shut down my system and got my coat and pocketbook.

"Are you two dressed up to go somewhere special?" Michelle asked, when we got back to the front door. "Or is that how you always dress, Thaddeous?"

"Not hardly," he said with a shy grin. He was much more likely to be found in jeans than in a suit. I was surprised he had a suit with him at all, but I imagined that his mama had insisted he bring it "just in case."

"A friend of mine died over the weekend," I told Michelle.

"That's terrible! I'm so sorry. Was it a close friend?"

"Not anymore. I knew Philip in college," I said, which was true, if not complete.

She made sympathetic noises.

"We're going to get something to eat," I said, "then go for visiting hours at the funeral home."

"Where are you going for dinner?" she asked.

"I thought we'd walk over to Legal Seafood."

"Oh, I love Legal Seafood. Their scrod is out of this world. And the lobster . . ." She sighed as if remembering, then looked at her watch. "Well, I guess I'd better get going, too."

"Have you got plans tonight?"

"No," she said, looking directly at Thaddeous. "I guess I'll just go home and open a can of soup."

I waited a few seconds, wondering if Thaddeous would get the hint. He didn't, so I said, "Why don't you come with us?"

She was still looking at Thaddeous. "Are you sure you two wouldn't rather be alone? I mean, you probably haven't had a chance to talk yet."

"Shoot, we've got plenty of time for that," Thaddeous said. "No need for you to eat by your lonesome if you don't want to."

"Well, if you insist. Just let me run to the ladies' room first." She scooted down the hall.

"Sure you don't mind?" I asked Thaddeous.

"Now why would I mind taking two pretty ladies to dinner?" he said.

It wasn't exactly a declaration of interest, but I thought he might at least be curious, especially since his last romance had ended badly. Michelle was awfully pretty, and Thaddeous didn't often see a woman with such dark, glossy hair and big, dark eyes in Byerly. I was fairly sure Michelle was interested in him, especially when she returned with makeup freshened and hair glowing from a vigorous brushing.

Thaddeous held the door for us, then took our arms as we walked down the sidewalk. I noticed that Michelle walked a little closer to him than I did, but couldn't tell if Thaddeous encouraged it or not.

When we got to Legal Seafood, Michelle talked Thaddeous into ordering lobster, which surprised me. We had seen lobsters in an aquarium at the airport, and Thaddeous had said he'd as soon eat road-kill as "one of them ugly things." He enjoyed it, too, obediently eating only the parts Michelle told him to eat.

Michelle spent most of the meal quizzing Thaddeous about how long he was going to stay and where he had been so far. Then she moved on to Thaddeous's job, family, and, of course, girlfriends. Some people might have been offended at such a concentrated interrogation, but then, Aunt Nora or Vasti would have asked even more personal questions. Thaddeous took it in stride.

Michelle seemed pretty satisfied by his answers. I had never pictured Thaddeous dating a Northerner, but it had worked out for me, despite dire predictions by some of my cousins. Come to think of it, Thaddeous had been a bit doubtful about Richard at first, too. If things worked out between him and Michelle, I was going to have to remind him of that.

Chapter 8

After dinner, Thaddeous and I walked Michelle to the subway, then caught a taxi to the funeral home in Cambridge. I had never been to a Northern visitation, so I wasn't sure what to expect, but the receiving room looked pretty much like what I'd find in any funeral home. Maybe the fixtures were a bit more formal than those in either of the places in Byerly, but the Hickory funeral homes were just as nice.

Unlike many of the visitations I'd been to, the coffin was closed. I was just as glad—seeing Philip once after his death had been plenty enough for me.

There weren't many people in the receiving room yet, and I didn't see Philip's estranged wife Colleen or anybody who looked like they could be his family. At the far end of the room I spotted a cluster of the people I had known at MIT who had gone on to work at SSI with Philip.

Jessie, a plump redhead who won't believe that freckles are cute on her, saw us and came right over. "Laura, I'm so glad you could come. Are you doing all right?"

"I'm fine, thanks. Jessie Boyd, this is my cousin, Thaddeous Crawford."

They exchanged pleased-to-meet-yous. "I'm afraid you

picked a bad time to come up," Jessie said. "The weather, and now this."

"I'm just glad Laurie Anne wasn't alone when she found out about your friend," he said.

"Come talk to everybody," Jessie said, and started to draw us toward the SSI crowd.

"I should pay my respects to Philip's family first," I said. "Which ones are they?"

"Colleen is in the ladies' room," Jessie said with an expression that told me she was peeved at Colleen for some reason. "His parents and his brother aren't here yet. I guess it took them longer to drive from Worcester than they'd expected."

"His family's late?" Thaddeous whispered to me as we followed Jessie.

"I don't think they were very close to Philip. He said they traveled most of the time. High-society types."

Despite the circumstances, I was glad to see the people I had spent so much of my time at college with. It had been several years, and now I felt silly for letting Philip stop me from keeping in touch.

As big a part of my life as they'd been in college, none of them had met any of my family, and it took a few minutes to introduce Thaddeous to everybody.

"Thaddeous, this is Vinnie Noone. He's chief executive officer at SSI," I said.

"Vincent," he gently corrected me, and shook Thaddeous's hand. In college, Vinnie had dressed as sloppily as the rest of us, but as Vincent, he was wearing a stylish pin-striped suit with black shoes so shiny I could see myself in them.

"This is Inez Parra, the chief operating officer."

I hoped Thaddeous wouldn't ask what the difference was

between the two positions, because I didn't know myself. Maybe they didn't, either. According to Jessie, though Vincent and Inez had been quite an item in college, they now argued constantly about who was in charge of what.

Inez had seemed wonderfully exotic to me in college. With her olive skin and sleek black hair, she was very different from the people I had grown up with. Though slender and not very tall, she didn't look at all dainty, especially with her nails painted deep red.

"Here are Dee and Dominic Henniel. They're programmers."

Dee and Dom both had round bodies and heads, with round glasses and short, curly brown hair. Tonight, with Dee in a dress and Dom in a suit, it was easy to tell which was which, but when they both wore jeans and rugby shirts, like they had in college, I had trouble sometimes. Their names, their figures, and those striped shirts had inspired Philip to call them Tweedledee and Tweedledum. I had giggled over it at first, but I thought it was mean when he used those names to their faces.

Murray was apparently growing impatient with the formalities. Without waiting for me to introduce him, he thrust his hand at Thaddeous and said, "Murray Wexelbaum, QA."

"Quality assurance," I explained. "Murray makes sure that the software does what it's supposed to do." Murray had been balding since college, and his Coke-bottle-bottom glasses made him look more than a little like an owl. He had never been high on my list of favorite people, but when it came to abrasive, annoying, nitpicking people, he was right at the top. I swear that he walked so precisely that each stride was the same length. Of course, most of those traits come in handy when performing the endless measurements and tests a good QA process requires, but they didn't make him fun to hang out with.

I didn't know the last person in the group, so Jessie introduced her. "This is Sheliah Turner, our new technical writer. Well, relatively new. She started a few months ago."

"A year ago, actually," Sheliah said, "but compared with everybody else, I'm still the new kid on the block. Are you one of the MIT crowd?"

"I'm afraid so," I said, wondering how many tales of glorious college living she had heard. She looked a year or two younger than the rest and was blond and very cute. I wondered what Philip had thought of her.

"So, Laura," Vincent said, with that air of forced joviality I remembered from college, "how are things at your firm? GDS, isn't it?"

"GBS," I said. I don't know who it was who decided that computer companies should go by initials, but half the places in Boston were named out of a can of alphabet soup. "Going pretty well. I'm doing a lot with PC interface design these days." I told myself that I'd have to explain that bit of jargon to Thaddeous later on.

"Really? We've got some plans along those lines in the new release of StatSys. If you've been considering making a change, we'd be happy to have you on board."

"I hadn't really thought about leaving GBS," I said.

Inez came in with, "Vinnie, this is a wake, not a job fair. Laura doesn't want to talk about business now."

"Just making conversation," Vincent said.

"Ha!" was all Inez said, and Vincent excused himself to go to the men's room. To me, she said, "That man has no blood in him, Laura, no heart." Then she added, "Speaking of not having a heart, here comes the grieving widow."

I had to admit that Colleen wasn't exactly dressed like a widow. Her dress was black, but it was also short, and snug across the bosom. I knew that she and Philip had been estranged, but I'd have thought she'd want to show respect, if not grief. Then again, maybe it was the only black outfit she had. I certainly wouldn't have felt like going shopping for new clothes at a time like that.

"That's Philip's wife," I said to Thaddeous. "We should go speak to her." Thaddeous nodded, but nobody offered to join us.

Colleen took a quick look at the coffin at the end of the room, then turned away and went as far as she could in the other direction.

"Colleen?" I said.

It took her a moment to recognize me. "Laura?"

"Hi, Colleen. Thaddeous, this is Colleen Dennis. Colleen, this is my cousin, Thaddeous Crawford."

"Nice to meet you, Thaddeous."

"I'm sorry for your loss," Thaddeous said solemnly, and I knew Aunt Nora would have approved.

"Thank you." Then, to me she said, "I hear it was at your place that Philip died." I must have winced, because she added, "Sorry. Jessie told me he was found behind your apartment." She looked over at the SSI contingent. "Jessie's the only one who bothered to call me."

"The group always did rely on Jessie to take care of the social amenities," I said diplomatically.

"Yeah, right. They're all so self-righteous now because I made Philip leave and he ended up in that alley. It's like they've forgotten all about trying to kick him out of his own company." Then, as if realizing how that sounded, she said,

"I'm sorry, I know I sound like a bitch. I'm having a tough time with this."

"I understand," Thaddeous said, though I didn't think he did. "If y'all don't mind, I think I'll step outside and smoke myself a cigarette."

As he went, Colleen said, "I guess I shocked him. I'm not exactly your typical widow."

"Thaddeous knows that you and Philip were estranged," I said.

"That's putting it mildly. The fact is, I'd made up my mind to get on with my life, and his dying doesn't affect me. Not much, anyway." Then she shook her head. "Who'm I trying to kid? I feel awful." She pulled a ragged tissue from her purse and jabbed at her eyes angrily.

I thought about putting my arm around her shoulders, but circumstances with Philip being what they were, she had never been a particular friend of mine. Instead, I just said, "It's okay, Colleen. I know it's awkward—everybody knows it. And everybody deals with grief in his own way."

"I wanted Philip out of my life, but not like this. I didn't want him dead."

"Nobody thinks you did." When she didn't respond, I added emphatically, "I know you didn't."

She took a deep breath. "Thanks." Then she looked at the entrance. "Oh, jeez, here they come."

"Who?" I turned and saw a couple in their late fifties, accompanied by a younger man who looked vaguely familiar. "Who are they?"

"Philip's parents, and his brother, Dave."

"Really?" Now I realized why the younger man looked familiar—he favored Philip. They weren't at all as I'd imagined them. From the way Philip had talked, I had expected furs and silk, not wool and cotton. They were as pale as the rest of us who lived in sun-starved Massachusetts, even though Philip had joked about their Palm Springs tans. I felt oddly angry at him. He had made fun of my family, but from the looks of his, they didn't have a bit more money than mine did.

"I have to say something to them," Colleen said. "It's just so damned weird." She hesitated. "Would you come with me?"

It was weird for me, too, both because I had dated Philip and because I had never met these people, but I said, "Sure."

"Thanks!" She took hold of my elbow, maybe to keep me from changing my mind.

"Hello Mom Dennis, Dad Dennis," Colleen said. She gave them quick hugs that they returned just enough to be polite. The look Dave gave her made it plain that he wouldn't put up with even that much.

Colleen pushed me forward. "This is Laura Fleming. Philip must have told you about her."

"Hi," I said, holding out my hand. "I knew Philip in college."

Mrs. Dennis took my hand and clasped it for a moment. "I remember Phil talking about you. I hadn't realized you still lived up here. I thought you went back to the plantation in North Carolina."

I swallowed. Apparently what Philip had told his parents about me was about as accurate as what he had told me about them. I couldn't wait to hear what my folks would say about our home place being referred to as a "plantation." "I just fell in love with Massachusetts," I said, which was honest enough. "I'm so sorry about Philip."

Mrs. Dennis nodded, her brow wrinkling in pain. "I never would have guessed he'd go like that. Out in the snow, like some poor homeless person."

Colleen flinched, and I didn't blame her.

"Couldn't you have left him enough money to get a hotel room, Colleen?" Dave asked loudly.

Colleen's cheeks got red. "Look, Dave, this is hard for me, too. Your brother and I hadn't been getting along for a long time, and you know it. But when I asked him to leave, I made sure he had money in his pocket."

"You listen to me, you—" Dave started to say, but his father put a hand on his shoulder.

"Now is not the time, Dave. Why don't you take your mother to see Phil?"

Dave looked like he wanted to argue with his father, but he relented and took his mother's arm to go toward the coffin.

Colleen said, "Excuse me," and strode angrily away, leaving me and Mr. Dennis standing there.

"I'm sorry about that," Mr. Dennis said.

"Don't worry about it," I said. "I know people aren't at their best at a time like this. If it means anything to you, I do think Colleen feels terrible about what happened."

"I'm sure she does. She's not a bad woman, and I can't blame her for Phil's and her problems. It's just that the timing was so . . ."

"Awkward." That seemed to be the right word to describe the whole evening.

He nodded. "Dave is feeling a fair amount of guilt himself right now. He and Phil argued the last time Phil came to visit, and they never made up. That's probably why Phil didn't come to us when he was in trouble."

I had wondered about that. My family were the first people I'd turn to if I ever needed help. "Philip came over to my apartment that last day, wanting to stay with me," I confessed. "I'm afraid I had to turn him down. I'm married now."

I was afraid that he'd get angry, but he just patted my arm. "Colleen explained it all when she called. You don't have to justify yourself to me, dear. It was very nice of you to come tonight." Then he went to join his wife and son.

What he had said should have made me feel better, but instead I felt worse. Maybe I didn't have to justify what I had done to him, but I sure wished I could justify it to myself.

With the coast clear, Colleen came back. "Sorry about that," she said. "I just don't know what to say to them."

It had been a dirty trick, but considering the stress she had to be under, I was willing to let it go. "I take it you and they don't get along."

"They treated me all right, I guess, but we were never crazy about one another. Philip said they tried to talk him out of marrying me, and it was hard for me to forget that."

Knowing Philip, I had to wonder if he hadn't just made it up to cause trouble, but it didn't seem like a good thing to bring up at his wake.

"Then," she said, "when I called them to tell them about Philip, Dave got on the phone and wanted to know what I was going to do about the money."

"What money?"

"Philip's share of our money. Only now it's my money, because we were still married. We hadn't talked to lawyers or anything. Dave wanted to know if I was going to give them half of everything. Like I'd even had a chance to think about it."

"It does sound like he was rushing things," I said.

"What do you think? Should I?"

"I can't answer that, Colleen." In fact, I wouldn't touch the question with a ten-foot pole. Money is always a ticklish issue, and I didn't have a clue as to what would be appropriate or fair under those circumstances.

"I'd be within my rights to keep it all, wouldn't I? If the company goes public, like Philip said it was going to, we could be talking about a lot of money."

"All I can say is that you might want to take some time and think it over before you make up your mind."

"I guess you're right," she said, and looked over as somebody came in. "Well, look who's here," she said. "I wouldn't have thought *he'd* come."

"Who?" I said, looking at the man she was glaring at.

"Didn't you hear who they brought in to take Philip's job? Don't you remember him from college?"

I looked at him harder, and then it dawned on me. "Is that Neal?" I hadn't seen him since college, but he didn't look all that different, just grown up. He had been almost a child prodigy when he came to MIT, enrolling at age sixteen and well on his way to a doctorate by twenty-one. "Excuse me, Colleen. I want to say hello."

Neal was talking to Vinnie when I came up. "Neal?" I said.

He turned, and after only a short hesitation, smiled and said, "Laura?" He gave me a quick hug, and said, "You look great."

"Thank you. You look pretty snazzy yourself." His head had looked just a touch oversized before, but he had grown into it and filled out elsewhere as well. It was the first time I had ever seen him in a suit, and I was glad to see that he had traded in his black plastic-rimmed glasses for more stylish wire frames. "I had no idea you were back in town."

"We brought him back," Vincent said. "Neal is going to help bring SSI back into step with the industry."

Neal looked embarrassed. Being brought in to take over for Philip in the company Philip had cofounded must have been difficult for him, even before Philip's death. Philip and Neal had been college roommates.

"Is this your husband?" Neal asked, looking at Thaddeous, who came in then to join us.

"No, this is my cousin, Thaddeous Crawford. My husband is spending the month in England."

They shook hands.

"What have you been up to, Neal?" I said.

"This and that," he said. "Nothing spectacular. How about you?"

I briefly caught him up on the past few years and we chatted for a few minutes. Then Neal excused himself to speak to Philip's family and Vincent went with him.

"He seems like a good fellow," Thaddeous said, kindly not adding that he was considerably more pleasant than the rest of the MIT crew.

"I always liked Neal," I said. He had been troubled but nice. I'd have to tell Thaddeous the story of how Neal had left MIT before finishing his doctorate. He had been putting the finishing touches on his dissertation when his hard drive crashed. Hard. Somehow his backups had been corrupted, too, and though he was probably the best programmer I ever met, he couldn't get his data back. This was before viruses were widely known, but all of us at MIT knew about them. All we could ever figure out was that some hacker had created something deadly, and somehow it had gotten onto Neal's system.

If Neal had been a little older, or maybe more mature, he might have been able to roll with it. As quickly as he'd done the work the first time, surely he would have been able to repeat most of it before the deadline MIT sets on doctoral students.

But he wasn't very mature, despite his brilliance. Rocketing through MIT in about a third of the time it usually took had cost him. I had often wondered how it would have turned out had he come to one of us for advice or support, but Philip was out of town when it happened and Neal didn't tell any of the rest of us what he was planning. He just packed up his things and went home to California. I hadn't seen him since, and as far as I knew, nobody else had, either. I'd have to ask Jessie how they had found him. In fact, there were a whole lot of things I was going to have to ask Jessie.

After all the other surprises I had had that night, I shouldn't have been surprised when the next person to come in the door was Detective Salvatore. "Thaddeous, look who's here."

"Isn't that that policeman?"

"What policeman?" Jessie asked, as she came up behind us.

"Detective Salvatore, the one who questioned us about Philip," I said. "Didn't you talk to him?"

"Only over the phone," she said. "What does he want?"

"Maybe he's just paying his respects," I said, but I had a hunch that that wasn't all. Chief Junior Norton in Byerly doesn't go to the funerals of people who die there unless she knew them or their deaths were suspicious. And Salvatore hadn't known Philip.

Thaddeous must have been thinking the same thing. "I guess he's doing a little investigating."

"Philip's death was an accident, wasn't it?" Jessie asked.

I said, "As far as I know."

"Then why is he here?"

I didn't have an answer for her, and even if I had, I wouldn't have had time to give it to her before she said, "I have to tell Vincent," and walked quickly away.

"Why is she so upset?" Thaddeous asked.

"Beats me," I said. "Maybe she's afraid this will cause bad publicity for SSI." It was probably rude of us, but Thaddeous and I couldn't help watching as Salvatore spoke to the Dennises for several minutes, and afterward, to Colleen. Then he turned and saw us, and came our way.

"Mrs. Fleming, Mr. Crawford. How are you enjoying Boston, Mr. Crawford?"

"Nobody calls me Mr. Crawford," Thaddeous said. "I'm Thaddeous. And I'm having myself a big time. This is one fine city. You've got some fine-looking women, too."

I'd have to repeat that comment to Michelle. "I'm kind of surprised to see you here," I said to Detective Salvatore. "Does this mean—?"

"It doesn't mean a thing, Mrs. Fleming. I'm just being nosy. I've been a cop for a while now, and this case is kind of unusual. We get people who die of exposure every winter, but usually it's derelicts, not successful computer programmers like Philip Dennis."

"I guess I was his last resort." I really hated having to say that, but it looked as if it was true.

Salvatore said, "Wouldn't his family have taken him in? They're in Worcester, but he could have gotten there somehow, or they could have come to get him."

"His father said that he and his brother had been fighting, so that might be why he didn't call them."

"Maybe," Salvatore said.

"Detective Salvatore," Thaddeous said, "you sound like a man who needs convincing."

Salvatore chuckled. "I guess you're right, Mr.—Thaddeous."

"Philip's death was an accident, wasn't it?" I asked, not sure if I wanted to hear his answer. "That's what you said it looked like."

"It still looks like it."

"Had he been drinking?"

"Definitely beyond the legal limit," he said.

"And he hit his head?"

"Absolutely."

I looked at him. "So what am I missing?"

"Maybe you're not so much missing something as I'm seeing something that isn't there. He'd been drinking, but not enough to pass out."

"Might be it was enough to make him slip and hit his head," Thaddeous said. "Especially with the snow and all."

"That's probably what happened," Salvatore agreed. "Only that blow to the head bothers me, too. I just wish I knew what he hit his head on." He was looking at me closely when he said that, and I suddenly realized he was being awfully chatty. I've known Junior Norton for years, and I don't think she'd have told me that much unless she had a darned good reason.

I lowered my voice. "Do you think Philip was murdered?"

"Why would I think that?"

The logical next question would be did he think I'd done it, but I didn't ask that one because I didn't want to hear his answer.

Salvatore kept looking at me, and I made myself look right back at him. Then he kind of nodded. "So who are the people from the company where Mr. Dennis worked? I'd like to meet them."

I hesitated at first, feeling like a stool pigeon. But then I decided I was being silly. He was a cop—he could find out who was who pretty quickly, with or without me. I pointed out Vinnie and Jessie, who were talking urgently, and gave him their names. Salvatore thanked me and headed in their direction.

"Is there anybody else you'd like to talk to?" Thaddeous asked.

"To tell you the truth, what I'd really like is to get out of here."

"Let's do it."

I nodded at Colleen from across the room and she half-waved in return. Then we found a phone to call for a cab.

Maybe I should have forced myself to stay longer, but I hadn't been able to help Philip when he was alive, and I sure couldn't help him now.

Chapter 9

I could tell on the way home that Thaddeous had something to say, but the idea of talking with a taxi driver listening bothered him. So I wasn't surprised when as soon as we got back to my apartment, he asked, "Are you all right?"

"I'm fine."

He didn't say anything for a few minutes, just let me look at the day's mail and check the phone machine for messages.

"You want something to drink?" I asked.

"Sure."

"Coke or iced tea?"

"Coke would be fine."

I got him a glass and poured myself some tea. Then we sat down on the couch and I reached for the remote control. "Shall we see what's on TV?"

"Are you sure you don't want to talk?"

"I'm fine."

"The hell you are! Laurie Anne, I know I'm not Richard, but I am here and I can listen pretty good, even if I can't come up with something from Shakespeare to say. Now, if you don't want to talk, that's all right, but don't tell me that you're fine when I can see that you're not."

"You sure are Aunt Nora's son, aren't you?" She had always been able to pull my troubles right out of me.

He didn't say anything, just waited me out.

"Okay, I'm feeling pretty down about Philip, but I don't want to spoil your vacation."

"How many times have you spoiled your trips back home when somebody needed help?"

"True," I admitted. In fact, I'd have been offended if anybody in my family had hidden trouble from me, and I owed it to Thaddeous to treat him the same way as I would want to be treated. "I talked to Richard about it last night, and I know it's nuts, but I still feel guilty about Philip. If I had let him stay here, he'd still be alive."

"I don't know about that," he said. "Like as not I'd have killed him myself. Or at least thrown him out."

"Thaddeous!"

"Laurie Anne, you're a smart woman about most things, but sometimes you trust people too much. This character shows up at your door after he's broken up with his wife, knowing that your husband is out of town. You can't tell me that he didn't have something on his mind."

"I didn't think about that," I had to admit. I had been more worried about keeping Philip out of my life than out of my bed.

"Of course you didn't—you're a good person. It doesn't sound to me like this Philip was."

"He wasn't all bad," I said. "I know all I've talked about are the bad parts, but there was some good in him." I tried to come up with an example. "I think there was. Lord, Thaddeous, I'd hate to think that I was a complete fool for dating him."

"I know you were never any kind of a fool, but I have to say that he doesn't sound like much of a catch. So why did you go out with him?"

I thought about it. "I think I must have been halfway in love with him the first time I met him. I'd only been up here a few weeks, and I hadn't made a whole lot of friends, so I was eating alone in the cafeteria. Again. Philip sat down at the next table, and I saw his sweatshirt. It had a computer joke on it, and I said something about it."

"A computer joke?"

"Just the kind of in-joke you see at MIT. It said:

C:DOS
C:DOS:RUN
RUN:DOS:RUN
RUN:RUN:RUN

Thaddeous looked blank.

"Don't worry—only a computer geek would get it. Which is what I was, so I laughed. Then we started talking, and he moved over next to me, and we talked some more, and before I knew it, I had missed half of my next class."

"What did you talk about?"

"Everything. Computers, and Cambridge, and MIT, and where we were from. Philip seemed so sophisticated compared to the other people I knew."

"Compared to folks in Byerly, you mean."

"I suppose. He had seen so much more of the world, and I couldn't believe that he'd be interested in *me*."

"Laurie Anne, that doesn't sound like you."

"It wasn't me, not really, and it certainly isn't me now. You've got to remember how it was then. In Byerly, everybody knew me. I was the smart one, the one who got the best grades and the highest test scores and all that. And I was different from anybody else, because I knew about computers. Up here, I was just another face in the crowd. Lots of people at MIT had better grades and test scores than I did, and from much bigger schools than Byerly High School. They knew more about computers, too. Nobody knew my family, and nobody knew me, and nobody cared. Until I met Philip, and he introduced me to the group. All of a sudden I had lots of friends."

"Those folks I met tonight?"

I nodded. "They all seemed to think a lot of Philip and kind of followed him around. I felt so lucky to be his girlfriend. Of course, I realized later on that he picked out folks who were misfits, just so he could be their leader. Like he picked me."

"You weren't a misfit."

"I sure thought I was. I talked funny and I dressed funny—talk about country come to town." He started to object, but I went on. "Except when I was with the group, and with Philip. He had this way of making me feel intelligent and attractive and unique and all kinds of good things." I remembered the first time we'd made love. I'd been so inexperienced, and he'd been so sweet to me. But I didn't want to talk to Thaddeous about that.

I said, "Philip really seemed to be going somewhere. He had all these plans for his future, programming and making money and having a great big house in Cambridge that he could fix up."

"His future? What about yours?"

"Sometimes he included me, but sometimes I wasn't sure. And we did break up a few times."

"Because of him and other women?"

"No. I didn't find out about that until later. We'd break up because he'd decide we were getting too serious and he wasn't ready for it, or because I was too dependent on him. Once I broke up with him because he was rude to a friend of mine, and when I called him about it, he hung up on me."

"Good for you!"

"Yeah, but I'd fall for him all over again. First I'd be miserable for a while, but try not to show it. Then he'd come back and tell me what a horrible person he was and how he didn't deserve me, and I'd take him back." I hated to admit the next part, even to Thaddeous. "I was always so grateful he came back."

"Laurie Anne," he said sadly.

"I know, I was stupid."

"Hey, I don't have any room to talk. I've made a fool of myself more than once."

"Anyway, we dated during my freshman and sophomore years, but during my junior year I finally got over him. I had other friends by then, and I was tired of the way he'd build me up, then cut me down again. We broke up for the last time not long after I met Richard. Then I started dating Richard, and you know how that ended up."

"Happily ever after."

"You bet," I said, smiling at the thought of my husband. "When I was little, I had had all these fairy-tale ideas about love and romance, but when I met Philip, I decided those ideas were childish. With Richard, I realized that the fairy tales were right all along. I know that sounds pretty silly."

"Not to me it doesn't. I just hope I find a fairy-tale princess of my own."

"You will." I thought about suggesting Michelle for the job, but decided that it wasn't a good time. "You'd think that after all he did to me, I'd be glad that he's gone. Or at least not care. But he did teach me a lot, if not always the best way. There are probably worse people I could have hooked up with." That was damning him with faint praise. "And he did introduce me to Richard—they met at a play." Of course, Philip had never dreamed that Richard and I would hit it off as well as we had, but he had done us a favor nonetheless. "So I guess I'm just doomed to feeling guilty over him dying the way he did, even though it wasn't my fault."

"Well, that's fine as far as it goes, and I'm sure glad you realize that it's not your fault. But I want to know what you're going to do about it."

"About what?"

"About feeling guilty."

"Do you think I need therapy?" I said, surprised that he would suggest it. Folks in Byerly were usually leery of psychologists.

"What I think is that you need to find out what happened to Philip. That police detective seemed to think something was fishy about his death, and I don't know but what I do, too. If he had money in his pocket, why didn't he go stay at a hotel or the YMCA? And why did he go off drinking and then come back here?"

"I don't know."

"I can see him having himself a few beers and deciding he was God's gift to women. Some men are like that. But if he decided to come see you again, why did he go down that alley instead of knocking at your front door?"

"That's a good question. They're all good questions."

"Then I think you ought to see about finding out some answers, and maybe that guilt will go away."

It was tempting, but I had to say, "I don't think it would work."

"Why not? You've found out answers to questions like that back in Byerly."

"But this isn't Byerly. I can't call Detective Salvatore like I do Junior, and I can't go see Aunt Nora or Aunt Maggie to find out what they know about people. Boston is a whole lot bigger than Byerly—I don't even know how much bigger it is. And that's not counting Cambridge or any of the other towns around here. We're talking millions of people."

"But how many of those people did Philip know?"

"What do you mean?"

"Did he know everybody in Boston?"

"Of course not," I said.

"So you wouldn't have to worry about everybody in town, just the people he knew. Like his family, and his wife, and those folks at the visitation tonight."

"Yes, but—"

"I've heard that the police always look at the people a murder victim knew, and purt-near all of the time, that's where they find the killer."

"*If* he was murdered," I said. "Salvatore didn't say that he was."

"He didn't say that he wasn't, either."

I drank some more tea. Thaddeous was right about Salvatore. It was clear that he thought something was up, and if an experienced Boston police detective had questions, chances were, he had good reason. If his experience and my instincts said the same thing, maybe I should listen. "I suppose it wouldn't hurt to ask a few questions."

"Uh huh."

"Philip's family is all the way in Worcester, and I don't think he saw much of them, so I'll hold off on them. And I don't know Colleen well enough to call her out of the blue. Besides which, like you said, the police always start with the family, so the Dennises and Colleen are where Salvatore is most likely to look. And he's going to be better at working out their alibis and tracking down life insurance policies, and so forth."

"Uh huh."

"But what he won't be as good at is getting to know Philip the way I did. Or rather, the way his friends did. Those folks at SSI, no matter how badly they'd been getting along, saw Philip more than his family did and probably more than Colleen did. And I can talk to them in ways no police detective can."

"Uh huh."

"It wouldn't hurt to talk to Jessie and see what's going on over there."

"Uh huh."

I looked at him and saw his expression. "Aren't you full of yourself?"

He just grinned.

"Well, if I've got to play detective again, I need my sleep. So you can get your own bed ready tonight. And stop grinning." Despite my saying that, he was still grinning like the cat who ate the canary when I left the room.

Chapter 10

I called Jessie the next day, but with the funeral that afternoon, she was too busy to have lunch with me. Instead, we agreed to meet the day after.

I thought about going to the funeral myself but decided against it. First off, I had a meeting I didn't want to miss, and second, I felt like my decision to look into Philip's death was going to be a better farewell than attending a funeral service. Third, it was awfully cold that day, with a harsh wind, and I just couldn't stand the idea of standing by a grave, shivering.

Thaddeous spent the day wandering around Boston, cold or no cold. He went to the Boston Tea Party ship to toss tea into the harbor, and to the Computer Museum. Though he didn't actually admit it, I think he went into the Children's Museum, too, which is right next to the Computer Museum and has plenty in it for adults to look at. Then he met me at the office.

I wasn't a bit surprised when Michelle let it be known that she had nothing to eat at home and no plans. She didn't know that I'd heard her turning down dinner with her mother. Thaddeous didn't seem to mind. When Michelle said she was up for Italian food, we let her pick a place in the

North End. Thaddeous got his first taste of cannoli, and while he said he preferred Aunt Daphine's apple pie to the ricotta cheese–filled pastry, he didn't leave a crumb on his plate.

It was still early after we ate, so we went to rent a video to watch at my house. I found it interesting that Michelle thought every movie Thaddeous suggested sounded wonderful, and she hadn't seen any of them that he hadn't . . . even those I knew she had.

The next day Jessie and I met for lunch about halfway between our two offices. I waited until the waitress took our orders before saying, "All right, Jessie, what's going on? Inez and Vinnie at each other's throats, Neal back in town, Philip and Colleen broken up, and now this. It hasn't been *that* long since I talked to you."

Jessie shook her head, her short, red curls shaking with her. "It's been a nightmare, Laura. I've been meaning to call you just to have someone to talk to, but I haven't had a chance."

"Then talk to me. When did Neal come back?" I thought it might be better to start with something less drastic than what had happened to Philip.

"Isn't it great to have him around again?"

"How did y'all find him? I thought that even *you* had lost track of him." Jessie had always been the group's source for phone numbers, addresses, and such.

"He'd been living in California, but Vincent found him over the Internet. Then we brought him here for an interview and offered him the job, and he went back just long enough to get his things."

"I'm surprised he was available, as good as he is."

Jessie lowered her voice. "He's had a hard time getting jobs because of what happened when he left MIT."

"You mean, not getting his doctorate? But he still had his bachelor's degree. And didn't he get a master's?"

"It wasn't the degree. It was other problems. He had a nervous breakdown after he got back to California."

"You're kidding. That poor guy." I thought about how young and fragile he'd seemed in college. "He seems fine now."

"Being back with the group is just what he needs."

That I found hard to believe. "So what's going on with Inez and Vinnie?"

"Same old, same old. It all goes back to when they broke up."

"That was years ago." Of course, the two of them had been pretty serious even before I'd started dating Philip, and their relationship had kept going after graduation and the founding of SSI. I had always thought they were perfect example of opposites attracting. Vinnie was such a WASP, while Inez was almost a stereotype of the fiery Latin woman. The only thing they had seemed to have in common was their fascination with computers, but that and the way their personalities complemented each other had seemed to be enough. "Did they really quit dating because of his family?"

Jessie shrugged. "Vincent would never talk about it, but that's what Inez said."

At the time, Jessie had told me that Vinnie's family, wealthy folks from Wellesley, hadn't minded their son playing house with Inez, but when he'd started talking about marriage, they'd started talking about disinheriting him. I had met his parents and brothers at graduation and immediately recognized them as the kind of people my Aunt Maggie would have called "highfalutin." Muriel, the wife he ended up with, was blond, blue-eyed, and just as highfalutin.

I said, "It was a tacky thing for him to do, but he's been married to Muriel for nigh onto four years now."

"I don't think Inez has ever forgiven him. You remember how she was at the wedding."

Richard and I had been there, but I hadn't expected Inez to show up. She did, wearing the shortest, tightest red dress I had ever seen. More heads turned when she walked down the aisle than when the bride did. Her escort, no doubt selected for his smoldering bedroom eyes, hadn't left her side the entire time. Shoot, she was nearly in his lap during the ceremony, and their dancing at the wedding had been enough to make me blush.

Jessie said, "Inez and Vinnie kept it pretty businesslike before the wedding, but afterward, it got real nasty around the office. They had always clashed over product design, just because they had such different ideas. Now every meeting was a battle—the two of them going after one another while the rest of us tried to stay out of the line of fire."

There was a short interruption when the waitress brought Jessie's chef's salad and my club sandwich. Then I said, "I can't believe they still act like that."

"It gets worse. Last week Muriel showed up at the office wearing a maternity dress. Vinnie hadn't even told us they were expecting."

"Did Inez notice?"

Jessie nodded. "And we had a staff meeting scheduled for that afternoon."

"It must have been awful."

She looked a little embarrassed. "It would have been, but I told Inez I had my period and asked if we could reschedule so I could go home. I thought it would help if everybody had a little time to cool off."

That was just like Jessie. Always doing her part to keep the group together, despite itself.

She went on. "About the only thing they've agreed on during the past year was that Philip had to go."

"Was he really that bad?"

"You don't know the half of it. You remember how Philip always liked being in charge?"

"How could I forget?"

"Well, he hasn't gotten any better. I mean, hadn't. He refused to make any changes to StatSys."

"You mean he didn't make updates?"

"Not substantial ones. It's great code, we all know that, but it's seven years old. You know how outdated code gets in seven years."

My own company's product rarely goes nine months without an update, and we roll out a complete new version every year and a half. That's in addition to bug fixes and changes required by changing technology.

"Why didn't he want to change it?" I asked.

"All he'd say was, 'If it ain't broke, don't fix it.' We've been losing customers like crazy. They wanted better graphics, a more user-friendly front end—all the buzz words. Do you know how hard StatSys was getting to sell? Another six months and we wouldn't have been able to give it away."

"I'm surprised you lasted this long," I said. I'd lost track of the computer companies who'd gone under by not keeping up.

"The only way we've kept going is by Dee and Dom putting together add-on packages. Philip didn't argue with those, as long as we didn't touch the core code. That way, we could put out new versions occasionally. But the add-ons are super kludgy because they have to work with the core code.

We were spending more time working around the core than we were developing new facilities. It was driving us all crazy."

"Why didn't you tell Philip?"

"We did, over and over again. We showed him sales figures, industry forecasts, everything we could think of."

"He wouldn't listen?"

"He'd listen, but he wouldn't do anything other than play games and create viruses. He said sales was Vincent's and Inez's department. It was awful, Laura. We were scared for our jobs. If SSI goes down, it takes all of us with it."

"I'm sure y'all could find other jobs," I said, knowing that it wasn't much consolation.

"Maybe," Jessie said, "but it wouldn't be the same."

For Jessie, losing SSI would have been like losing a member of her family. Maybe worse, because she had only her parents, and from what I remembered from dorm room conversations, they weren't exactly warm people.

An inner voice told me that this made an awfully good motive for murder. Could Jessie have killed to keep her "family" together? I tried to push the thought away because I didn't want to think of my old friend as a murderer, but I knew that if Philip was murdered, the murderer probably was an old friend.

"Anyway," Jessie said, "about a month ago, Vincent and Inez said flat out that we were going to have to fire him."

"But Philip was one of the founders. How do you fire a founder?"

"That's the problem—we couldn't. Not without a majority vote, anyway."

"A majority vote from whom?"

"From the board of directors. All of us founders were directors. We vote on all the big decisions."

I couldn't imagine a worse way for SSI to make business decisions than to have the seven of them arguing over them. "You voted on whether or not to fire Philip with him sitting there?"

"Of course not. But Vincent conducted a couple of straw polls just to see if we could get him out. We couldn't."

"Who was holding out?"

She suddenly looked more interested in her salad. "It was a secret ballot."

I knew what that meant. Jessie herself must have been one of the holdouts. She was loyal to a fault—at least, to the group. Once somebody was no longer with the group, the loyalty disappeared. I knew that from personal experience.

When Philip and I had broken up, the group had sided with him. To tell the truth, he could be a lot of fun. There were lots of fights, but life was never boring around Philip. Still, I had considered Jessie a close friend, and it hurt when I realized that she was more interested in preserving what was left of the group than in being with me. But that was long in the past, and I knew I shouldn't be moping about it now.

Jessie went on. "It was three for keeping him and three for firing him. Philip's own vote would have been the tie-breaker, so there was nothing we could do."

"But Philip knew you were trying to fire him. He told me so."

"He found out in the middle of the vote. Vincent had spoken to all of us except Philip, and after giving us some time to think it over, sent our receptionist around to collect our ballots. Philip saw her going from desk to desk and wanted to know what she was doing. She wouldn't tell him, but she was in Murray's office when Philip caught her, and Murray couldn't resist telling Philip what was going on."

"Murray never was very tactful."

"Murray was sure that Philip was going to lose the vote, so he didn't see any reason not to rub it in. But when Vincent counted the ballots, he found out it was a tie."

"Did Philip know?"

"Of course. He barged into Vincent's office and demanded to know the results. Then the two of them had a terrible fight."

"I can imagine." I thought about the last time I broke up with Philip. Actually, we'd been broken up for a month and a half, but he thought that we'd be getting back together. Only I wasn't about to take him back, and I told him so.

At first he wouldn't believe me, or maybe he couldn't believe me. It was like it had never occurred to him that anybody would dump him. He kept apologizing for whatever it was we'd fought about, saying, "I'm sorry, it won't happen again," over and over again, like I was just trying to make sure that he was really sincere.

When he finally figured out that I was serious, he got angry, really angry. Not violent, thank goodness, but awfully ugly. He must have heard about my being with Richard, because he started saying horrible things about him, and then he started in on me. That's when I slammed the door on him, but I could hear him ranting for endless minutes longer, screaming at my closed door and cursing his way down the hall.

That was just me, and I'd have been fooling myself to think I was that important to him. SSI was his life. I knew just how he must have reacted when he found out that they wanted to get rid of him.

"They decided to hold another vote the next week, so Vincent spent the whole week trying to convince everybody to vote to fire Philip," Jessie said. "He said the company wouldn't survive the year if we didn't. At the same time, Philip was trying to convince everybody to vote to keep him. It was awful."

I nodded. Weighing loyalty against the good of the company, friendship against the loss of a job—it wasn't a choice I'd want to make. "What happened when you voted again?"

"It was weird, Laura. I saw Philip and Vincent the morning before the vote, and both of them were sure that they were going to win. Not just being cocky, but completely convinced. But when they counted the ballots, the vote hadn't changed. Three to three."

"And Philip's vote made it four to three. So he won."

"Yes and no. Knowing that three of us wanted to fire him was nearly as bad as all of us wanting to. He was *so* mad. He walked out of the office and didn't come back for the rest of the week." She added sadly, "It was the quietest few days we'd had at SSI in a long time."

"What happens to SSI with Philip gone?"

"We should be able to pull through," Jessie said, looking more cheerful. "Vincent had an idea a while ago that would help us raise capital so we could put money into development and get back into the market."

"You mean going public?"

"Yes," she said, looking surprised. "It's supposed to be a secret. How did you know?"

"Colleen said something about it at the wake. Since she and Philip were still legally married, his share of SSI passes to her."

"I'll have to talk to Vincent about that. We hadn't thought about her having control of Philip's share. At least she won't be able to vote. Anyway, Vinnie wants to go public, and the rest of us agreed that it was a good idea. Except for Philip, of course. He said he didn't want stockholders telling him what to do."

"That sounds like Philip."

"We haven't voted on it yet. I think Vincent was afraid he'd run into the same deadlock if we did, so he's been trying to make doubly sure that he had support first."

I nodded, thinking that this gave Vincent a particularly powerful motive for murder. With Philip out of the way, Vincent could go ahead with his plans.

"Plus," Jessie said, "Vincent was worried about what Philip would do if we voted for the public offering despite him."

"What could he do?"

"Sabotage. We were sure that he'd do something to the system, even with us watching. You know how sneaky he was. Vincent was sure that he had viruses set to destroy the code, maybe only needed a key command to blow it all up."

"You're right," I said. When it came down to it, destruction was what Philip had been best at.

"We're supposed to vote soon, and with Philip gone, I think it will pass. Vincent and Inez are definitely for it, and I know Dee and Dom are ready to get down to some serious development. They're tired of doing trivial programming while the technology keeps changing. And Murray is hoping that we'll get enough money coming in that he can get a real QA staff instead of having to do it all himself."

"What about you?"

"Oh, I'll vote for it. Anything to keep us all together."

The word "anything" sounded ominous, considering how things had turned out. "What about Philip and Colleen splitting up? When did that happen?"

"I didn't even know they were having problems," Jessie said. "I guess Philip didn't want to admit there was anything wrong. The first I heard was when she threw him out of the house."

"And now she inherits everything from him," I said, not being very subtle.

"It can't be much. It's not like there've been a lot of profits from SSI lately. Plus, they bought that house in Cambridge and it's been expensive fixing it up the way Philip wanted."

"At least there's his life insurance," I said. "SSI does provide life insurance for its employees, doesn't it?"

"Yes, but Colleen doesn't get any of it. We directors named the company as beneficiary in our policies. Vincent's brother the lawyer recommended it."

I nodded, mentally taking Colleen off of my list of suspects. Maybe Philip had money or property I didn't know about, but I didn't think so. He'd been as poor as Job's turkey when were dating.

"I guess she gets the house, anyway."

"For what it's worth," Jessie said. "They owe an awful lot on it. I thought Philip was biting off more than he could chew with that place, but you know how Philip was."

"He and Colleen were still in an apartment that last time I saw them. You remember, at your party a few years ago. I hadn't spoken to either of them since then. Which is why I was so surprised when he ended up at my apartment that day. Jessie, why didn't Philip stay with one of the group?"

She looked uncomfortable. "He wanted to. Well, not with Vincent or Inez or Murray, of course—he was barely on speaking terms with them. He did call Dee and Dom, but they turned him down. Then he called me, but I've got three cats and he's allergic. He wanted me to board them, but with all the cat dander in the apartment, that wouldn't have helped. Then he called Neal, but he wasn't home. That's when he called me to get your number and address." She looked uncomfortable. "I thought he was just going to call you."

"It's not your fault he showed up," I said. Though I wished she hadn't given him my address, it was way too late to worry about it. "Colleen said she and Philip had been having problems for a while."

"Well, she didn't talk to us." Jessie's tone of voice made it plain that she considered this a personal affront. "When we started SSI, we thought she'd come and work with us, but she said she wasn't interested. After a while, we never saw her. She didn't even come to company parties anymore. Philip said she didn't have time for us."

"People do grow apart," I said. And miscommunication messes up lots of friendships, especially when the one doing the communicating is Philip.

Jessie sniffed. "She never was a real part of the group, anyway. Not like you were."

I wasn't sure if that was a compliment, or a complaint that I had grown away, too. "I appreciate the thought, Jessie, but I just didn't feel comfortable hanging around anymore. Not with Philip there, and especially not with the way he treated Richard." The rest of the group had been fairly cool to Richard, too.

She reached over and patted my arm. "We should never have let Philip get away with that, Laura. You were as much our friend as he was. It must have been lonely for you."

Part of me wanted to tell her that it had been very lonely, or would have been without Richard, but it was too late for her to apologize now. And part of me wanted to tell her that it hadn't bothered me a bit, that I had been glad to get away from them. But what I said was, "It was a long time ago. We were younger, which my Aunt Maggie says is another way of saying that we were stupider."

"It doesn't have to be like that now. We'd love to see more of you. Richard, too. Maybe you could come work at SSI." Before I responded to that, she added, "Things would have been different if you had come to work with us at the beginning. You always brought out the best in Philip."

Great! Now SSI's problems were my fault because I hadn't been there. "I was never invited to join SSI," I pointed out.

"You could have if you'd wanted to," she said airily, though it certainly hadn't felt that way to me at the time.

Admittedly, I hadn't wanted to work at SSI, and from the way things had turned out, it was clear that I had made the right decision, but it had bothered me at the time. And later, as we said our goodbyes, I realized that it still bothered me.

Chapter 11

I told the whole story to Thaddeous over takeout pizza that night, explaining the background he didn't know.

When I was done, he said, "It seems like we've got lots of reasons for murder."

"We? The night before last, it was just *me.*"

"You didn't think I was going to let you do this by your lonesome, did you? Richard would pin my hide to the wall, right next to his sword."

"Could be," I admitted. "Anyway, I'm glad for the help." I wasn't sure how much help he could be, so far away from his home territory, but then again, I wasn't sure how much I'd be able to do, either.

"Good enough." Then he hesitated. "I was thinking. We don't need to tell my mama about this, do we? Not right away, anyway. I don't want her worrying about me."

"Great. When she finds out, she's going to want *my* hide."

He just smiled and went on. "Like I said, everybody at that office had reason to want Philip out of the way. Especially Vincent—he sounds right ambitious to me. And Jessie might be more caught up in this company than she ought to be."

"I think so, too, but since she all but admitted to voting to keep Philip, why would she kill him? Come to think of it, who else was voting to keep Philip? From what Jessie was saying, they all wanted him gone. Maybe she'd vote for him to keep from breaking up the group, but what about the others?"

"They're your friends—you tell me."

"Well, Vincent and Inez were the ones behind getting rid of Philip in the first place, so surely they voted against him. And with the way Murray told Philip about the vote, he must have voted against him, too.

"Philip called Dee and Dom when he needed a place to stay, so he must have thought they had voted for him, but why would they have? Programming was always the most important thing to those two. Voting for Philip would mean that they couldn't do the kind of work they wanted to do."

"So what you're saying is that nobody wanted him there, but somebody was voting to keep him."

"Three somebodies. It doesn't make sense."

"Could Philip have stuffed the ballot box?"

"I don't think so. He didn't know about the first ballot in time, and I feel sure Vinnie would have kept him from fiddling with the second one."

"Do you suppose Jessie knows who voted what?"

"She might, but I don't think she'd tell me even if she did. Her first loyalty is to the group, and SSI." That meant I couldn't use my best source of information.

I sighed. I was like a fish out of water up here. In Byerly I knew almost everybody, and if I had to get to anybody I didn't know, somebody in my family could help me out. I had friends in Boston, but they were too scattered. "It's a shame I'm not like Michelle," I said.

"Why is that?"

Was it my imagination, or had Thaddeous's ears pricked up when I said her name? "It's just that she's real good at talking to people. She can get information out of you without your hardly noticing it. And she's got connections all over Boston, like your mama does in Byerly. Come to think of it, I wonder if she knows anybody at SSI."

"Mama?"

"No, Michelle. If she knows the receptionist over there, it sure could help. It was the receptionist who collected the ballots. Don't you think she'd have kept track of how everybody voted? And if the receptionist knows, Michelle can get it out of her."

"Do you think Michelle would help us?"

"I bet she would." I had once made the mistake of mentioning some of the incidents Richard and I'd been mixed up in, and every time I came back from Byerly, she grilled me to find out everything that had happened. "I know she'd do it if *you* asked her."

"Me?" Thaddeous said, sounding genuinely surprised. "Why would that make any difference?"

"I think she's sweet on you."

He shook his head. "I can't believe that, Laurie Anne."

"Then why is it that she hardly spoke to me when the three of us went out to dinner? She was too busy talking to you."

"She's just interested in people."

"There's interested, and then there's *interested*," I said. "Why don't you come to the office for lunch tomorrow, and we'll both ask her to help?"

"All right."

"And you could ask her out while you're there."

"I imagine she's got plenty of boyfriends."

"Then why has she been flirting with you?"

"She's just being friendly."

"Thaddeous, I've seen her act friendly. *This* is flirting."

"Do you really think so?"

"Lord, yes!"

He fiddled with his plate. "I'll think about it."

That was as much pushing as I could get away with. I finished my last piece of pizza and said, "So, what did you do today?"

"I went to that museum at Harvard you told me about."

"The one with the glass flowers? Aren't those the most amazing things?"

We spent the rest of the evening talking about Harvard and museums, and watching TV.

When I asked Michelle to go to lunch with me the next day, she accepted even before I told her that Thaddeous would be joining us. To make sure that we'd have plenty of time to talk, we didn't go anyplace far, just to the snack bar in the basement of our building.

As soon as we got our food and found a table, I said, "Michelle, we've got an ulterior motive for inviting you to lunch."

"Yeah?" she said, looking at Thaddeous significantly.

"You remember I told you that a friend of mine had died over the weekend?" I said. "Well, I know this sounds crazy, but we think he was murdered, and we want to find out who did it." I explained how I knew Philip, why it was we thought he had been murdered, the little I had found out so far, and what we wanted her to do. I ended with, "If you can find a connection to SSI and talk to the receptionist about those ballots, it could be just what we need."

"Let me get this straight. This guy Philip, who you used

to date but who you don't even like anymore, shows up on your doorstep and tries to bully you into taking him in. When you give him the bum's rush, he gets himself killed. Now you want me to help you find the killer?"

"Actually, all we want from you is a way to talk to that receptionist. After that, you don't have to be involved."

"Are you crazy? You think I'd pass up on a chance to help out with one of your cases?"

"But you said—" Thaddeous started to say.

"I was just getting things straight. I know Laura has done this kind of thing in North Carolina, but I never thought she'd get involved in anything up here. I mean, this is Boston, not Byerly. People don't go around solving their ex-boyfriends' murders."

"They don't often do it in Byerly, either," I admitted.

Thaddeous said, "Laurie Anne just wants to do the right thing. Even Yankee—even Northerners try to do the right thing, don't they?"

"Of course we do," Michelle said. "It's just that we've got a different idea about what the right thing is." She waved all that aside. "But it doesn't matter what your reasons are; I want to help. There's only one condition: I'm not going to just get you to this receptionist and then disappear. If I'm in, I'm in all the way."

"That's mighty nice of you, Michelle," Thaddeous said. "We can sure use the help."

Part of me wanted to say that in the past I had done just fine without her, but I had to admit that without my family and Richard to work with, we probably did need her.

"Of course, we'll have to remain in constant contact," she said. She was looking at Thaddeous when she said that, not at me. Maybe she wasn't so interested in finding a murderer as she was in finding her way into my cousin's affections.

"Absolutely," I said. "So do you know anybody at SSI?"

"No, but I bet somebody I know does. Or somebody I know knows somebody who does. Don't worry—I've got a network the *Boston Globe* would kill for. As soon as I get back to the office, I'll make some calls."

Lunch hour was nearly over by then. Thaddeous wanted to spend the afternoon shopping for souvenirs for folks back in Byerly, so I gave him directions to Downtown Crossing, the shopping district in the middle of town. Filene's Basement alone would probably keep him occupied for the rest of the day.

"That's nice, him looking for something for his mother," Michelle said to me as we went back to the office.

"He's always been real generous," I said.

"Will he be able to find her something nice? Some men are no good at buying for women."

"Thaddeous is. He's got wonderful taste, especially in jewelry. You should see the brooch he bought Aunt Nora for Mother's Day a few years ago. And this year, he got her earrings to match." Okay, I happened to know that Michelle had a weakness for jewelry, so I was stacking the deck.

"He's kind of shy, isn't he?"

"He can be," I admitted. "He's been burnt a few times in the past."

"I know how that can be."

She'd gone through several relationships since I had known her, so I imagine she did know.

By then we were back at the office, and as Michelle settled in at her desk, she said, "Let's see what I can do."

"Thanks, Michelle."

"My pleasure. Maybe we should get together for dinner, in case I find out something this afternoon. If you and Thaddeous don't have other plans, that is."

"Sounds good to me." Of course, I didn't have any idea that it was me she was interested in having dinner with.

Chapter 12

By dinnertime, Michelle had found a connection to Roberta, the receptionist at SSI. Michelle's friend Priscilla knew Roberta and had agreed to set up a lunch with her the next day. Michelle was going along, too.

Of course, Michelle didn't need to go to dinner with us to tell us that, which only strengthened my suspicions that she had designs on my cousin. The shy grin on Thaddeous's face when he saw her told me that he had ideas of his own.

"How did the shopping go?" Michelle asked.

"Tell you the truth," Thaddeous said, "I never made it to those stores y'all told me about. I was going to, but I got to thinking that it wasn't right for me to be off enjoying myself while y'all were doing all the work."

"Thaddeous, it's not your fault that you don't know anybody in Boston," I said.

"Of course not," Michelle added.

"But I want to do my part. After all, it's my doing that Laurie Anne's got herself mixed up in this mess." Before I could object, he went on. "We wondered just where it was that Philip went after he left here that day. Detective Salvatore said he'd been drinking, which means he either went drinking at somebody's house or he went to a bar. Since Laurie Anne said he was on foot when he left here, I thought I'd check out the bars within walking distance and ask if anybody had seen him."

"But Thaddeous," I said, "there must be more than a dozen bars around here." If anything, that was an understatement.

"There are right many more than I expected," he said. Then he grinned, and for the first time I realized that his face was flushed. "You know, folks back home are always saying that Yankees are unfriendly, but that just ain't so. I'd buy me a beer, start to talking to the bartender, and it wasn't no time before they were falling all over themselves to speak to me."

"It's that accent," Michelle said knowingly. "It just charms people."

I wasn't so sure it was the accent. Wasn't there an old saying about one drunk loving another? "Thaddeous, how many bars did you go into?"

"I'm not rightly sure."

"You didn't drink at all of them, did you?" I asked.

"I had to. It wouldn't have been polite otherwise."

"Now, that's what I call going above and beyond the call of duty," Michelle said.

"Of course, I didn't finish all the beers," Thaddeous admitted.

"A good thing, too," I said. Michelle might think it was funny, but all I could think of was what Aunt Nora would say if she ever found out her little boy had spent an entire afternoon bar-hopping. "Did you find out where Philip went?"

He shook his head. "And I think I hit all the likely places."

"You're sure they really hadn't seen him?" I said. "Maybe they were just blowing you off. Remembering a customer from several days ago would be asking a lot." And while I didn't want to admit it, sometimes Bostonians weren't the most friendly people.

"I think they were straight with me. With the snow that night, pretty much everybody said it was slow and they thought they'd have remembered him. So I guess I was wasting my time and money."

"Don't you worry about that," Michelle said soothingly. "You did good."

I said, "You know, if Philip didn't go to a bar, then it's that much more likely he went off with somebody."

"Like somebody from SSI?" Michelle asked.

I nodded. "And since as far as I know, nobody has owned up to seeing him that day, that makes SSI look pretty promising." I would loved to have left it at that, but my pessimistic side had to say, "Of course, he could have grabbed a cab or gotten on the subway and gone to a bar in another part of town."

Michelle waved away my objection. "Why would he do that and then come back to your place? That's nuts! We're making progress here, and you know it. We should celebrate."

"I don't know," I said doubtfully. "I think Thaddeous has celebrated enough already."

But Michelle waved that away, too, and before I knew it, the three of us were on our way to Durgin-Park, a restaurant famed both for prime rib and for incredibly rude waitresses. Knowing that the waitresses Thaddeous was used to were friendly to the point of intrusiveness, I was wondering how my cousin would react to a waitress wearing a button that said MEANEST, but I needn't have worried. Whether it was the company, the novelty, or the afternoon's beer, Thaddeous had a great time. The more the waitress made fun of him, the more he laughed.

After dinner, he insisted on the three of us taking a horse-drawn carriage ride. He was having so much fun, I didn't have the heart to tell him that I had heard that pulling a carriage amidst all the gasoline fumes in Boston isn't good for horses. Our horse looked like she was well taken care of, at least. I did try to make up a reason to bow out so he and Michelle could be alone, but I couldn't, so I settled for making sure he sat next to her.

I learned a long time ago that Boston isn't a perfect city. There's crime, and dirt, and ugliness—all the things you'd expect to find in a big city. But there's magic, too, in the cobblestone streets and lights reflecting on the harbor and the sleek, tall buildings sitting right next to historic churches and landmarks. And magic was all we saw on our ride that night.

Chapter 13

Michelle had lunch with Roberta, SSI's receptionist, the next day, and wanted to see Thaddeous and me that night to tell us what she had found out. Since it was cold and cloudy, instead of going out again, we met at my apartment and ordered in Chinese.

I think it was the first time Thaddeous had ever had Chinese food, and he looked a little dubious about it. But after encouragement from Michelle, he gave it a try. I don't think he loved it, but he didn't hate it, either. And he got a big kick out of the fortune cookies.

My fortune said, "The pen is mightier than the sword, but take the sword anyway, just in case," and Michelle's said, "A journey of a thousand miles begins with a single step." Thaddeous didn't want to share his, but I grabbed it out of his hand and read it out loud, "Romance is right around the corner." If I hadn't known better, I'd have thought that Michelle had arranged it.

With dinner out of the way, I asked Michelle, "What did you find out?"

"I found out that Roberta doesn't deserve to call herself a secretary. Would you believe that she collected those ballots without even trying to see who voted what?"

"Are you sure?" I said. "Maybe she just didn't want to tell you."

Michelle nodded emphatically. "I'm sure. I had Priscilla steer the conversation toward office politics right off the bat, dropping hints like crazy, but even then it took Roberta forever even to come out with the story. It's got to be the most exciting thing that's happened at her office in a year. You'd think she'd want to talk about it."

"Is she that discreet?" I asked.

"She's not discreet—she's dense. I asked if she hadn't snuck a peek. Anyone would have, I told her. She just looked at me like she didn't know what I was talking about. 'Why would I have done that?' she asks. Can you believe that? The ballots weren't even sealed—just folded over." She tossed her hair. "Priscilla or I or any other secretary would have known exactly who wrote what, even if they had been sealed."

Thaddeous asked, "Didn't this Roberta even have a guess? Maybe from how they acted when they gave her the ballots?"

Michelle looked even more disgusted. "It never occurred to her to wonder about it. I'm telling you—this is the most dense woman I have ever met."

I said, "You tried. I'm just sorry you had to waste a lunch hour."

Michelle tried to look innocent, but a tiny grin snuck out. "Well, I wouldn't say it was completely wasted."

"What did you find out?" I demanded.

"After I was sure that Roberta knew nothing about the ballots, I asked her about what had gone on between the two votes. You know how you said that Vincent and Philip were trying to drum up votes?"

I nodded.

"Well, I asked Roberta if she knew what it was either of them said. Or how the conversations went. I mean, if Philip went to talk to this Dom person and came out with a smile, chances are that Dom had told him he'd vote for him."

"That's pretty smart," Thaddeous said admiringly.

"Did you get anything?" I wanted to know.

"It's hard to tell. Roberta heard only parts of a few conversations, so you tell me if any of it means anything."

"Let's hear it."

"Okay, she heard Philip talking to Vinnie. Pardon me, *Vincent*. Vinnie is a good enough name for my uncle and my grandfather, but apparently not good enough for Mr. CEO. Anyway, Roberta went by Vincent's office a couple of days after the first vote. The door was closed, but Roberta could hear Philip yelling something about Vincent's rat."

"His rat?" I said.

"That's what she said. His rat. Does that mean anything to you?"

I shook my head. A computer has a mouse, but I never heard it called a rat, and there's a rat-tail hairstyle, but Vincent didn't wear one. "Maybe Philip was calling Vincent a rat for voting to fire him," I said. "What else?"

"Next is Inez, and she's more promising. Roberta heard her yelling at Philip that he'd better not tell anybody, and that nobody would believe him if he did."

"Tell anybody what?"

"You got me. Inez must have some secret or another. Next was Murray. Roberta heard Murray laughing at Philip, followed by Philip yelling at Murray, and Murray laughing some more. Roberta said Philip was apeshit!"

"I'm not surprised. Nothing got Philip madder than being

laughed at." One time I laughed at him myself when he slipped and fell in the snow. I didn't mean to be mean, and I could tell he hadn't hurt himself. Even so, Philip hadn't spoken to me for days afterward. "But that would have been a motive for Philip to kill Murray, not the other way around."

"That's what almost happened right there in the office. Roberta was sure that Philip was going to hit Murray, but he just stormed out."

"One thing about Philip," I said. "I never knew him to resort to physical violence."

"He sounds like a coward to me," Thaddeous said. "A man's got to fight sometimes."

"A *real* man does," Michelle said, looking at Thaddeous.

This was starting to sound like a Kenny Rogers song. "Anything else?" I said.

"That's it." She sighed. "Roberta is hopeless. How can you take care of your people if you don't know what they're up to?"

That was the best rationalization for snooping I had ever heard, but considering I was snooping myself, I didn't have any room to talk.

"So what do you think? Does any of this help?" she asked.

"Maybe," I said. "We don't know who voted what, but we do know that people voted differently from what we'd have expected. If you hear about an election that didn't go the way you'd expected, what's the first thing you think of?"

"Payola," Michelle said at the same time Thaddeous said, "Blackmail."

"I don't think Philip could afford to pay enough for it to

be worth losing a job," I said, "but I can see him trying to blackmail people into voting for him. When he was over here, he said something about 'rattling cages' to get people off his back. And what Inez said to him sure sounds like he was trying to blackmail her."

"If you ask me, blackmail is about as low as a man can get without digging a hole," Thaddeous said.

I had to agree. Our Aunt Daphine had been tormented by a blackmailer a while back, and I didn't like the idea of anybody having to go through what she had.

Thaddeous asked, "Do you think he was trying to blackmail the entire company?"

I said, "He wouldn't have to. He had three votes already. So all he'd have to do is go after the other three, or make sure that the three votes he had didn't change."

"But how would he find out anything he could blackmail people with?" Michelle wanted to know. "It sounds like nobody trusted him."

"Maybe nobody trusted him these days," I said, "but he'd known these folks ever since college. People in college tend to tell each other secrets, and people do things in college that they might not want known about afterward."

"Not you, Laura," Michelle said, in mock shock.

"No, of course not," I said, batting my eyes. "Other than having been a transvestite, a Satanist, and a communist, I'm as pure as the driven snow."

That broke them up, which made me think that maybe my reputation was a little *too* squeaky clean.

"You'd better not let Vasti hear you say that," Thaddeous said. "She's likely to believe you, and she'll have it spread all over Byerly in no time."

"Anyway," I said, trying to get us back on the subject, "Philip was good at getting confidences out of people. He'd confess something first, and then you'd tell him something. Even though I have to wonder now how many of his confessions were made up out of whole cloth, at the time it was very effective."

"You think he planned to blackmail people? That long ago?" Michelle asked.

"I don't think so—he just liked knowing things about people."

"So you're thinking that one of those folks he was trying to blackmail killed him instead," Thaddeous said.

I nodded, and Michelle's eyes got bigger and rounder.

"Jeez," she said, "if only Roberta had heard more of those conversations. I should have gotten more out of her."

"You did just fine," Thaddeous said firmly. "Better than anybody could be expected to do in their first try at undercover work."

"Undercover work," Michelle said, with a slightly different emphasis. "I like the sound of that."

While they made eyes at one another, I thought about something. "Maybe undercover work is just what we need."

Thaddeous said, "Meaning what?"

"Meaning a prospective employee at SSI might hear more than an outsider. When I talked to Vinnie at the visitation, he halfway offered me a job, and I think he was serious. Jessie said something about it, too. Maybe I can get an interview over there, and see what I can find out. Prospective employees are supposed to ask questions."

"That's not a bad idea," Michelle said.

"In fact," I said, "I think I'll call him the first thing Monday morning and set up an appointment. Only I'd better call him before I go to work."

"Why's that?" Thaddeous asked.

"I'd rather not call from the office. *Our* secretary finds out everything that's going on, and I don't want the boss to find out that I'm interviewing."

Chapter 14

I hated having to wait two days to call Vincent, but the next day was Saturday. The three of us tried to come up with something useful to do, but the only suggestion was Thaddeous volunteering to make sure he hadn't missed any bars. I quickly vetoed that.

Instead, Michelle and I were forced to show Thaddeous more of Boston. Okay, it wasn't that bad. We spent Saturday afternoon at the Science Museum, looking at exhibits and watching artificial lightning bolts, and exploring the museum shop, which has some of the best toys I've ever seen. Even for big kids like us.

Saturday night, Michelle insisted that we take in some of Boston's night life, and though I was afraid it would be awkward for two women and one man to go out, the clubs Michelle picked were so crowded that you couldn't tell who was dancing with whom anyway.

Sunday morning we had brunch, but then I begged off. If I was going to interview the next week, I had to put together a résumé and make sure I had a clean suit to wear. Even if I didn't really want the job, I had to go through the motions.

Thaddeous and Michelle went to Downtown Crossing, the shopping zone Thaddeous had neglected for his detective work. I had a hunch that Michelle was checking out Thaddeous's gift-buying talents, but I was happy they were having a good time together.

With them gone, I had a chance to call Richard and catch him up on all that had happened. It wasn't that I wanted to ask for his approval before I went looking for Philip's killer, because that's not the kind of relationship we have. But I did want to use him as a sounding board, and make sure I wasn't going off half-cocked.

As it turned out, Richard had just returned from a matinee performance of *Hamlet* and promptly launched into a description of it.

"It was wonderful, Laura," he said. "A traditional performance, in Elizabethan dress, with sets that were as close as they could get to period. And what a Hamlet! I never saw such aching indecision on anybody's face."

"It does sound wonderful," I said.

"What about you and Thaddeous? Are you having a good time?"

"Absolutely."

"You're not still feeling guilty about Philip, are you?"

"Not exactly."

There was a pause. "You're up to something, aren't you?"

"Actually, we are." I told him how I had decided to try to find out how Philip had died, and what we had done to get started. When I was finished, there was a long silence, which wasn't a good sign. Richard isn't a silent man.

"Are you still there?" I finally asked.

"Just struggling with my Neanderthal instincts."

"I beg your pardon?"

"I'm trying to resist the urge to tell you to stay home and out of danger. And it's not easy."

"Would it help if I told you that I have every intention of being careful?"

"Probably not," he said. "That would require me to be rational, and Neanderthals were not known for their rationality."

There was another long silence. Then I heard him breathe deeply and say, "Good luck. Let me know if there's anything I can do to help."

"Thank you, Richard." If he had tried to *order* me not to look into Philip's death, I'd have done it anyway, but I honestly don't know how I'd have reacted if he had *asked* me not to. I was grateful that I didn't have to find out. "I'm just glad you don't think I'm nuts for wanting to do this."

"Why would I think you're nuts? To do so much for Philip after the way he treated you is incredibly noble. I'm proud of you."

"Thank you." There was one of those silences that would have been filled with a hug, a kiss, or at least hand-holding if we had been in the same place.

Then Richard said, "Now, despite those sentiments, I am going to be Neanderthal enough to say that I wish I were there with you."

"I'd rather you were here, too, but I don't think this will wait until you get back. I know I couldn't live with it until then."

"Of course you couldn't," he said. "Would it be unforgivably Neanderthal of me to say that I'm glad that Thaddeous is there with you since I can't be?"

"Would you be glad if a female relative were here?"

"Absolutely. Especially if it were Aunt Maggie. No offense to Thaddeous, but she's probably tougher than he is."

"Then no, you're not being Neanderthal. Just concerned."

To distract him from worrying, I then told him about Michelle's obvious interest in Thaddeous. "The problem is, while it's plain to me that Michelle likes Thaddeous and that Thaddeous likes Michelle, Thaddeous hasn't figured out that Michelle likes him, and Michelle can't figure out what's taking him so long."

" 'The course of true love never did run smooth.' *A Midsummer Night's Dream*, Act I, Scene 1. Laura, you're not playing matchmaker, are you?"

"Of course not."

He didn't say anything.

"I haven't had time."

"You're not using this murder thing just as an excuse to get the two of them together, are you?"

"No, but it is a good way to make sure they spend some time together, don't you think?"

"I'm out of town just over a week and my wife is investigating a murder and matchmaking. I don't know which worries me more."

Chapter 15

When I called SSI the next morning, Vincent said he'd be tickled to death to talk to me about a job. Well, actually he said stuff like "enthused" and "eager to discuss possibilities," but I knew what he meant. He'd have met with me right away, but I put him off until Tuesday morning so I could come up with an excuse to take time off from my real job.

Michelle actually had plans of her own that night, so Thaddeous and I stayed home and went to sleep on time for a change. At least, Thaddeous did. I sat up and worried about the interview. I always do that when I've got a job interview.

I don't like job interviews. You try to write a résumé with no typos, wear something fashionable yet businesslike, show up early but not so early that you look anxious, answer questions with the answers they want to hear, and ask for enough money but not so much that it scares them.

At the same time, you're trying to figure out whether or not this is the kind of place you want to work at. Would they give you interesting projects to work on, and respect your opinion, and not expect you to work twenty-hour days, and maybe even give you a pat on the back when you do a good job?

This time, I guess I was nervous out of habit. It was the

first interview I had ever gone on for a job that I flat out didn't want. All I wanted was to see what I could find out about the inner workings at SSI.

A woman who had to be Roberta was at the front desk when I walked into SSI the next morning. "Hi!" I said. "My name's Laura Fleming, and I've got a nine-thirty appointment with Mr. Noone."

She looked up at me dully for a minute, so I repeated it.

"I guess I should let him know you're here." She called Vinnie, then said, "He'll be right up." She went back to her computer without saying anything else.

No wonder Michelle hadn't been impressed. In the two or three minutes it took for Vinnie to come get me, Michelle would have found out my marital status, number of children, town of residence, and favorite TV show.

Vinnie was again dressed to impress, this time in a dark blue suit with an artsy patterned tie that was just this side of flamboyant. "Laura, good to see you again."

"Thanks, Vinnie—Vincent." As sensitive as I am about people calling me Laurie Anne, the least I could do was call him by the name he preferred.

"Let me show you around," he said.

The office was quietly plush, with gray walls and burgundy carpeting. Roberta's desk was separated by a door from the rest of the office. Beyond that was a corridor lined with doors. Vincent opened the first two to show me a conference room and a smaller room set up for product demonstrations. The next few doors were offices, with name plates outside. I saw Jessie talking on the phone in one office and Murray sitting behind stacks of paper in another. Two neighboring offices were marked "Vincent Noone" and "Inez Parra."

At the end of the hall was another door that led into the work area. No offices here, just a big space broken into cubicles with four-foot-tall partitions. From where I was standing, I could see Dee, Dom, Neal, and Sheliah working away—there wasn't a whole lot of privacy.

There was a trash can overflowing with pizza boxes just inside the door, and the carpet was mottled with stains. Instead of the tasteful corporate art in mauve and cool blues I had seen in the public areas, the walls back here were covered with Star Trek posters and white boards filled with arcane notations.

As if he could guess what I was thinking, Vincent said, "We like the programmers to be comfortable."

"Uh huh," I said. Most of the computer companies I know of spend time and money to dress up the areas customers see, but don't bother in the rooms behind the scenes.

"Shall we go to my office and talk?" Vincent said.

He led me back the way we had come to a corner office, complete with windows on two sides and sleek Scandinavian furniture. Vincent's extravagantly framed MIT diploma was hung above a photo of him in cap and gown. Next to that was a photo of Vincent and three other young men, all wearing college sweatshirts. Vincent's was from MIT, of course, and the other three were from Harvard, Yale, and Dartmouth.

"Your brothers?" I asked him. When he nodded, I added, "That's an impressive collection of degrees. Your parents must be proud of y'all." Quite a difference from my family. I was the only one in my generation to go to college.

There was a small, round table in one corner, and Vincent waved me toward one of the chairs next to it and took the chair opposite. "Did you bring me a résumé? Just a formality, of course," he added, letting me know we were all friends here.

I pulled a copy out of my rarely used briefcase and handed it to him. We talked business for a few minutes, with my explaining projects I had worked on and his letting me know how that experience would apply to plans at SSI.

The only tricky part was when Vincent asked why I wanted to leave my current job. I had given this a lot of thought on the way over, wanting to sound sincere without bad-mouthing my company. The computer industry isn't that big—anything I said here just might find its way back to my boss.

I said, "I'm not sure I want to leave. It's just that I've been at GBS for several years, and I wanted to get a feel for what else is available. It never pays to get stuck in a rut."

"I understand," Vincent said. "I hope you see SSI as a promising alternative." He put down my résumé. "This looks good, which is no surprise. I knew you were going to be an excellent worker all those years ago at MIT. And you have the potential for management, unlike many of our comrades with the brass rat." He fingered the MIT class ring he was wearing.

I murmured an appropriate thank-you before what he said sank in. The symbol on the MIT class ring is actually a beaver, which makes sense for a school that turns out so many engineers and applied scientists, but somewhere along the line, folks started calling it a brass rat, and that's what most MIT graduates call their degree. According to Roberta, Philip had threatened Vincent with something to do with a rat. Could it have been his brass rat?

Fortunately, Vincent had gone into a monologue about the goals of SSI, so he didn't realize I wasn't paying attention to him. I focused in again just as he ended his spiel with, "Are there any questions you'd like to ask?"

This was the opportunity I had been waiting for. "A couple. I've been hearing rumors that you're planning to take SSI public." I added, "Not from anybody here at SSI," when he raised his eyebrows. "I just wondered how that would affect the office."

"Well, I had been trying to keep the planned stock offering quiet, but it *is* difficult to keep secrets. The fact is that the only effects I expect are good ones. We're hoping to expand dramatically, in all areas. You'd be the first of many new hires, and I'd like very much to have you in a supervisory position. Though we have very good programming talent here, there's little interest in management."

In other words, Vincent wanted to move on to bigger things than day-to-day supervising. I couldn't blame him for that, and management did sound appealing.

At least, it would have, had I not had other reasons for being there. "This may not be any of my business, but I'm a little concerned about something Philip said. He told me he was being pushed out of the company. Can you give me some background on that?"

He leaned back in his chair, not looking surprised by the question, but not looking happy about it, either. "That was awkward," he admitted. "We were old friends, but Philip wasn't willing to let this company grow in the direction it needs to."

Meaning that like Jessie told me, Philip hadn't wanted to update StatSys.

"Nobody was sorrier than I was when I realized that we were going to have to force him out, but he had made some alarming threats about what he might do if SSI went public."

That also fit in with what Jessie had said.

Vincent went on. "I personally spoke with everyone here, and we all agreed that there was really no other choice. And of course, with the recent tragedy, it's a moot point now." He looked regretful on cue, just like a funeral director on duty. "Does that reassure you?"

"To tell you the truth, Vincent, I'm surprised it took as long as it did. Maybe we're all old friends, but friends and business don't always mix."

Vincent smiled, obviously relieved. "I just hope that's not true in this case. I want you to come to work at SSI, Laura."

There weren't any more questions I felt I could legitimately ask, so we talked money for a few minutes. I had thought the salary I was requesting was high, giving me an easy way out, but Vincent didn't even blink. So I had to leave it at, "I'd like some time to think about it."

"Could you let me know by the end of the week? I don't wish to rush you, but we *are* eager to get things moving."

"Absolutely."

We shook hands, and he showed me out. Jessie was off the phone and looked up as we passed by. I was going to have to call her soon to let her know what was going on. At least, part of it.

Chapter 16

It was nearly lunchtime when I got back to my side of town, so instead of going into work, I stopped at a pay phone in the lobby of our building. "Michelle? This is Laura."

"It's about time!"

"Has Thaddeous called?"

"He's up here waiting for you."

"Why don't the two of you meet me downstairs for lunch so I can tell you what happened?"

"We're on the way."

I got to the snack bar first, got soup and a sandwich, and found us a table. When I saw them coming, I couldn't help but notice that they made an awfully cute couple.

Now stop that, I told myself. I was getting to be as bad as my cousin Vasti. These were two adults, and they were certainly capable of arranging their own affairs. Just because Michelle was interested in Thaddeous, that didn't mean he was interested in her. It's just that I could tell that he was interested by the way he opened the door for her, escorted her to the table, helped her off with her coat, and held her chair for her. Not that Thaddeous isn't always a gentleman, but he never has that look in his eye when he holds a chair for his mama.

"So? What did you find out?" Michelle asked.

"Vincent offered me a job."

"Don't you dare leave GBS!"

"I'm not going to leave," I said, "but after the money he offered me, I *am* thinking about asking for a raise."

"It's blood money," Michelle said. "He feels bad about killing Philip right behind your apartment."

"Silly me, I thought he might be interested in my programming skills."

"Oh, Laura, everyone knows you're a dynamite programmer. I just don't trust this Vincent character."

"I'm not sure I trust him myself," I admitted, "but that doesn't mean he killed Philip."

"What else happened?" Thaddeous said.

"That's about it," I said. "Vincent confirmed a lot of what Jessie told me, but he didn't tell me anything new. There is one thing I might have figured out. Remember how Roberta said she had heard Philip and Vincent talking about a rat?"

"They don't have rats in that building, do they?" Michelle asked.

"Not live ones, but they've got plenty of brass rats."

"I don't get it."

I held out my hand with my MIT class ring. "See my ring? That critter on it is called a brass rat."

They inspected the carving on the ring.

"It doesn't look like a rat to me," Thaddeous said. "More like a beaver."

"It *is* a beaver," Michelle said. "Look at the tail."

"You're right, it's a beaver. But everybody at MIT calls it a brass rat."

"How come?" Thaddeous wanted to know.

"Why are North Carolinians Tar Heels? Why is Boston the Hub?"

Both of them started to answer at once, defending their native state or city, but I managed to talk over them. "People just call it that. I don't know why."

"So you're saying that Vincent and Philip were arguing over a ring?" Thaddeous said, looking doubtful.

Michelle asked, "You think Philip stole Vincent's ring, or maybe Vincent stole Philip's?"

"Detective Salvatore said that Philip was wearing his class ring when they found his body, and Vincent still has his, too. But I bet that class ring is involved somehow." I had to admit that it didn't sound like a whole lot from the morning's work, but it was all I had. "So how did you end up on this side of town?" I asked Thaddeous.

He said, "As a matter of fact, I found out something myself this morning, and wanted to tell you."

"He's such a good detective," Michelle said, as proudly as if she had taught him herself.

Thaddeous just grinned, and said, "I saw that neighbor of yours this morning, the one who told us about the police finding Philip's body."

"John?"

Thaddeous nodded. "He was having trouble with his car, so I went out to try to give him a hand. Only it turned out he has a problem with his starter, and I couldn't help him with that. So he called Triple A and asked me in for a cup of coffee while he waited."

"Really?" Richard and I had been living a floor above John for four years without ever having seen the inside of his apartment. Of course, we had never tried to help him with a dead car, either.

"Anyway, we got to talking about Philip. The police questioned John about him, too. They asked when he had last been in the alley, and it turns out he went back there that night to take his trash to the dumpster just after it started snowing. He's sure Philip's body wasn't there then."

"We already knew he wasn't there all night," I said. "There wasn't that much snow on him."

Thaddeous said, "The thing was, Salvatore wasn't completely sure he wasn't with you that evening. He talked to John after he talked to us and asked him if he'd seen Philip visiting you before."

"I hadn't seen Philip in ages," I said indignantly. "He'd never been in my apartment before that day."

"Calm down," Thaddeous said. "That's just what John told him. At least, he told him he'd never seen him around. Salvatore even asked if John had heard anything from your apartment the day Philip died."

"Had he?" I asked, wondering just what John had been hearing from above us for the past four years.

"He heard some of the argument with Philip, but he also heard the door slam when Philip left. And he didn't hear him come back."

"Good," I said. "That proves that Philip went somewhere else after he left my place. And hopefully the police don't suspect me."

"That's what it looks like," Thaddeous said. "I told John I sure appreciated him speaking up for you like that. Folks back home are always saying that Yankees don't look after their neighbors, but that's just not so."

"Of course we do," Michelle said.

As for me, I was feeling guilty. I wasn't even sure of John's last name, and I had never paid attention to his comings and goings. Richard and I were going to have to get to know him.

Thaddeous said, "I got a chance to return the favor a little while later. Triple A came, and I went back to your place. When I went outside again, somebody had gone into your building and pulled out a couple of folding chairs that belonged to John. He'd left them leaned against the wall outside his door, and now they were sitting in the street."

"In the street?" I said.

"Yep. Smack dab in the middle of the place where John's car had been parked. Kids, I guess. So I picked them up and put them back were they belonged."

Michelle and I looked at each other. I had seen John carefully shovel out that parking space after the snowstorm, and thought about explaining to Thaddeous that it was customary for Bostonians to claim their parking places by placing lawn furniture or sawhorses in them. But I didn't want to make him feel bad. So I just said, "That was nice of you."

Michelle said, "I want to know why Philip was behind your apartment like that." Then her eyes got big. "Maybe he was a peeping Tom. Or maybe he was stalking you. You read about that in the papers all the time. He could have been waiting for you to come out so he could grab you."

It was a nicely creepy theory, but I had to shake my head. "I don't think so, Michelle. If he wanted to grab me, he'd have had a much better shot at it from the front of the apartment. I almost never go back in the alley, and he'd have no reason to think that I did."

"Then he was watching you through the rear window so he'd know when you went out and came back."

"My apartment has only one window on that side, and it's in the bathroom." Before she could do anything with that, I added, "It's six inches wide, and way up high in the shower.

Besides which, it's translucent glass, not clear, so about all he'd see is the shadow of the very top of my head. I don't think that'd be enough for even the most dedicated stalker. And that's if he could figure out which window was mine, which would be tough, considering he never saw anything of my apartment other than the living room." Whatever reason Philip had had for returning to my apartment, it hadn't been to leer at me from a distance.

Thaddeous said, "I saw some cars parked there when we were back there with Detective Salvatore."

"Philip didn't have a car," I said.

"But whoever he was with might have had one," Thaddeous said.

"Maybe, but why would they be coming back to see me?"

"Maybe they weren't. Maybe the other person only brought Philip back there so he or she could kill him, and then leave the body there to frame you. Come to think of it, do we know Philip died back there?"

"Detective Salvatore didn't say anything different," I said.

"I'm not nearly so interested in why he was back there as I am in where he went before that and who he was with," Michelle said. "And I'd like to know where those SSI people were that afternoon."

"You and me both," I said. "Unfortunately, I couldn't very well ask Vincent about that."

"Can you talk to Jessie again?" Thaddeous asked.

"I think she'd get suspicious. If she thought I suspected one of them of murder, she'd clam up in a heartbeat."

"Assuming that she's not the murderer herself," Michelle pointed out.

"She's the one who told Philip where I live," I said, "mean-

ing that she knew he was going to be there." She'd said she
thought he was just going to call me, but if that was so, why
had she given him my address?

Michelle said, "So she picked him up outside your door,
and then brought him back later to kill him. It all fits."

"Mightn't she have killed him to protect her friends? Either from the blackmail or from losing their jobs?" Thaddeous said. "Or maybe he was blackmailing her, too."

"It's possible, but at this point, *anything* is possible. We
just don't know enough. What we need is a reliable inside
source at SSI. Only we can't enlist anybody because they're
all suspects. Unless . . ." I thought about it for a minute.
"Maybe I should take that job."

"Oh, no, you don't!" Michelle said.

"I wouldn't really quit, but I could take some time off and
tell Vincent that I've quit. How would he know the difference? He's already offered me the job, so he'd have no reason to check my references."

"I don't know if it's a good idea for you to be spending so
much time with a bunch of murder suspects," Thaddeous said.
"If anything was to happen to you, Richard would have my
hide. If Mama didn't beat him to it. For all we know, those
folks were all in it together."

Now, that was a really creepy notion, but I didn't believe
it. "Thaddeous, as much of a pain as Philip was, it still took
the group months to decide to try and fire him. It would have
taken them *years* to agree to kill him. And nobody's going to
try anything in broad daylight, in the middle of an office."

Thaddeous quit objecting, and Michelle and I concocted
ways to deal with our boss and contingency plans in case Vincent called about me. To keep from messing up my insurance, I'd claim that I was covered through Richard's job. I

was a little fuzzy about duplicate tax forms, but Michelle was fairly sure that I wouldn't get into trouble as long as Uncle Sam got his share. Like I told Thaddeous, trying to find a killer didn't scare me nearly as much as messing with the IRS.

As soon as Michelle and I got to the office after lunch, I went in to talk to my boss. He wasn't too difficult about my taking time off, especially when I used Thaddeous's visit as an excuse and the fact that I had just finished a big project as justification. I promised that I'd be gone no longer than two weeks, and that I'd work at home if anything urgent came up. Under the circumstances, I decided not to ask for a raise right then.

My message light was blinking when I got back to my desk. Jessie had left voice mail, wanting to know if it was true that I was coming to work for SSI. I called her back and told her that I was seriously considering it, but I wanted to talk to Richard before I decided for sure. She was delighted by the idea.

At first, that made me think that she couldn't have killed Philip. If she had, the last one she'd want around would be the person she'd tried to frame. Then I started thinking like Michelle, wondering if maybe Jessie didn't just want a better opportunity to get at me. Between trying to sort that idea out and keeping my voice low to make sure nobody suspected I was taking anything but a normal vacation, I got off the phone quickly.

Actually, I hadn't just been stalling with Jessie. I did want to talk to Richard. So after dinner that night, I left Thaddeous alone with the TV and went into the bedroom to call him. With the time difference, my seven o'clock phone call was going to wake him up at midnight, but I didn't think he'd mind too much. It turned out he wasn't in bed yet because he had just returned from a performance of *King Lear* that he had enjoyed even more than the *Hamlet*.

Once he finished telling me why, and I allowed as how I would have liked to have seen it myself, he said, "How goes the investigation? Got the miscreant under lock and key?"

"Not yet," I said. "Lots of suspects, a few motives, but no conclusions. I do have some ideas about where to go next." I told him about my plan to infiltrate SSI. "What do you think? Will it work?"

"It might," he said, "but I'm not sure exactly what it is you'll be looking for."

"I'm not exactly sure myself. It's just that I'm sure that SSI is the key to what happened to Philip, or rather, somebody at SSI is. This just seems like the best way to be around them all enough to figure out who it was."

"If the murderer is at SSI, won't he or she think it suspicious if you go to work there?"

"I don't see why. None of them knows about the kinds of things we've done in Byerly."

"Not even Jessie?"

"Nope, I never told her about it. We really haven't told that many people up here. Michelle knows, but that's only because Michelle can get anything out of anybody."

"Then maybe Michelle should go undercover. Not," he added quickly, "to impugn your deductive abilities."

"I did think about that, but they need a programmer, not a receptionist. Besides, there's a certain snobbishness in computer companies. Programmers usually don't hang around with administrative personnel. Or maybe it's vice versa." My own friendship with Michelle was unusual. "Either way, I think it'll be easier for me to talk to the folks at SSI than it would be for Michelle. Plus, Thaddeous would have a conniption if I suggested putting her in danger."

"So the budding romance is beginning to bloom."

"Maybe not blooming yet, but something's going on."

"Now, tell me why it is Thaddeous would keep Michelle away from SSI, but I shouldn't keep *you* away from there?"

"Because I'll be very careful. Besides, I've known these people for years."

"Hadn't Philip known them even longer?"

It was an uncomfortable question, but he had a point. "Yes."

"And you still think one of them killed him?"

"Yes. Though I'd love to be proved wrong."

"Well, until you are proved wrong, don't forget that somebody there might be a killer. No clandestine meetings in dark offices, no after-work outings except in public, no eating gifts of food unless they're factory sealed, no accepting ticking packages—the usual precautions."

"I promise."

We moved on to other matters, but not for very long. As eager as Vincent had been, I was pretty sure that he'd want me to start at SSI as soon as possible, probably before the end of the week. That meant that I had a busy day ahead to take care of loose ends at GBS so I could go to SSI with a clear conscience, and I needed a good night's sleep.

I called Vincent before I left for work the next morning and gave him the good news. I knew he wouldn't ask why I hadn't given two weeks' notice. One benefit of working for computer companies is that they frequently don't expect or even want a person to work out his notice. Since a system can easily be damaged by a disgruntled employee, and since people who quit tend to be disgruntled, it's safer to pay out the notice and let the person leave.

Vincent was gratifyingly enthusiastic and wanted me to start immediately, but I talked him into waiting until the next day. I wanted a little time before walking into the lion's den.

Chapter 17

the whole way. But Maria's enthusiasm, and warmth, made a great impression on me, I must run into her. Wanting to tell her that I wanted to talk now with a thinking, but the local was

I was at SSI bright and early Thursday morning, only to find that nobody was at the front desk. "Hello?" I called out.

A bleary-eyed Roberta came in from the back. "Can I help you?"

"Hi. I'm Laura Fleming."

There was no hint of recognition in her face.

"I'm supposed to start working here today."

"I forgot. Vincent hasn't come in yet." She looked around as if hoping somebody had posted instructions. "I guess you can wait for him up here."

"All right," I said, not the least bit impressed. Not only would Michelle have recognized me immediately and known that I'd be starting work, she'd also have taken me to my desk and shown me around.

Roberta didn't bother to try to make conversation with me, just worked on something at her PC. She didn't even offer me coffee.

After about ten minutes, Inez came in and went to Roberta's desk. "Any messages?"

"Not yet."

"Good morning, Inez," I said.

Inez turned and saw me. "So you are coming to work here."

Not exactly a warm welcome. "I thought so. Did you and Vincent not discuss it?"

"Vinnie deigned to send me a memo. I take it that he isn't here yet."

I shook my head, and realized that she was the only one at SSI who still used the name "Vinnie." I didn't think it was because it was a pet name.

She said, "Typical. Why don't you come on into my office? I need to talk to you anyway. You want some coffee?"

I followed her to the break room to get coffee, then back to her office. I was tickled when I noticed that Inez's office was the exact same size as Vincent's, with the same furniture. The difference was that she only had one window, not two, and I just knew that it had started a fight.

I couldn't help but think of my Aunt Nellie's three daughters. They were triplets, and when they were children, if one of them got more or less of anything than the others, you'd have thought the world was coming to an end. I wondered if Vincent and Inez had measured each other's offices to ensure that the dimensions were the same.

Inez sat behind her desk and motioned me toward a guest chair. "Look, Laura, I don't want you to think that I'm not glad you're here. I think you'll be a great asset. It's just that Vinnie should have consulted me before hiring you. I don't even know what it is you're supposed to be doing."

"From what he said at the interview, I think I'm supposed to work with Neal. Neal is going to concentrate on the code and let me work on the user interface."

"Okay, that makes sense. I was afraid he wanted you to

work on something stupid." She looked at my expression and laughed. "You must be wondering what you've let yourself in for."

"It had crossed my mind," I admitted. "I've never started a job by telling the chief operating officer what I'll be doing."

"Well, SSI isn't like other companies. Vinnie refuses to stay off my turf, and that makes it hard for the rest of us. Mother of God, how did I ever put up with him when we were dating?"

It sounded like a good time for girl talk. "I know what you mean. I can't figure out how I put up with Philip for over two years."

"I never did understand that," she said. "He was so full of life and noise, and you were so quiet."

"I wasn't *that* quiet," I said, stung by her description, probably because it was too accurate.

"You know what I mean. Compared to Philip."

"Compared to Philip, *you* were quiet."

"You're right. If he had just grown up to be the man he started out to become, it would have been very different around here. As it was . . ." She shrugged.

"Is it true that y'all were trying to fire him?" I said.

"How did you hear that?"

I looked toward Vincent's office, which was bound to give her the wrong impression, and said, "Maybe I shouldn't say." It wasn't quite a lie, but it was darned close.

Inez looked disgusted. "Some people should learn to keep their mouths shut. Yes, we did want to fire him, and he was fighting us every step of the way."

This next part was iffy, but I tried it anyway. "Is it true that he tried to blackmail people?"

She looked startled. "Vincent told you that?"

Instead of answering, I just looked uncomfortable.

"Okay, don't say. I suppose you could call it blackmail. Philip threatened to tell people that he and I had slept together." She held up one hand. "Not while the two of you were together, that I swear. And before he was with Colleen. Never do I touch another woman's man."

An interesting distinction, considering the period she was talking about. "But weren't you and Vincent still . . . ?"

She shrugged her shoulders. "It was just the once—I was drunk. Besides, what difference does it make now? Philip thought I wouldn't want Vinnie to know, but I don't care one way or the other. Why should I?" Then she lowered her voice. "Did Vinnie tell you what Philip had on him?"

"Actually, it wasn't Vincent who told me," I said, improvising quickly. "It was Philip. And he didn't give me any details."

She looked disappointed.

I changed the subject a little. "You could have knocked me over with a feather when Philip showed up at my door. He didn't try that on you, did he?"

"He knew better. The last time I saw him was when he left here that day."

"I wonder if he went to anybody else's apartment that day. You live in Boston, don't you?"

"Off Newbury Street. Not all of us have rich families to buy us houses in Lexington, like Vinnie does. Why do you ask?"

"You know Philip died behind my apartment, don't you? After I wouldn't let him stay with me, he went somewhere else and then came back. I figured that since your place was so close, he might have gone to see you."

"He knew better," she repeated. "When he threatened

me, I told him I'd send my cousins after him if he ever bothered me again. You have to be tough with a man like that. No offense, Laura, but that was always your problem with Philip. You were never tough enough."

I really didn't appreciate her telling me why my relationship with Philip had failed, certainly not after all this time. Which is why I got nasty and said, "Is that what happened with you and Vinnie?"

I regretted it immediately. Inez didn't say anything at first, but the temperature in the room went down several degrees. Finally she said, "That was totally different. Vinnie was the one who needed to be strong, not me."

"I'm sorry," I said. "I shouldn't have brought it up. Everybody knows it was Vincent's loss."

She thawed a little. "Just remember that you can't trust Vinnie, not at all."

"I'll be careful," I said, which was true enough. At this point, I didn't trust anybody at SSI.

"Good. If you have any problems, you come to me."

"I will. Thanks, Inez."

Her phone rang then. "This is Inez. Yes, Laura's in here, Vinnie."

I hid a grin. Vincent's office was next door, but he'd called rather than come within range of Inez.

She went on. "A great welcome you gave our new employee. Did Muriel keep you up late last night?" I don't know what he said, but she smiled and it wasn't a very nice smile. "No? Better luck next time. Those headaches can't last forever . . . sure, I'll send her in. 'Bye, Vinnie."

She hung up the phone. "Vinnie wants to talk to you. But remember what I said—don't trust him."

I nodded. Paw once told me that hate wasn't all that far

from love, so that if the loving went away, hate was real quick to slip in. I guess he wouldn't have been surprised by the way Inez and Vincent were acting.

Either Vincent hadn't been all that upset by Inez's remarks, or he had pulled himself together quickly. As soon as I tapped at his open door, he came toward me with his hands outstretched. "Laura, *mea culpa, mea culpa, mea maxima culpa.* I meant to get here early to get things ready for you, and somehow I overslept."

"Don't worry about it," I said. "I know this past week has been rough on you, what with Philip's funeral and all."

"That's no excuse for not making you feel welcome. Let me show you where you'll be sitting. At least I had enough sense to have Roberta get your desk ready yesterday afternoon."

I would have wondered why Roberta hadn't shown me to my cubicle when I'd come in if I hadn't already figured out that she wasn't exactly a ball of fire. And she had put the necessities at my desk: a stapler, pads, pens, and yellow sticky notes.

"I think you'll be happy with your workstation," Vinnie said, patting the top of the PC.

"Looks great." It was a nice system—better, in fact, than the one at my real job. And the cubicle was bigger, too.

"What do you want me to do first?" I asked. "Do you still want me to concentrate on the user interface?"

"Absolutely."

"How far has Neal gotten on the design specifications?"

He hesitated. "Not too far, I gather. Since Philip's . . . accident, he's mostly been trying to get into the code."

"Password protection? Surely somebody here had the password."

"If it were just a password, it would be no problem. Unfortunately, Philip left us other gifts."

"Viruses?" I guessed. There were lots of ways to destroy code and data with bombs and viruses. They can even be set to go off later, making sure that backups are corrupted, too.

"Philip had a unique sense of humor."

And he had been very territorial. That made me think of something else. This cubicle was the only vacant one I saw. "Vincent, this wasn't Philip's desk, was it?"

Vincent hesitated a minute, which answered my question for me. "Well, yes. Is that going to be a problem?"

"I guess not. If Philip is going to haunt anyplace, it's more likely to be the alley behind my apartment than it is this cube."

Vincent gave a half-chuckle, meaning that he wasn't really amused but didn't want to say so.

"And," I went on, looking right at Vincent, "if Philip had any unfinished business on this earth, I imagine it would be more blackmail."

Vincent's face went blank. "How did you hear about that?"

"Something he said that afternoon at my apartment."

Now he stiffened. "Oh?"

"Nothing specific, just threats about rattling cages."

He relaxed visibly. "Well, Philip wasn't one to admit defeat. And he was getting desperate." He checked his watch, either a Rolex or an excellent imitation. "Go ahead and get comfortable. When you want to get started, talk to Neal so you two coordinate efforts. And if you have any questions or problems, come straight to me. All right?" He was gone before I could answer.

I almost hoped that I did have a problem so I could see who jumped first to solve it: Inez or Vincent.

It didn't take me too long to settle in. I played around with my computer enough to see that the software I'd be likely to need had already been installed and arranged my desk to suit me. Then I was ready to talk to Neal.

Neal's desk was down the hall in a corner, so two of his walls were real ones rather than cube walls, and he had a window. I tapped on one of the walls, and he said, "Come in."

Like many programmers I know, Neal kept his work space dark. There was a little light coming from the window, and a string of tiny white lights outlined a three-foot-tall potted tree, but the overhead lights were switched off and the main source of illumination was the glow of his computer screen.

"Good morning," I said.

"Good morning," he said, with the most genuine smile I had received all day. "Have a seat. Vinnie—I mean, Vincent, said you were starting today."

I sat in a chair next to the desk. "It's hard to get used to calling him that, isn't it?"

He nodded. "I try, but I keep blowing it. It's been weird, being with him again. With all the MIT group. It's just like before, only . . ."

"Only different," I finished for him. "I know what you mean. Didn't it feel strange, coming back to Boston? Or were you already in the area?"

"No, I was in California. Mountain View."

"And you left that for this," I said, waving at the window. It was gray and cold, a typical Massachusetts February day, and unlikely to get much better until April.

Neal grinned. "I got tired of wearing shorts all the time. It was either come back here, or throw out all my sweaters."

"I know what you mean. If I ever went back to North Carolina I'd have to throw out a lot of clothes, too. What kind of work were you doing out there?"

"This and that," he said. "Keeping my hand in."

I remembered what Jessie had said about his having had a nervous breakdown, and inwardly fussed at myself for asking. "How did they find you?"

"On the Internet. Someone had heard there was an opening here and posted messages asking if anybody knew anything about the company. He mentioned Vincent's name, and I thought I'd get in touch. We spoke over the phone, he asked me to come for an interview, and here I am." Then his expression turned serious. "Vincent told me there was a strong possibility that Philip would be leaving the company, but he didn't tell me that he was trying to push him out. Or that I was here to replace him. I didn't find out about any of that until I got here."

"That was a dirty trick," I said. "Would you have come back here if you had known?"

"I'm not sure, Laura, I'm really not. On one hand, Philip used to be my roommate and I felt bad about getting his job. But on the other hand, somebody would have taken the job if I hadn't. And I guess I was smug about them wanting me. I was never asked when SSI was formed. I heard about it from some people at MIT and let it be known indirectly that I was interested, even after what happened with my dissertation, but Philip never called. So maybe I took the job out of spite."

"I don't think so," I said. "You never were a spiteful guy."

"And you always did say the nicest things."

"Thank you. Tell me, did Vincent talk to Inez about hiring you?"

"Did they pull that on you, too? 'He should have consulted me,' " he said, in an exaggerated imitation of Inez's accent. Then he did a good version of Vincent saying, " 'If you have any problems, come straight to me.' "

I couldn't help but laugh. "Those two are something, aren't they? Has it been rough working for them?"

"Not really. Even though they don't agree on how the company should be run, most of the time they do agree on how StatSys should work. Vinnie doesn't get into the guts of the product, actually. As long as it looks good, he's happy."

"I guess that's good," I said doubtfully.

"Don't worry—Murray pays attention to the guts."

"I bet he does. I saw a T-shirt the other day that reminded me of him. It said, 'Does anal retentive have a hyphen?' "

We both laughed at that.

Then I said, "Vincent wants me to work with you, but he didn't tell me what you've done so far."

Neal grimaced. "I haven't done much of anything. I was just getting started on some product design when Philip . . ." He hesitated for a second. "Before I went any further with that, Vincent asked me to decompile StatSys so I can check out the code."

"Decompile? That must have taken forever. Why didn't you just look at the source code?"

He looked exasperated. "We can't find it. Philip was the only one who had a copy because he wouldn't let anybody work on it but him."

"Jessie told me he'd been pretty territorial."

"Paranoid is more like it. He hid the code so well that I've given up trying to track it down. He had a password-protected directory that was supposed to contain the source code, but when I finally got into it, it was all garbage text. I don't know if I set off some sort of booby trap or what, but I have gone through every bit and byte on his hard drive and every disk in this office—there's no source code to be found."

"Are you kidding me? Why on earth would he do that? Just to be a pain?"

"Who knows? I finally decompiled the code, and ever since then, all I've done is try to make sure the system is clean. Booby traps, viruses—you name it, it's in there. There were a couple of loops that could have tied up the CPU for a day or more. Philip would have put up barbed wire if he could have. I want to make sure everything is clean before I go any further."

"I don't blame you. Do you want to talk about what we need in an interface? That way I can do prototype design while you finish up with this."

We got down to technical issues for a while. Neal had no problems with the way Vincent had suggested we divide up the work. In fact, he preferred it that way. A lot of programmers I know are like that—they like the nuts and bolts of software but don't like to worry with how it will be used. I'm just the opposite. Nuts and bolts are fine, but if nobody can use the result, it's a waste of time, as far as I'm concerned. I must take after my Aunt Maggie—I've heard her say the same thing when talking about high heels.

The planning part of a project is always fun to me, and I got so involved in our conversation that I almost forgot what I was really there for. It wasn't until we had been talking for well over an hour and Neal mentioned something about Philip's original design that I suddenly remembered that I was talking with a man who might very well be a killer. I found it hard to keep my mind on product design after that, so I told Neal that I'd had as much as I could take for my first morning.

Okay, I told myself as I sat down in front of my PC, now I was ready to get back to my real reason for being at SSI. So where did I start?

Chapter 18

That's the question I kept asking myself as I formatted screens for the rest of the morning. Oh, I knew what it was I wanted to find out—I just didn't think I could get away with asking. So, Dee, how did Philip rattle your cage? Was it a reason to kill him? How about you, Dom? Murray? Philip may have acted like the south end of a northbound horse, but even he wouldn't have been obnoxious enough to ask something like that straight out.

Finally it was lunchtime. In the cube across from me, I heard Dee say, "Dom, are you hungry?"

He shook his head without looking up from his screen.

Maybe I could handle this one-on-one. "Dee, are you going out for lunch?" I asked.

She looked at the back of her husband's head. "I guess so."

"Want some company?"

She shrugged, which I took as a yes. "Great!" I said with false heartiness. "You can show me the good places to eat." I grabbed my pocketbook and coat.

We didn't talk much on the way to the restaurant, but not from lack of trying. It's just that every time I attempted to start a conversation, Dee grunted or nodded and that was it. Maybe it was the cold wind, or the number of people we had to thread our way through. Or maybe she just didn't want to talk.

To Dee's credit, she did find us a good place to eat. It wasn't much to look at, just one of the dozens of pizza and sub shops in Cambridge, but my cheese steak sub was one of the best I'd ever had.

I was glad the food was good because the conversation still wasn't going anywhere. Maybe I shouldn't have been surprised. Dee never had been much of a conversationalist. She and Dom had always seemed to split duties between them, and he was the talker.

Even though I was trying to eat slowly, I was halfway through my sub when I finally said something that got a little bit of a rise out of her. I looked out the window at the back of the neon sign that read PIZZA • GRINDERS and said, "You know, for the longest time when I got up here, I wondered what a pizza grinder was. I finally asked Philip, and he laughed like it was the funniest thing he'd every heard. I think it was Jessie who finally explained that the signs meant they had pizza *and* grinders." I never did get an explanation for why it was everybody called the sandwiches steak subs, no matter what the signs said. "Then he made fun of me about it for I don't know how long afterward. Just like my cousin Linwood."

Dee grunted. "That sounds like Philip."

Except for ordering, that was more words than she had said at one time since we left the office, so I wasn't about to let it go. "I know I shouldn't speak ill of the dead, but he did have a mean streak, didn't he?"

"You're telling me," Dee said.

"Oh?" I said, hoping she'd elaborate. After a minute, it was clear that she wasn't planning to. "What did he do to you?"

"Don't you remember 'Tweedledee and Tweedledum'?"

I nodded. "That was pretty mean." I didn't want to admit that I had laughed myself when he said it the first time. Okay, I had her talking about Philip. Now all I had to do was bring up the subject of blackmail in a way that wouldn't get her back up. "He wasn't exactly trustworthy, either. One time I told him something in confidence and he told people," I said, trying to dredge up an example. Fortunately, Philip had supplied all kinds of bad examples.

I said, "Two girls I knew were applying for a job in the chemistry lab. One of them got it, and Philip was there when she told me. She made me promise not to tell anybody, because she wanted to break it to the other girl herself. But Philip got to the second girl first, and I don't know what he told her, but the second girl never spoke to the first girl again. And they'd been friends since high school."

"Philip never could stand to see anybody else happy."

This time Dee's voice sounded downright nasty. "It's probably none of my business, but you say that like he did something really awful to you."

She didn't answer at first, just looked at me without blinking for the longest time. I tried not to look away, but I realized that Dee had awfully cold eyes. Finally she said, "He told you, didn't he?"

"Told me what?"

"About us."

I hadn't known that Dee and Philip had an *us*, but I thought she might say more if I acted like I knew more than I did. So I said, "You mean the time you and he . . . ?"

Dee took a fierce bite out of her sub. "I should have known he'd tell you. He swore that he'd never tell anyone else, that it was just between us. I don't know why I believed him. You two must have had a good laugh over it, too. Poor ignorant Dee, not knowing what to do, and Philip having to teach her."

Was she talking about what I *thought* she was talking about? "Dee, I wouldn't have laughed about a thing like that. And I don't think he told anybody else."

"You're probably right, because then he wouldn't have been able to play with me. Saying things to Dom that went right over his head, and then winking."

"What a rotten thing to do." Philip and I had been intimate, but he'd never tried to hold it over me like that. Of course, I told Richard all about my relationship with Philip. From what Dee was saying, she hadn't been so honest with her husband. "Dom doesn't know?"

"Of course not. Dom and I were already engaged when it happened."

I tried not to let anything show on my face.

Dee went on. "Dom wanted to wait until after the wedding, but I was afraid I wouldn't know how to ... I should never have spoken to Philip about it, but it was late one night and I'd been drinking, and Philip offered to show me some things. We didn't mean to go that far, but it just happened."

Knowing Philip, he certainly had meant to go that far. Getting Dee drunk and then talking her out of her virginity right before her wedding night was just the kind of thing he'd have enjoyed. And hadn't Inez said she'd been drunk the time she'd slept with Philip? How many women had he used that trick on?

I felt sick to my stomach, both because of what Philip had done and because of how I had tricked Dee out of the information. I still had a good piece of my steak sub left, but I wadded up the wax paper around it. I wasn't hungry anymore.

Maybe it had spoiled my appetite, but the subject seemed to make Dee hungrier, and she took another big bite. "Teasing me all these years was bad enough, but that bastard threatened to ruin my marriage."

"What?"

"He threatened to tell Dom all about it if I didn't vote to keep him at SSI."

"That son of a bitch! What did you do?"

"I told him I'd do it. The funny thing was that I had voted for him the first time anyway, and probably would have the second time. I wanted to change things at SSI, but not by kicking people out. But after Philip threatened me, I had to vote for him. I couldn't risk him going to Dom."

"What would Dom have done?"

"He'd have left me. At least, I think he would have." She looked away. "Maybe he wouldn't have cared, things being like they are."

"Are you two having problems?" I asked, honestly concerned this time.

"Maybe we've just been together too long. He doesn't talk to me anymore—maybe we don't have anything to talk about. We don't even have sex, not that I can blame him for that." She looked down at herself with a look of pure disgust, then looked at me with those cold eyes again. "I suppose you and Philip had a big laugh over me, over how fat I am and how I looked in bed."

Okay, I'd found out what I needed to know and had made Dee feel bad in the process. I couldn't turn around and be honest now, because that would just humiliate her further. The only way I was going to be able to repair some of the damage was to lie. Like Paw always told me, a white lie never hurt nobody.

"To tell the truth," I said, though the truth was the last thing I had on my mind, "that's not how it was at all. You see, I was pretty inexperienced myself before I dated Philip." Which was a fancy way of saying that I had never gone further than one French kiss with a boy in Byerly. "He implied that you were substantially more skilled that first time than I *ever* was." If I was going to lie, I might as well make it a whopper. "Imply, hell, Philip said flat out that you were one of the best he was ever with."

She put down her sub. "Get out of here."

"Really," I insisted. "He didn't get into details, but he said—well, I don't want to sound ugly, but he said you were a great lay."

Dee didn't look like she minded my putting it that way. In fact, she almost smiled.

I went on. "I was so jealous I nearly turned green. Then I wanted to ask you if you had any advice, but I was too embarrassed. I mean, who wants to admit that her boyfriend still fantasizes about another woman?"

For a second, I was afraid that I had laid it on too thick with that last part, but Dee didn't seem to think so. She kind of stared into the distance, as if remembering that night with Philip. Then she kind of shook herself. "He never told me that."

"Of course not," I said quickly. "Philip never told people the truth to their face. But that sure explains why he kept teasing you about it. With things going sour with him and Colleen, maybe he was hoping to rekindle the old flame."

"You're full of shit," she said, but she sounded almost affectionately. "I've got to get back to the office."

Nothing more was said, but I noticed something when we

got to SSI. Dom was still glued to his terminal, but Dee came around behind him and gave him a great big hug and whispered something in his ear. Dom didn't react at first but then turned to look at her. And I swear she fluttered her lashes at him.

Chapter 19

I got back to work on StatSys, but I gave only part of my attention to it. The rest I used to try to figure out ways to approach the other folks at SSI. The upshot was that I didn't get anything done for SSI or for myself.

Neither Vincent nor Inez had told me what my official hours were to be, but by five-thirty, I was ready to get out of there. Nobody questioned me as I headed for the door, so I figured it was okay to leave. I was standing at the elevator when Murray came by.

"Hello, Laura," he said. "Are you leaving early, too?"

I guess that meant I was supposed to work later. "I think I've enjoyed myself as much as I can stand for one day."

Richard usually grins when I say that, and he's heard it I don't know how many times before. Murray just nodded.

"Do you think we could meet tomorrow?" he said. "I hear you and Neal were discussing plans for the next release, and I want to give you my feedback."

I bristled, which was silly. Why should I be possessive about a project I wasn't even planning on completing? It's just that Murray always rubbed me the wrong way. I made myself say, "That would be fine. It's always good to get input." And Murray just loved giving input.

"Great. You're not taking the elevator, are you?"

Since the down button was lit and I was standing there, I thought it was pretty obvious that I was. "Why?"

"I always take the stairs for exercise," he said virtuously. "We desk jockeys can't be too careful." He started for the door to the stairs.

I thought about going with him, both because I probably could use the exercise and because it would be a way to talk to him privately, but then I remembered Richard asking me to be careful. I just couldn't imagine that accompanying a suspect down six lonely flights of stairs would be considered being careful. So I said, "See you tomorrow," and headed home via elevator and subway.

I was feeling pretty full of myself because of what I'd found out, and when I found Thaddeous waiting at my apartment, I started to tell him about it. But he stopped me in midstream. "You may as well hold your horses. Michelle's going to want to hear it, too."

"You asked Michelle over?" I asked, a little put out by his inviting somebody to my apartment.

"Not exactly. She kind of invited herself. I hope you don't mind."

Now I was just amused. "No, it's no problem. I'm glad y'all are getting along so well."

He didn't say anything, but I could tell he was working real hard at not grinning. I went into the bedroom to change clothes and to give him a chance to grin without my seeing it. I don't know who he thought he was fooling, but if he wanted to pretend that I couldn't figure out what was going on, that was all right with me.

When Michelle got there, we decided we could talk while we ate, but we couldn't agree on a restaurant. So we went to the food court at the Prudential Center, picked three different places to get dinner, and found a table isolated enough that I felt comfortable telling them what had happened that day.

"That's incredible!" Michelle said. "In just one day, you found not one but two women who wanted to kill Philip. Which one did it?"

I said, "To tell you the truth, I can't see that either of them would have."

"Are you crazy? Philip sleeps with two women and then threatens to expose them, and you don't think either one would have killed him for it? Thaddeous, tell her she's crazy."

"It does seem like they've got good motives," Thaddeous said. "Especially that Inez. I could tell when I met her that she was a hot-blooded woman."

"She's got a temper, that's for sure," I admitted. "And I can see her breaking a few dishes, but not hitting somebody like that."

Michelle said, "Didn't you say it wasn't the blow to the head that killed Philip? Maybe Inez didn't mean to kill him. Suppose Philip goes to Inez's apartment after he leaves you and they get to drinking. Later on they go back to your place."

"Why?" I wanted to know.

"I don't know why. Just say that they did. And Inez gets mad at Philip and hits him. She doesn't realize how badly he's hurt, so she leaves him there, thinking that he's going to wake up in a few minutes. The next day she finds out he's dead. There's no point in her coming forward, so she just keeps quiet. Couldn't it have happened that way?"

"It could have, but I don't think it did. I just can't see that Philip threatening to tell about a one-night stand would make her want to hit him. Why would she care if people knew now?

She didn't sound like she was all that mad at Philip. Annoyed, maybe, but not hit-him-upside-the-head mad. And she told me about it without a whole lot of prodding, which doesn't make sense for a secret worth killing over. Blackmail works only if the victim cares about the secret coming out."

Thaddeous said, "Maybe she didn't care, but that doesn't mean that she didn't get mad about him threatening her. From what you've said, once you get on her bad side, you stay there. Look at how she's held a grudge against Vincent."

"If Vincent had been the one to show up dead, she'd be my first suspect," I said, "but I still can't see her killing Philip."

"Okay, then it wasn't Inez. It must have been Dee. She had an excellent motive." Michelle looked directly at Thaddeous. "You can bet that if anybody tried to come between me and my man, I'd do something drastic."

"She looks like she's strong enough to have done it," Thaddeous said.

"She probably is," I agreed, "but why would she? She voted for Philip, just like he wanted her to. So he didn't need to expose her and she didn't need to kill him."

Thaddeous said, "The thing is, a blackmailer doesn't usually stop after he's found himself a victim. Philip could have held that over her for the rest of her life. This way, she doesn't have to worry about it coming out later."

"But like I said about Inez, if Dee had been willing to kill to protect her secret, she wouldn't have told me so quickly," I said. "Of course, she thought I already knew."

"Oh, my God! She's going to come after you next!" Michelle said.

"Michelle! She's not coming after me." At least, I didn't think she was. "Besides, I just thought of another reason why she couldn't been the murderer—Dom. They go everywhere together. How could she have snuck away from him long enough to kill Philip?"

Thaddeous asked, "Mightn't he be in on it, too?"

"Only if she told him about that night with Philip herself, meaning that she'd have no motive. Unless she made up some other reason to make Dom want to kill Philip, and I don't think she's that kind of sneaky."

"It's got to be one of them," Michelle said, clearly exasperated with me.

Before I could say anything, Thaddeous came to my rescue. "Not necessarily. We've got to take our time and look at all the suspects before we go making up our minds. Maybe it was one of them, but maybe it was somebody else altogether."

"I guess you're right," she said reluctantly.

I nodded. Even though my gut feeling was that neither Inez nor Dee had killed Philip, both of them were still in the running. So was everybody else at SSI. That meant I was going to have to spend at least one more day sharing an office with a killer.

Chapter 20

Though Murray had said something about us meeting the next day, I wasn't expecting to find a note on my desk the first thing in the morning that said, "Ten o'clock okay? My office.—Murray." Since I had no plans for the morning, I decided I might as well get it over with, both for Murray's reasons and my own. So at ten o'clock, I took my coffee cup and a pad and tapped at Murray's office door.

"Come in."

Since the job of a quality assurance person is to oversee all the details in a product, from spelling to calculating numbers to formatting, I always expect them to carry this attention to detail over to other realms. So it's always a shock when I find a QA person in a messy office, even though every one I've ever met has had stacks of printouts and disks all over everywhere. Murray was no exception.

Murray was typing furiously at his keyboard.

"Is this a bad time?" I asked.

"No, I'll be with you in a minute."

Five minutes passed, then five more, and he was still working hard.

I said, "I can come back later."

"Almost done."

And, in fact, it was only two minutes later when he finished up and turned to me. "Shall we get started?"

Since I had been ready to get started for fifteen minutes, I thought it was a silly question. I said, "Neal and I didn't come up with anything definite yesterday, but I have some notes about what we have in mind."

"Actually," Murray said, "I'd like to go over the QA log first." He scrambled around in the tallest stack on his desk and pulled out a thick sheaf of papers. "I understand you'll be addressing user interface issues, so I thought we'd limit this meeting to those."

"Fine," I said. So much for the informal discussion I'd thought we were going to have.

For the next thirty minutes, Murray read out items from his voluminous log, detailing each suggestion or correction. Admittedly, some of the items needed a little clarification, but with most of them, I could just as easily read them myself.

After a while, I was having a tough time keeping my eyes open. "Look, Murray, wouldn't it be easier if you just gave me a printout of the log and let me take a look at it? If I have any questions, I'll get back to you."

He looked doubtful. "You're sure you'll get the changes into the next release?"

"Murray! Do you think I'm going to ignore you?"

"Philip always did."

Finally, a topic that interested me. "Really?" I said.

"Look at these dates," he said, shoving a page at me. "I first logged these errors almost three years ago, and Philip never corrected them."

He sounded very indignant, and I didn't blame him. Sometimes QA suggests things that are tricky to do or that wouldn't be a good idea, but some of those items wouldn't have taken two minutes to fix.

"That's crazy," I said.

He relaxed a little. "That's what I said, but nobody listens to me."

"Well, *I'm* listening." I felt bad being so emphatic when I wasn't planning on staying at SSI any longer than I had to, but I thought he needed to hear it. And I promised myself that I would take care of some of the errors while I was there. "I can't believe Philip treated you so badly."

"Philip never wanted anyone doing quality assurance in the first place—he said that it wasn't needed. As if he were perfect. And he said if I was any good as a programmer, I wouldn't be satisfied being a proofreader."

"I swear I think Philip went out of his way to be nasty. Is that what he said when he tried to get you to vote for him?" I was hoping if I made it plain that I knew about Philip's attempts, Murray wouldn't question how I had found out, and it worked.

"Oh no, he was all sweetness and light. A week earlier, I hadn't been good enough to correct his spelling, but now I was the finest computer professional he'd ever met. He said my talents were being wasted, that he'd make sure I was authorized to hire as big a staff as I wanted. Or if I'd rather, I could move to development and work with him because I was the only one who could keep up with him. As if I'd just forget all the other things he'd said to me over the years."

"He didn't really think you'd swallow that, did he?" I said, but Philip probably had thought Murray would believe him, just like he'd thought I was going to let him stay with me.

"Who knows what he thought? I just laughed at him. Then

he tried to use guilt on me, talking about how long we'd been friends." He snorted. "I'm Jewish, for God's sake—my mother can out-guilt Philip any day of the week."

I had to laugh.

Though I'd liked to have talked more, Murray said, "I'm glad we had this meeting, Laura. I'll get that printout to you ASAP."

It was a clear dismissal. So I said, "Good enough. If I have any questions, I'll get back to you." He thought I meant questions about the QA log, and I did, but that wasn't all I meant.

Chapter 21

Later that morning, I ended up talking to Sheliah the technical writer about some new product features. Since we were still together when noon came around, I asked her if she had plans for lunch, and we decided to go to a deli and bring back sandwiches.

As we walked back to work, I was looking forward to spending time with somebody who wasn't a suspect in Philip's death. After all, she wasn't one of the MIT group and hadn't been on the board of directors, meaning that she wouldn't have been involved in the voting. But then I realized that I had been assuming that the vote had had something to do with Philip's murder. I didn't know that for sure. So I couldn't cross Sheliah off my list just yet.

We got back to the office and spread out our food on the break room table. Then, after a quick look around to make sure nobody else was within earshot, I said, "It must have been weird for you, coming into an established group of friends here at SSI."

"More so than I had expected it to be," Sheliah said with a grin. "I've worked at small companies before, but never one that was so . . ."

"Inbred?"

She nodded. "Roberta and I are the only ones who weren't at MIT."

"What do you think of the group? From an outsider's perspective."

She hesitated a minute, not meeting my eyes. Then she said, "Look, I know you've been friends with these people a long time, and I don't want to offend you."

"It's nice of you to worry about that, but I wouldn't have asked if I hadn't really wanted to know what you think."

"Okay, since you asked . . . I think they're a bunch of nerds. Inez not so much, and Neal isn't too bad, but the others . . . I've worked with computer geeks before, but these guys take the cake."

I thought about Murray's thick glasses and Dee and Dom's indifference to fashion. "I guess they *are* kind of stereotypical."

"You said it. It's like they never graduated from college. Vincent is so busy trying to act like a boss that he has no clue about what's really going on, and Dee and Dom haven't got one whole personality between them. Jessie's so worried about everybody being happy that she can't get anything done. Inez is enough on the ball that she could probably make something of the place if she didn't spend so much time fighting with Vincent. Murray has some good ideas, but when people don't instantly do what he wants, he whines."

She had to stop then to get her breath, and I said, "I'm not saying that you're wrong, but if they're that bad, why do you stay?"

"Well, the recession is supposed to be over, but jobs are still tough to come by. And they're treating me decently, all things considered. It's just that I still feel like a new hire, even after a year here."

I nodded, remembering how nobody at Philip's visitation seemed to remember just how long it was she had been working with them.

"I think you're already more a part of the company than I am," she added.

"Do you think so? I've kept up with Jessie, but I haven't really been around the others that much since college."

But Sheliah said, "It's like you've never been gone. It's the same with Neal, and he got here only a week or two before Philip died."

She'd been the one to mention Philip, but I was more than willing to take advantage of it. "What was your take on him? Philip, I mean. I hear he was pretty awful to work with."

"Well . . ." she said, clearly ill at ease.

I thought I knew why. "You heard that he and I used to date, didn't you?"

"Jessie told me."

"It's ancient history. Really. I was just curious about him. Didn't you ever have the urge to find out how an old boyfriend turned out?"

She grinned. "Lots of times. I always hope I'll find out that they're miserable."

Philip certainly had been miserable the last time I saw him alive, and it had gone downhill from there. I was tempted to warn her about getting what she asked for, but instead I said, "Knowing Philip, I don't think I could ever have worked with him."

"It wasn't an ideal situation to come into," she admitted. "First off, SSI hadn't ever had a real technical writer. The programmers documented the pieces they knew, and then Jessie prettied it up and stuck it in a binder. No consistency, no graphics, no index, no actual document design. It was awful. And Philip didn't think we needed anything better. He was completely against my being hired."

"Really?" If Philip had tried to keep Sheliah out or get her fired, that could have been a reason for her to want him dead.

"They had to have a board meeting about it, but fortunately, everybody else voted for hiring me. Vincent was really set on online documentation and jazzing up the manual, Inez and Murray wanted to cut down on technical support calls, and Dee and Dom thought they had better things to do with their time than write documentation."

"What about Jessie? She hates fights."

"She hated doing the manuals herself even more, so she went along with the others. Philip was stuck with me."

"Getting product information out of him must have been like pulling teeth."

"You're telling me! I don't think I'd have minded as much if he had told me up front he wasn't going to help, but what he did was worse. You see, I didn't find out he'd voted against me for a long time. He was always nice to my face. He'd come to meetings and tell me what a great job I was doing and how much better the manuals were. But he never had time to answer my questions or return review copies. It took me six months to realize that. And he was so slimy. Telling me how nice I looked, and how he bet I had lots of boyfriends."

"He harassed you?"

She looked half-embarrassed, half-angry. "Nothing overt. Just slimy. I told Jessie about it a couple of times, and she kept saying she'd take care of it. But she never did. I'd have been glad to see him leave the company. Not like what happened, of course."

"I don't blame you."

"Now I think we've got a chance to turn things around at SSI."

I couldn't resist teasing her. "Even with a bunch of nerds?"

"I knew I shouldn't have said that. Maybe they're nerds, but some of the best software design comes from nerds. I'm really encouraged that we've brought you and Neal on board."

"I'd have thought that the last thing you'd want to see is another MIT refugee, let alone two of us."

"You two are different. Neal is brilliant, one of the best I've ever seen."

"You know he started college a couple of years early, and even then it showed. His professors had a hard time keeping up with him."

"As for you, you've worked elsewhere, not just at SSI. So you've got new ideas. But SSI will accept you because of your history. The best of both worlds."

"Thank you," I said. Even though I wasn't planning to stay at SSI, I was glad she thought I'd have been an asset.

"Now can I ask you a question?" she said.

"Ask away. I've certainly asked you a slew of them."

"Why didn't you come work for SSI with the others?"

"Because I wanted a real job, for a real company, in the real world," I said. "I was fairly sure StatSys would be successful, but I knew SSI would be a seat-of-the-pants company for a long time. I wanted stability."

"Makes sense."

"Besides," I added ruefully, "working with my ex-boyfriend didn't sound like a good time. You say he was slimy with you—I can't imagine how he'd have been with me."

"I can understand that."

"And honestly, the biggest reason is that nobody asked me." I shrugged. "Things worked out for me better going elsewhere."

"It might have done them good if you had come into the company in the beginning."

"Why's that?"

"I've heard stories about the MIT days, and your name comes up a lot." She grinned. "I felt like I knew you even before we met. Anyway, it sounds like you were the practical one, the one to bring them all back down to earth. If you had been around, SSI might not be doing so badly now. You might even have been able to keep Philip under control."

"I doubt that," I said with a laugh, "but I appreciate the compliment." I had never really considered the role I had played in the group, but I thought that Sheliah might have put her finger on it.

It was nearly time for us to get back to work by then, but there was one more question I wanted to ask. "I hear Philip was trying real hard to keep his job."

"He sure was. He even asked me to put in a good word for him. As if I'd have had anything to say about it, or as if I wanted him to stay."

"Did he threaten you?"

She looked surprised. "He insulted me when I told him to forget it, but I was used to that. Why? Did he threaten other people?"

I fudged. "You know he came over to my apartment the day he died."

She nodded.

"Well, he said something then about 'rattling cages' and

making SSI keep him, but he wouldn't say anything more. Philip loved to drop hints."

"What a loser!" Then, as if remembering his death, she added, "I really do feel sorry about what happened to him."

"Me, too," I said. Though I was starting to wonder why.

After we cleaned off our table and headed for our desks, I realized that I hadn't spoken to a soul at SSI who was going to miss Philip. Even those I didn't suspect of killing him were glad to see him gone. Sheliah had known him a relatively short time, but the nicest thing she could come up with for him was pity. As for me, after all I'd heard about Philip since I'd come to SSI, I was having problems feeling even that much for him. I wasn't sure if that said something about Philip, or about me.

Chapter 22

After about the third time I passed by Dee and Dom's cube that afternoon, I finally noticed that not only was Dee not there, but her computer screen was dark. Since I hadn't spoken to Dom yet, I thought this was as good a time as any. So I stuck my head in and said, "Knock, knock."

He stayed glued to his screen.

"Dom? Dom? Hello-oo?"

There was still no response.

I stepped inside and lightly touched his shoulder.

"What?" he snapped, turning around.

"Sorry. It's just me. I'd forgotten how engrossed you get in your work."

He grinned sheepishly. "I do kind of lose track. That's why I like sharing a cube with Dee. Otherwise, I'd be here all day long and probably half the night, too."

"Where is Dee? She's not sick, is she?"

He grinned wider, but now he looked more like a wolf than a sheep. "We didn't get much sleep last night, so I talked her into taking a sick day so she could get some rest."

Remembering how she had been acting with him the previous afternoon, I didn't think I needed to ask for any details. With Richard out of town, the last thing I needed to hear about was other people's marital bliss. Instead, I said, "Everybody needs a day off once in a while. So how's it going? I haven't had a chance to visit with you."

"By all means, come visit." He pulled Dee's chair out for me. "Have Vincent and Inez put you to work yet?"

I nodded. "User interface."

He grimaced. "I hate doing that stuff. I know it's important, but it's just too fuzzy. Give me the code any day." He waved at the screen behind him, filled with rows of characters that were nearly incomprehensible to me, despite my years in programming.

"You can keep that mess. Troubleshooting code makes me crazy. Spending three hours to find out that I've left out a comma is too much like work."

"Better that than staying up all night trying to figure out which font is the easiest to read. And picking colors! What a pain."

"That goes to prove what my grandfather always said. If everybody liked chocolate the best, they wouldn't bother making all those other flavors."

He grinned again. Like Dee, Dom was mostly round: a round face in a round head on top of a round body. He looked a lot like the snowmen I used to draw before I saw a real one, and his grin was pure Pillsbury Doughboy. I hated to spoil the mood, but I did have an ulterior motive for talking to him.

I said, "At least you're not like Philip. He refused to believe software needed well-designed screens or field names that made sense. If a user didn't understand the product, it was the user's fault, not the product's."

As I'd expected, Dom's grin melted right off his face. Philip had had that effect on people when he was alive, and it had only gotten worse since he'd died.

"Philip had a different idea of what a product should be," Dom said diplomatically.

"Philip had different ideas about a lot of things."

He looked at me curiously. "Was it terrible, having to identify his body?"

I started to say something noncommittal, but since I was there to pick Dom's brains, I thought that the least I owed him was an honest answer. "It was pretty bad. I've seen dead people before, but not in a body bag. He wasn't gross, but he was very clearly dead." I shivered without meaning to.

"Hey, I'm sorry. I shouldn't have asked."

"It's okay. I know people have been curious about that, and I think I'd rather they asked outright than tried to be subtle."

"Subtlety never was my strong point."

"Mine, either." My next question proved it to me once again. "I still wonder what he was doing back behind my apartment."

"I thought he'd gone over there to ask you for a place to stay."

"He had, but he went somewhere else before ending up in the alley. Nobody knows where." I looked at him closely as I asked the next question. "You didn't see him that evening, did you?"

"Not me," he said, and he sounded sincere. "The last time I saw him was here at the office. At least, I guess I saw him that day. I know he was here, but . . ." He looked at his computer screen. "The Red Sox could have paraded down the hall, and I'm not sure I'd have noticed."

"Sometimes losing yourself in work comes in handy. Especially the way it must have been around here for the past few months."

"You mean the attempted coup?"

"The coup?"

"That's what I've been calling it. Vincent's and Inez's campaign to get rid of Philip."

"Did you not approve?" I was already fairly sure that Dom had been one of those to vote for keeping Philip, but confirmation would be nice.

"At first I didn't. Philip was with SSI from the beginning, after all. It didn't seem fair to ask him to change just because Inez and Vincent had new ideas about how to run the place. And I was afraid that once he was gone, those two would really go after each another. If nothing else, Philip kept them distracted. So I voted for him to stay." I nodded, but before I could ask anything else, he added, "The first time, anyway."

"Only the first time? I heard that the vote was the same both times."

"The same numbers. I guess somebody who voted against him the first time changed his mind."

"I guess so," I said, trying to sound nonchalant. I was sure that Vincent, Inez, and Murray had voted against Philip in that first vote. That meant that one of those three had switched sides. "Why did you change your mind, if you don't mind my asking?" For some reason, when you offer to back down, people are a lot more likely to answer, even if the question is none of your business.

Dom said, "Partly because Vincent started talking about the new direction we'd be going in, and the programming sounded like it would be more interesting than what I'd done before. And I was worried about SSI going belly up. I knew Dee and I'd be able to get other jobs, but I'm comfortable here. There's a lot of garbage going on, but there's garbage anywhere."

"Better the devil you know than the devil you don't."

"You bet. So I was thinking about changing my vote, but I wasn't sure yet. Then Philip came by, and he was pretty convincing, too. He talked about loyalty and how we'd been friends for years. And he said that if Inez and Vincent got rid of him, then they could get rid of me and Dee anytime they wanted. He had some good points, so I told him I'd think about it.

"Then he got Dee to go talk to him alone, and he said something to upset her. She wouldn't tell me what, but I could tell. I could understand his not wanting to lose his job, but he didn't have any business picking on Dee. You know how sensitive she is."

Actually, I had never thought of Dee as sensitive, but naturally her husband would see her differently. I nodded sympathetically.

"After that, I decided the hell with him. I didn't want him bothering Dee anymore." Then he lowered his voice. "What gets me is that the way I figure it, Dee must have voted for him despite his being an asshole. That's how sweet and forgiving she is."

Again, that was a part of Dee's personality I'd never seen, but I said, "That was nice of her." Of course, I knew her real reason was the threat Philip had been holding over her head, but I didn't mind letting Dom think the best of his wife.

It was then that I glanced outside his cube and saw a shadow the right size and shape to be somebody standing outside, listening to our conversation. Whoever it was moved away just then, and I wasn't sure if there really had been somebody there or if somebody had just walked by. It did make me uneasy enough to want to change the subject. We talked about programming for a little while and then I went back to my own cube.

Though Dom had answered all my questions, now I had a whole new batch. If he was telling me the truth about how he'd voted, either Inez, Vincent, or Murray had changed sides to vote for Philip. Which one, and why?

And who had been outside Dom's cube? I didn't think I'd told any one person enough for anybody to figure out what I was up to, but if somebody had overheard me asking Dom the same kind of questions I'd asked him or her, it wouldn't take a whole lot of brains to put it together. If that shadow had been the murderer, would he or she be worried enough to come after me?

Chapter 23

I should have realized that something was cooking that afternoon, but I got involved in working through the suggestions from the QA log and didn't pay any attention to the rest of the office. After seeing that shadow outside Dom's cube, I was afraid somebody might be getting suspicious, and I thought I ought to play possum for a while.

So it wasn't until around five that I noticed that the office seemed quiet. I leaned over to look into Dee and Dom's cube, but there was no one there, and I didn't hear Neal or Sheliah tapping away at their keyboards, either. The whole office had that empty, after-hours feeling, and it was starting to give me the creeps. Which is why I jumped when my phone rang once, meaning somebody was calling me from inside the office.

I picked it up. "This is Laura."

"Laura, this is Jessie. Could you come into the conference room for a minute?"

"Sure." Since it was rather late in the day, I saved my work and shut down the computer first. If whatever she needed me for took long enough, I'd be able to go home afterward, and goodness knew I was ready to go. I figured that not even Murray could say anything about my leaving early, since it looked like almost everybody else had already gone.

When I opened the door, the conference room was dark, and I stood there a minute, trying to decide if I should go inside or run as fast as I could. Then the lights came on, and there was a yell of, "Surprise!"

I know I must have jumped back three feet, because everybody started laughing. And I do mean everybody. All of the SSI crowd was there, even Dee, which meant that she must have come into the office just for this.

"We got you!" Jessie crowed.

"You sure did. What's this for?" I asked.

"A welcome home party," Jessie said, pointing at a white cake that said just that in red icing. "Well, sort of. Welcome back to the group."

"That's so sweet," I said.

"There's pizza on the way, too," Neal said, "so I hope you don't have plans for dinner."

Jessie handed me a can of Coke and said, "We tried to get your cousin so he could come, too, but he wasn't at your apartment."

"I'll call him later. I think he's got a date tonight." If not, I felt sure that Michelle would take care of him.

"In town less than a week, and he's already got a girlfriend?" Inez said with a raised eyebrow.

"I introduced him to a friend of mine, and I think they've hit it off," I explained.

"You should have told me he was available," she said. "It's impossible to find a good man in this town." She looked pointedly at Vincent.

Vincent promptly announced, "I'll go downstairs to wait for the pizza."

Inez grinned.

"Come sit down," Jessie said to me, ignoring the two of them. "This is like old times, isn't it?"

"It sure is," I said. I did think about Philip, but wasn't about to bring that up. "I can't believe you guys did this."

"It was Jessie's idea," Dee said, but I could have told her that. This kind of thing was always Jessie's idea. Jessie's own birthday was forgotten most of the time, but she made sure nobody else's ever was.

"Thank you, Jessie," I said, toasting her with my Coke.

She looked embarrassed. "No big deal."

Inez said, "So tell us about Richard and what he's up to. Does he know you're working here?"

Answering her took a few minutes, and then Vincent came back up with the pizza and we dug in.

Everybody looked settled in for a good long stay, and as the guest of honor, I didn't think it would be very nice for me to leave. So as it got close to the time I would have left work, I went back to my desk long enough to call my apartment, and when there was no answer, I called Michelle at GBS.

Fortunately, she hadn't left yet, and I explained that I was going to hang around SSI a while longer.

"I've already talked to Thaddeous about getting together for dinner. You want us to meet you there?"

"No, that's okay. I don't know how long I'll be here." I lowered my voice to add, "Maybe I'll hear something useful."

"Yeah? Well, you be careful with those people. Only eat that pizza if they eat a piece first."

I wasn't sure how one would go about poisoning a pizza after it left the pizza parlor, but I said, "You bet. After pizza and cake, I know I'm not going to want anything else to eat. Why don't y'all go ahead? I'll see y'all at my place later."

Michelle said, "If you're sure you don't mind." I could tell that she didn't mind a bit.

While eating pizza, I tried to think of intelligent leading questions to ask. After all, with all my suspects together, it should have been an excellent time to try to dredge up some information. But I couldn't come up with any, and the truth was, I didn't want to do any investigating. It felt so nice to be welcome that I just couldn't bring myself to ask about alibis and motives.

I did try to pay attention to what everybody was saying, but even though we spent a lot of time talking about old adventures at MIT, Philip's name didn't come up. I don't know if it was reluctance to talk about a recently deceased friend, or guilt at how SSI had very nearly fired him, or something more sinister.

I finally relaxed and gave up thinking about the murder. Instead, I laughed at old jokes that were still funny only because we all knew them, listened to old stories that were interesting only because we all knew how they were going to end, and made fun of professors I hadn't thought of in years just because we'd always made fun of them.

And I had a good time, too, at least for a while. It was only after a couple of hours that I had a strong sense of déjà-vu. I looked around the room, thinking about how many times I had been with the group just like this. And even though everybody was older and it wasn't exactly the same set of people, it felt like I had never left, and for some reason, that really bothered me. I was relieved when the party broke up not long after that.

Chapter 24

Thaddeous and Michelle were still out when I got back to my apartment, and that was fine with me. It meant that they were having time alone and that I had some time to myself, too. The uneasy feeling from my surprise party was still with me, and I didn't think I'd be good company.

Richard and I have joked before that we're psychic about each other's moods, and maybe we are, because after I'd flipped through every TV channel three or four times, the phone rang.

"I call, in kindness and unfeigned love, to do greetings to thy royal person."

"Richard!"

"The one and only. Paraphrasing from *King Henry VI, Part II*, Act III, Scene 3, of course."

"Of course. How's it going?"

He reviewed the latest plays he'd seen, then I told him about my first couple of days at SSI. He wasn't at all happy to hear about the shadow I'd seen outside Dom's cube.

"Who do you think it was?"

"I don't know. The only ones I'm sure it wasn't are Dee and Dom. Which isn't much help, because I don't know that the eavesdropper had anything to do with Philip's death. He could just have been nosy."

"As the Duke of York warned, 'My liege, beware; look to thyself. Thou hast a traitor in thy presence there.' *King Richard II*, Act V, Scene 3."

"Don't worry. I've been careful, and I'll keep on being careful."

"You better be. I expect to find you hale and hearty when I return."

"You will."

"Okay. Now, so far we've got Philip leaving booby traps for Neal, blackmailing Dee, insulting Murray, harassing She-liah, and getting Dom mad. Not exactly a serene work environment, is it?"

"Not hardly. It's going to be so much better with Philip gone."

"Do you think that's the reason he was killed? To create a better atmosphere?"

"Actually, I think that one of his blackmail schemes back-fired."

"Does that mean you suspect Inez or Dee? Those are the only two being blackmailed."

"They're the only ones I know about for sure, but don't forget what Dom said about changing his vote. That means that somebody else changed sides, too. That had to have been another case of blackmail, because whoever it was continued to speak against Philip publicly."

"So you've eliminated the people who aren't on the board of directors."

"I'd like to," I said, "but I can't. Sheliah admitted that Philip had been sexually harassing her, and for all we know, it could have been worse than she said, meaning that she'd have a pretty good motive. She's not a big contender because I think it would have been easier for her either to quit or to report Philip to the EEOC.

"As for Neal, he knew Philip for years and they were roommates, so there could be something there. I don't know where he's been these past few years, so maybe he'd kept up with Philip while working in California. But until I know something, I'm going to put him on the second list, too."

"What about Roberta?"

"What about her? Michelle didn't mention her showing any particular animosity toward Philip."

"Maybe not, but I find it interesting that Roberta was the one to collect ballots both times, and that while the numbers should have changed the second time when Dom voted against Philip, they stayed the same. You're assuming that somebody else decided to vote for Philip, but what if Roberta stacked the vote herself, and then denied knowing who voted what?"

"That's twisty," I said admiringly, "but wouldn't she have just faked it so that Philip got all the votes?"

"Not if she wanted to get away with it. This way, nobody knows for sure who changed his or her mind."

"Are you thinking that Philip blackmailed her into doing this?"

"Or sweet-talked her into it. Or even bribed her. Maybe he didn't resort to blackmail right off the bat."

"Maybe not. I've just gotten used to assuming the worst of him."

"With good reason. He did threaten to ruin Dee and Dom's marriage. Do you think he'd have gone through with it?"

"I'm not sure. The threat is bad enough, but I think he'd

have had enough decency not to do it. At least, I hope he did."
Then I paused. "I thought I knew Philip, but now I'm not so
sure. I can't believe I ever dated him."

"It was a long time ago."

"I know, but it feels like it was just yesterday. Especially
after the party this afternoon. That really felt weird. At first
it was nice, like old times. The stories we used to tell, and the
same old jokes. I was thinking how sweet they all were. Then
suddenly it felt weird."

"Because Philip wasn't there?"

"Not just because of that. All of a sudden it was like I was
back in college, like a time machine had grabbed me and it was
seven years ago and these people were still the most important people in the world to me. Other than my family, anyway." I paused. "Shoot, there were times when they were
more important to me than my family was. God forbid my
family should ever hear me say that."

"College friendships can be very intense."

"This wasn't friendship. This was real darned close to ob-
session."

"This is upsetting you, isn't it? Why?"

I shrugged, forgetting that he couldn't see me. "I'm not
sure. Except that I'm not who I was then, and I don't want
to be. And I don't want to get sucked into that group of people again."

"You're not going to get sucked in. You're only going to
stay at SSI long enough to find out what you need to know,
and then you'll go back to your real life. Right?"

"Right."

"You don't sound convinced."

"I'm not." I struggled for a way to explain what I was feeling. "Paw used to say that you could judge a person by his

friends. He wanted me to be nice and polite to everybody, but he thought I should be extra careful about who I picked to be friends with. I suppose all kids hear something like that."

"Even Prince Hal heard it from his father. The king thought Hal was hanging around Falstaff too much."

"Did Hal ever feel ashamed of being friends with Falstaff?"

"Laura, you don't have anything to be ashamed of."

"I feel like I do. Then I feel guilty for being ashamed, because they aren't bad people. I just don't want to be close to them anymore."

"We all leave friends behind. People change, circumstances change. It's nothing to be ashamed of."

"It just struck me as such an awful reflection of who I used to be. You should have seen Thaddeous's face when I introduced him to the group. Not to mention what he must think of me for having dated Philip."

"Thaddeous knows you were a lot younger then. He's not going to judge you by the friends you used to have."

"Maybe not."

"Do you judge Thaddeous by his old friends? Let's not forget that he was in the Ku Klux Klan. Philip, for all his faults, never wore white sheets or burned crosses on people's front lawns."

"You know Thaddeous never would have joined the Klan if it hadn't been such a terrible time for him," I objected. A few years back, Thaddeous had thought a woman he cared for had been raped and killed by a bunch of black men. He was so angry and felt so helpless that he convinced himself that joining the Klan would help. "Besides, he only stayed in for a week."

"So? Your first few months at MIT were a terrible time

for you. And you only hung around those people for a few years."

"Okay, you've got a point."

"I'm starting to wish that you hadn't gotten involved in this, Laura. I've been worried about you being around these people because one of them might be a killer—now I'm worried because of how you're reacting to being with them."

"I'll be fine. Today was just weird, that's all."

"Okay, but let me say this again. One, you have nothing to be ashamed of for having been friends with these people. And two, you have nothing to be ashamed of for not wanting to be close friends with them now. All right?"

"All right," I said, and repeated, "I'll be fine." I could tell he wasn't convinced, but I knew it was late for him and talked him into getting off the phone. And I did feel better, just not all the way back to myself. I couldn't help but be ashamed of who I had been when I was an MIT freshman. Even worse, for all my talk about my having grown and being different now, sometimes I was afraid that I hadn't really changed at all.

Chapter 25

Michelle and Thaddeous showed up soon after that, in a much better mood than I was in. My outlook did improve when I saw that they were carrying pints of ice cream and hot fudge. As we ate way too much of it, I repeated what I'd told Richard. Like my husband, they were bothered by the eavesdropper outside Dom's cube, but I soothed them just as I had him. Then I said, "I don't have any idea of what to do next."

"Don't worry about it," Michelle said breezily. "It's time to party. I've got the weekend all planned."

I suppose I could have been offended about her taking over, but I wasn't. I'd done enough thinking for one week, so I was perfectly content to let her lead me and Thaddeous around Boston, and I was pretty sure that Thaddeous would be, too.

Saturday was spent at the Museum of Fine Arts, not the first place I'd have picked to take Thaddeous, but he seemed to enjoy it. I don't think he was terribly impressed by the Impressionists, but he did like the Egyptian exhibits.

Then we walked to the Isabella Stewart Gardner Museum, one of the most charming places in Boston. Isabella Stewart Gardner and her husband were wealthy, eccentric art collectors. After his death, Isabella became even more eccentric and collected even more art. She built a house to hold it all, and then made it into a museum.

Isabella had a good eye for art, but she also collected things just because she liked them. After Thaddeous wandered through the floors of Spanish masters, Sargent portraits, tapestries, and a Venetian sedan chair, he said, "I bet Aunt Maggie would have liked this lady. She liked digging for stuff, just like Aunt Maggie does."

I'm not sure if the aristocratic Mrs. Gardner would have welcomed the comparison of her lavish European buying trips to my great-aunt's thrift-store prowls, but Thaddeous might have been right.

I had a bad case of museum fatigue after that, but Michelle insisted on dragging us out to Harvard Square to look into shops and listen to the few street performers willing to brave the cold. Thaddeous got to look at the folks who hang around in the center of Harvard Square. There's always lots of leather, spiked and unusually colored hair, and pierced body parts to see.

I'll give my cousin credit: I knew he'd never seen people dressed that way before, but he didn't gawk. He looked, of course, but he wasn't a bit rude about it. I don't know that I could have said the same about myself the first time I went to Harvard Square.

We ate dinner at Bartley's Burger Cottage, one of Richard's college hang-outs and still our favorite place for hamburgers. The burgers are so huge that I've never had dessert there. Thaddeous made it through his burger and fries, but gave up on the onion rings.

Michelle was all for going dancing after that, saying we'd missed some places the week before, but I was worn to a frazzle and Thaddeous admitted that he was a mite tired, too.

So we went back to my apartment to watch videos. At least, they did. I fell asleep as soon as I got comfortable on the couch.

Sunday, Michelle had plans, so Thaddeous and I hung around the apartment and tried to come up with a plan to track down Philip's killer. The problem was, I had spoken to everybody at SSI at least once, and we didn't have any more idea of what to do next than the man in the moon.

"Now what?" I demanded of Thaddeous that evening, as we finished up the spaghetti we had made for dinner. It was just as well that Michelle hadn't come over—I wouldn't have dared cook anything Italian if she'd been around.

"It seems to me you've covered all the bases. Other than maybe Roberta."

"I don't think Roberta's even noticed that Philip's dead yet," I said. "But she's been at SSI plenty long enough to come up with a motive for killing him. That's the problem. Everybody's got a motive."

"Let's lay it all out," Thaddeous suggested. "Write it down and look at it."

I got a pad out of my desk and started at the top of the page. "Okay, in no particular order, we have Vincent, Inez, Jessie, Neal, Murray, Dee, Dom, and Sheliah."

"And Roberta."

"And Roberta." I thought about it. "Better add Colleen, too, but I think she's a long shot."

"Good enough. Now, what's Vincent's motive?"

"He wanted to take SSI public, and Philip was standing in the way. And something about his MIT class ring."

"The brass rat?"

I nodded. "I don't know what, but Philip was holding something over his head. I wonder if Inez would know."

"Wouldn't she use it herself if she did?" Thaddeous asked.

"You're probably right. Then let's move on to Inez. Same motive as Vincent. Philip was blocking her from what she wanted for SSI. And he was threatening to make their past public."

"Doesn't sound like much of a threat," Thaddeous said. "This ain't Byerly—who'd care? Unless she's got a boyfriend she hasn't told about her past."

"None that I've heard about, and I think I would have. Jessie knows everything, and tells most of what she knows."

"Then what about Jessie?"

"Philip was threatening the well-being of the group," I said, knowing it sounded silly. "She really is a mother hen. Or maybe a mother lion, when it comes to defending that group."

"It don't sound like much of a reason to kill to me."

"Not to me, either, but I think the folks at SSI are all the life Jessie has. So maybe saving it would be worth killing to her."

"Next is Neal."

"I don't have a motive for him."

"Did he and Philip get along when they were rooming together?"

"They always seemed to. Philip teased Neal because of Neal being so much younger, but Neal didn't act like he held it against him. And it's been a long time." I moved to the next name. "Murray."

"You said Philip put him down."

"A lot," I said. "Murray must have hated that. But Philip treated Murray badly for as long as I can remember—I don't know of any reason he'd suddenly decide to kill him."

"Sometimes a man will snap after a while. Daddy told me once about a man at the mill whose wife popped her chewing gum. He never said anything about it, not for years and years. Then one night he up and left her, without a bit of warning."

It sounded unlikely to me, but unlikely things did happen.

Thaddeous said, "Now Dee. Philip was threatening to tell Dom about their affair, and breaking up somebody's marriage is a pretty good motive."

I nodded. "As for Dom, he was angry at Philip for upsetting Dee, but it sounded like voting against Philip was enough revenge for him. Though if Philip did tell Dom about that night with Dee, mightn't Dom have killed him because of it?"

"Could be. Some people would say that Philip had it coming."

"I wouldn't go that far." But I put it on the list. "Sheliah."

"He'd been treating her badly at work. Could it have gotten worse than that? Like stalking?"

"I don't think so. Philip was slimy, but I don't think he was ever obsessed enough with anybody to go that far."

"Then there's Roberta."

"Nary a clue," I said.

"His wife Colleen?"

"Not for insurance, because she doesn't get any. She does get the house and whatever else they had without having to go through a divorce. I don't know what they had, so I don't know if it was worth killing for. I suppose I could go talk to her, but I don't know that she'd tell me if it was."

That made me realize something, and I looked at the list in disgust. "That's our problem, Thaddeous. Everything we've got, we've got from the people involved, and they've all got reason to lie. How can I trust any of it?" I ripped the sheet off of the pad and was ready to wad it up, but Thaddeous pulled it away from me.

"Now, simmer down, Laurie Anne. We've made a lot of

progress. What we've got to do now is confirm some of this information through an objective source."

I looked at him. That wasn't his usual way of speaking.

He grinned. "That's what Mama always tries to do if she hears good gossip."

A conscientious gossip? It sounded like a contradiction in terms to me, but I could see how it would make sense to Aunt Nora. "The problem is, any objective source would say that we're nuts for sticking our noses into this. Heck, we can't even be sure that Philip was really murdered. Maybe his death was an accident after all and I've just been wasting my time. All of our time."

"It seems to me any man who had as many enemies as Philip did had to have been murdered," Thaddeous said.

"People make enemies all the time without being killed. Look at Big Bill Walters back home. He's still alive and kicking."

"But Philip isn't," Thaddeous said.

He had a point. "What objective source do you suggest?"

"If this was Byerly, you'd call Junior and ask her what was what."

"Thaddeous, you don't think Detective Salvatore is going to tell me anything, do you?"

"Why wouldn't he?"

"Because he doesn't know me from Adam's house cat. For all he knows, I might have killed Philip myself."

"Now, we know he doesn't think that because the snow on Philip shows he died long after he left your apartment."

"Maybe, but there are ways I could have gotten around the snow." Then something clicked in my head. "Snow! Thaddeous, I am a complete idiot. The snow could tell us for sure if Philip was murdered!"

"How's that?" he asked, but I was already trying to figure out where I'd put Detective Salvatore's business card. I
finally found it in a stack of mail on my coffee table and dialed
the number, hoping that he was unlucky enough to have to
work on Sunday.

"Boston Police. Salvatore speaking."

"Detective Salvatore, this is Laura Fleming. We spoke
about Philip Dennis's death."

"Yes, Mrs. Fleming. What can I do for you?"

"My cousin and I were just talking about Philip," I said,
wondering if that sounded ghoulish, "and we wondered about
the condition of the snow around the body. I mean, wouldn't
there have been tracks in the snow? Couldn't they help you
figure out what happened?"

"We did consider that," he said with a tone of determined
patience. "Unfortunately, the tracks weren't all that clear.
Part of the alley had been plowed, presumably before Mr.
Dennis died, and there was a fair amount of melting before
he was found. So it was pretty muddy before we got back
there."

"Oh," I said, disappointed. Though I guess I should have
been relieved that the police knew what they were doing.
"Then you can't tell if he was alone or not?"

"Do you have reason to believe that he wasn't alone?"

"Not really," I said, not willing to admit what I'd been up
to. "It just seems he might have gone off with somebody, and
then they drove back. People do park back there."

"As a matter of fact, we found tire tracks that could have
been made around the same time as Mr. Dennis's death. But
we can't tell for sure if Dennis was in that car." He paused.
"You're sure that you don't have any reason to believe he was
with somebody else?"

Did I have anything concrete to tell him? I wished I did, but I just didn't. If he'd been Junior, I wouldn't have minded sharing my suspicions, because she wouldn't have laughed, no matter how silly they sounded. Well, not too much, anyway. But I didn't know Salvatore any better than he knew me. "No, I don't."

"Then the most likely explanation is that somebody parked back there, saw Dennis lying on the ground, and left. Either they thought Dennis was a bum sleeping it off, or they could tell he was dead and didn't want to get involved. Not everybody takes as much interest in crime as you do, Mrs. Fleming."

I didn't want to think about what might be behind that last sentence. "Have you learned anything else about the . . ." I'd nearly called it a murder. "About Philip's death? Was there anything in the autopsy report?"

"Nothing conclusive. Though we're still not sure what Dennis hit his head on."

"Doesn't that point to the idea of somebody hitting him? And then taking the weapon away with him?"

"Or her. It's possible."

He didn't say anything else for a long time. Hadn't Junior told me that sometimes the best way to get information from a suspect is to be quiet? If I'd been guilty, it just might have worked.

"Well," I said brightly, "I sure hope you find out what happened."

"I think I will," he said, which sounded vaguely ominous. "You be sure to call if you and your cousin think of anything else."

"I sure will. 'Bye now."

"Well?" Thaddeous asked.

"Philip was murdered," I said definitely. "At least, Salvatore thinks so."

"He said that?"

"No, but what he did say plus what he didn't say has me convinced. Of course, now he's suspicious of me again because of my calling him."

"I'm sure he knows better."

"It doesn't matter. I know I didn't do it, so he can't possibly make a case against me. I'm just glad he's still looking. And we'll do the same."

"That's what I wanted to hear." He looked at me expectantly for a few minutes. "Well, then, what do we do next?"

"Shoot, Thaddeous, I don't know." I felt very foolish, but before I could say anything, he reached over and patted my hand, just like his mother would have.

"Don't you worry about it," he said. "I feel sure we'll come up with something."

It was nice he had so much confidence in us, but I sure wished I felt the same.

Chapter 26

I did nothing useful at SSI the next day. Or rather, I did lots that was useful to SSI, but nothing that helped us learn about Philip's death. I was really hoping Thaddeous would call with a brilliant plan, but it just didn't happen. In fact, he wasn't even at my apartment when I got home.

The phone rang a little while later, and I picked up the receiver, expecting to hear Thaddeous. "Hello?"

"Laurie Anne?"

"Hi, Vasti. What's up?"

"How does it feel to be famous?"

"What are you talking about?"

"It's not every day that you get into a real, live book. Did that author not call you yet?"

"Vasti, I haven't got the slightest idea what you're talking about."

"Well, I was over at Aunt Nora's this morning to pick up cookies for my bake sale when the phone rang. Since her hands were full, I answered the phone, and it was a reporter."

"I thought you said author."

"Same difference. He's writing a book, isn't he?"

I knew I shouldn't have interrupted her. "Okay, a writer called. What did he say?"

"He told me about this book he's writing about true crime stories in North Carolina. I guess he heard about some of the things you and Thaddeous have been involved in, like Melanie Wilson's and Tom Honeywell's murders, because he asked all kinds of questions about how you came to solve them. He said he was sure y'all would get into his book, and he'd even mention that Arthur is your cousin by marriage and how he's running for reelection to the city council. Isn't that wonderful?"

I knew there were a lot of books about true crime stories, but I couldn't see how the murders Vasti was talking about would interest anybody enough to put them into a book. "Vasti, who was this guy?"

"I don't remember what he said his name was, but he's from Charlotte. Well, he lives there now, but he's not from there. Not with that accent."

"What all did you tell him?"

"Everything I remembered, of course. You want his book to be accurate, don't you? He said he'd call you, too, as soon as he'd done some more research. He likes to get his background work all done before he talks to the subject. Oh, no!"

"What?"

"He asked me not to call you because he wanted to surprise you. I up and forgot that part until right now!"

Just as she had forgotten what day Thaddeous was due in Boston. But just like that time, her spoiling the surprise might come in handy. "When did you say he called?"

"This morning."

"Why didn't you call me sooner?"

"I was busy getting the bake sale ready, and I didn't want to spend the money to call during the day."

"Of course not," I said.

"Don't you want to be in a book? I'd think you'd be glad to help Arthur in his campaign. It's not like you have to *do* anything, just talk to the man when he calls you."

"Vasti, I'm not about to tell my private business to some stranger, and I wish you hadn't, either. How do you know he was really a reporter?"

"He said he was."

"Not everybody is as honest as you are." Okay, there was a little sarcasm in my voice when I said that, but I'm sure it went right over her head.

"Why else would he call, if he's not a reporter?"

"I'm not sure. It's just that Thaddeous and I have been looking into something—"

"Another murder! That's wonderful! Now I know he'll put you in the book."

If there was a book. "Did he call anybody else in the family?"

"Aunt Maggie said somebody called her, but she didn't have time to talk to him. Can you imagine that?"

"Well, do me a favor. Tell everybody not to tell this man anything. If he wants to ask questions about me and Thaddeous, he can call us up here."

"I don't understand why."

"Vasti, it's hard enough getting people to answer questions as it is. This isn't Byerly, and folks are a little more private. The only reason we've been able to get away with it is that everybody just thinks we're curious. If they found out we'd done this kind of thing before, nobody would speak to us." Not to mention the fact that we could very well become targets. "Do you see what I'm saying?"

"I guess so," she said, sounding miffed.

It was time to add some soft soap. "I knew *you'd* understand. Do you think you can get the others to see it our way?"

"Of course I can," she said confidently. "Nobody's going to say one word when I'm done with them."

"That's great. One other thing. Can you call Hank Parker at the *Byerly Gazette* to see if anybody's talked to him? I don't know how this guy heard about me and Thaddeous, but I wouldn't be at all surprised to find out that he checked out the paper."

"You don't think this man was the murderer you're looking for, do you?"

"I don't know. What kind of accent did he have?"

"A Northern one."

"What kind of Northern accent? New York? Boston?"

"How would I know? I just know he talked funny."

I sighed, wishing Vasti knew more about accents. "I don't know if he's our guy or not, but I still smell a rat. Let me know if you hear anything else from him."

"All right. 'Bye, now."

I hung up the phone, feeling more than a little nervous. On Friday, I'd seen somebody listening in while I'd asked questions. On Sunday, I'd asked Detective Salvatore a bunch of questions. And on Monday, somebody had started asking questions about me. It didn't take a whole lot of brains to realize that I'd made somebody suspicious. Which led to the question of who it was. Though I knew I was being silly, I still went to the front door and put the chain on.

Chapter 27

I was as nervous as a long-tailed cat in a room full of rocking chairs, so naturally I jumped a foot when the doorbell rang. It was Michelle, and I buzzed her in.

"Have you applied for a bank loan recently?" she asked, as soon as she got in the door.

"No."

"I knew it! I told myself, there is no way Laura would be fooling around with a loan when we're in the middle of solving a murder. Not to mention the fact that your husband is out of town."

"Why? What happened?"

"Today I got a phone call from somebody wanting to talk to human resources. Lucky for us, Sharon is out for a couple of days to take her baby to see her folks in Rhode Island, so I asked if there was anything I could help him with. This guy said he was from the Bank of Boston and he wanted to confirm your employment record for some loan you had supposedly applied for. Which I knew you hadn't."

"Did you get his name?"

"I got a name, but no way do I believe it was his real one."

"What did you tell him?"

"I told him our cover story, that you had worked for us up until last week and that you'd gone to work at SSI."

"Did he believe you?"

"Of course he believed me. I'm a convincing person. I'm just glad that I took the call."

"You and me both. And by the way, you're not the only person to get a bunch of questions about me today." I told her what Vasti had told me.

"This is not good, Laura, not good at all. Somebody knows what we're doing."

"I'm afraid you're right."

"Where's Thaddeous?"

"I don't know. I haven't spoken to him since I left for SSI this morning."

"Oh, my God!" she said, her eyes getting big. "I've been trying to reach him since around ten—I thought he could meet me for lunch. That means he's been missing all day!"

I could tell she was starting to panic, and to tell the truth, I was getting close to that myself. "Calm down. I'm sure Thaddeous is fine."

"He could be lying in an alley somewhere. Or maybe shot. Or maybe—"

"Michelle! Stop that! Thaddeous is a grown man—he can take care of himself."

"And Philip Dennis wasn't a grown man?"

There wasn't much I could say to that. All I could think of was that Thaddeous could be anywhere. I didn't even know where to start looking. Should I call the police? The hospitals? What was I going to tell Aunt Nora?

I made myself take a deep breath, then said, "Look, it's just now six-thirty. I bet he got mixed up in the rush hour on the subway and got lost. The subway can be pretty confusing, and you know how men are about stopping to ask for directions." This last was a sexist generalization, but I was hoping it would calm her down.

It didn't.

"I don't know why I let you talk me into getting involved in this," she said. "It's making me a nervous wreck, is what it's doing."

I thought about reminding her that it was she who had insisted on joining as a full partner, but decided that it wasn't worth it.

"Let's give him until eight o'clock," I said. "If we haven't heard from him by then, we'll call the police." I'd heard that the police wouldn't actually start looking for a missing person until he'd been missing for twenty-four hours, but I knew I couldn't wait that long.

Michelle never would have been able to, either. I didn't think she was going to make it an hour and a half. She kept muttering things like, "I'm going crazy here," and "If he's even a little bit hurt, I'm going to call my third cousin Vito and find out if he really is connected."

Her worry for Thaddeous would have been touching if she hadn't been driving me up the blooming wall. The thing was, I didn't have anything I could tell her to make her feel any better, so I just let her complain.

Which she did for the next forty-five minutes, pacing up and down my living room, which really isn't big enough for a decent pace, talking the whole time. I'd thought she had a vivid imagination when she was coming up with possible motives for Philip's death, but that was nothing compared to the possibilities she came up with for Thaddeous's absence.

Finally, just before I'd have been forced to knock her upside the head just to save my sanity, the door opened and Thaddeous walked in.

"It's about time!" I said, but I was drowned out by Michelle.

"Where have you been? I've been pulling my hair out here."

At least he had the good grace to look embarrassed. "Sorry. It took me longer to get back than I expected."

"*What* took you longer that you expected?" she asked.

"Finding me an objective source."

"What is he talking about, Laura?"

"I don't know, but I'm fixing to drag it out of him if he doesn't tell us about it right now."

"Well, I'd better start at the beginning," he said.

That didn't surprise me. I'd never known a Southerner to start a story any other way.

"This morning, after Laurie Anne left, I got to thinking. Last night we were talking about how everything we knew could be lies, and that the only way we'd know for sure would be to talk to somebody objective. Now, Laurie Anne's been doing a real good job with the folks at SSI, but the one person she hadn't had much of a chance to speak to was Philip's wife, Colleen."

"You're not talking fast enough," Michelle warned.

He did try to speed up, but as with most Southerners, talking fast doesn't come naturally to him. "We've been wondering whether or not Philip had enough money for her to kill for, so I needed somebody who'd be likely to know, and who'd talk to me about it. Well, I don't know many people up here, but I did see Philip's family at the visitation. I even spoke to Dave a few minutes because he came outside to smoke a cigarette while I was there. We didn't say much, but from what he did say and what he said inside, I could tell he doesn't think a whole lot of Colleen."

"So you called him?" I said.

"No, I didn't think this was something you'd talk about on the phone. I went to see him."

"You went to see a complete stranger out of the blue?" I said. "And he talked to you?"

"Why wouldn't he?" he asked.

I thought about explaining to him what life in the big city was like, and how people wouldn't talk to just anybody the way they would in Byerly, but I decided not to. What he didn't know didn't seem to be hurting him. In fact, it seemed to be doing us a lot of good. "But Dave lives in Worcester. That's got to be fifty miles from here."

"About that. I looked in that guidebook you left me, and it said there was a train that went there, but I didn't want to have to mess with the schedules. So I rented a car and drove there."

"You couldn't have called one of us before you went shooting down the Pike to Worcester?" Michelle said.

"I wanted to surprise y'all," he said apologetically. "I thought I'd be home before y'all got here, but it took me right much longer to get there than I expected. And the traffic coming back was something fierce. I got stuck in one of those places where you go in a circle—"

"You mean a rotary?" I said.

He nodded. "I must have been in there a good fifteen minutes, just going round and round. I'd have called if I could have. Then I had to take the car back, and every phone I passed on the way back from the rental place was busy or broken. I'm awful sorry I upset you."

"You should be!" Michelle said, clearly not giving him an

inch. She glared at him for a full minute while he shuffled his feet.

Finally he said shyly, "I didn't realize you'd be so worried about me."

"Why wouldn't I be? You disappear when there's a murderer running around loose, and you expect me not to worry?"

I said, "We're just glad you're okay. Isn't that right, Michelle?"

"Hmmph," was all she said.

"Take your coat off and sit down, Thaddeous, and tell us what happened. Did you talk to Dave?"

"I sure did," he said, as he did what I'd told him to. "He's a pretty good fellow."

"I don't care if he's Prince Charming," Michelle said. "Did he have any dirt on his sister-in-law?"

I would have thought that Thaddeous would be offended, but he just grinned at Michelle like she was the cutest thing he'd ever seen. He was hooked, all right.

"I'll tell you," he said. "I got to Worcester—am I saying that right? Worst-er? Wooster?"

"It's Worcester," I said, pronouncing it the way Richard had taught me. "It rhymes with . . . you know, I don't think it rhymes with anything."

"You guys . . ." Michelle said warningly.

Thaddeous quickly went on. "I got to Worcester at around eleven o'clock, eleven-thirty. I looked Dave up in the phone book and got directions to his house, but when I got there, nobody was home. So I parked and waited."

"As cold as it was today?" I asked.

"It was a mite chilly," he admitted. "At half-past two, I went and found myself something to eat and warmed up in the restaurant. Then I went back over there. That's when I

saw Dave's truck pulling into the driveway. It turns out he's
an electrician, and he'd stopped by home in between jobs. It
took a few minutes to remind him of who I was and explain
why I wanted to talk to him—"

"What did you say?" I asked.

"I told him that I was in the neighborhood, and that Jessie
had asked me to speak to him because the folks at SSI were
worried about Colleen. I said that since the insurance money
went back into the company, they were afraid that she
wouldn't have enough to live on. Only they didn't want to ask
her themselves because they didn't want to embarrass her,
and wondered if Dave and his family knew how her finances
were."

"That's not bad," Michelle said, starting to thaw.

Thaddeous went on. "Anyway, I offered to take him out
for coffee if he had a few minutes, but he invited me in instead,
which was mighty nice of him."

Michelle said, "It's that Southern accent again. It charms
the socks right off of people." She was definitely thawing.

"So we went in and he fixed us coffee, and he gave me an
earful about Colleen."

"He doesn't care for her, does he?" I said.

"That's like saying Georgia doesn't care for Sherman,"
Thaddeous said. "He didn't like the way she treated Philip,
and the way she talked about his parents behind their backs
drove him crazy."

"Let me guess: it was Philip who told him what she
said."

Thaddeous nodded. "I suppose I could have tried to break
it to him that his brother wasn't the most truthful man on
earth, but Mama always says I shouldn't speak ill of the dead.
Especially not to a man's brother. Anyway, Dave said he

didn't think Philip had left Colleen two nickels to rub together, which was fine with him. He said she made Philip buy their house, which had cost more than they could afford, and that she caused Philip's problems at work, too."

"How did he know about the problems at SSI?" I asked. "I got the impression that he and Philip had been fighting for a good while."

"Dave didn't want to talk about that at first, but he finally admitted that Philip had called him maybe a week or so before he died. Philip wanted to borrow some money because SSI was doing so badly, but Dave wouldn't give it to him. Philip had already borrowed a lot from their parents, and he never paid the first penny of it back. Dave figured that lending him more would be throwing good money after bad. He told Philip not to bother talking to their parents again because Dave had made them promise not to lend him any more."

"Philip must have been fit to be tied," I said.

"You know he was. Dave didn't go into details, but there were hard words on both sides. That explains why Philip didn't go to Dave or his parents when Colleen threw him out."

I said, "It also explains why Dave was so rude at the visitation. He was probably feeling guilty about feuding with Philip the last time they spoke."

"He still feels bad, but like I told him, he wasn't the cause of Philip's being on the street. Philip had enough money to get himself a hotel room. I think Dave knew that, but he wanted to hear somebody else tell him."

"Well, it sounds like you've eliminated Colleen," Michelle said, "unless we can come up with a better motive than money."

"And Dave and his parents are out of it, too," I added. "If Philip owed them money, they won't get it now."

"Dave said his parents could really use it, too. Even if you don't count the money they loaned Philip over the past couple of years, they're still paying on his college loans."

"Dave did tell you a lot," I said.

"Once he got to talking, I couldn't have shut him up if I'd tried. I guess he needed to get some things off of his chest. Those two brothers had had problems their whole lives because Philip was so highfalutin and Dave was more down to earth."

I didn't have any problem believing that. It was ages before Philip actually admitted to being from Worcester, which has the reputation of being a blue-collar town. He'd just say he was from the western part of the state.

"Then I understand your being so late," Michelle said. "It was real nice of you to help Dave that way." She had warmed up enough to give him a peck on the cheek.

All Thaddeous said was, "It wasn't nothing," but he was grinning so wide I thought he was going to bust.

Apparently forgetting that I was in the room, the two of them made what my friends in junior high school used to call "cow eyes" at one another.

I let them bask in mutual admiration for few minutes before clearing my throat and saying, "I hate to interrupt, but I've got some news, too." First I told him about the phony loan officer who'd called GBS, and then I repeated the story Vasti had told me. "Why did Vasti have to be at your house when that man called? Aunt Nora wouldn't have spilled her guts like that."

"I don't suppose there's any chance it really was a writer, is there?" Thaddeous asked.

"I doubt it. A reporter appearing right now is too much of a coincidence. Besides which, what writer in his right mind would promise to push Arthur in a true crime book? Even if he did, a book couldn't be published in time for the election. This guy was up to something."

"Why would he be talking to folks in Byerly?"

"Checking up on me. And you, too."

"What about me?" Michelle wanted to know.

"I don't know, but if I were you, I'd warn my family not to answer any questions from strangers."

"Who do you think it was?" Thaddeous asked.

"All I know is that he had a Northern accent. Michelle, what about the guy you spoke to? What kind of accent did he have?"

"He didn't have an accent."

Thaddeous and I just looked at her.

"All right, what I mean is that he had a Boston accent. Hey, couldn't I call up everybody at SSI and see if I recognize the voice?"

I said, "You could try, but there's no way of knowing that whoever it was didn't get somebody to call for him."

"I suppose that means we can't even be sure that it wasn't a woman who got a man to call," Thaddeous said.

"I'm afraid not," I said. I guess it was a good thing that we had stirred somebody up enough to ask questions about us, because that had to mean that we were on the right track. But I didn't feel happy about it—I just felt worried.

Chapter 28

"Okay," I said briskly. "What do we do next?"

Thaddeous said, "I don't know, Laurie Anne. I'm fresh out of ideas."

I thought about what we'd found out as I got us all something to drink. "You know, there's still one loose end we haven't followed up on: Vincent's rat."

"No offense," Thaddeous said, "but I can't make hide nor hair of that rat. What in the Sam Hill does it mean?"

"I'm not sure," I admitted, "but I'm sure that it's got something to do with MIT." I fiddled with my class ring for a minute, and then I thought of something. "What you said about Philip and his brother has given me an idea. When I was in Vincent's office the other day, I noticed a picture of him and his brothers, all of them wearing sweatshirts from their alma maters. One went to Harvard, one to Yale, and one to Dartmouth. And, of course, Vincent went to MIT."

Thaddeous said, "They must be a smart bunch in that family."

"And very competitive," I said. "Vincent didn't talk about them much, but I remember meeting his family at graduation, and they really looked down their noses at MIT. The brothers kept making cracks about nerds. Even Philip couldn't shut them up. The fact is, MIT isn't nearly as prestigious as those other schools."

"It's done well by you," Thaddeous said loyally.

"I know it has, and I wouldn't trade my education there for anything, but to some people, MIT is still just a technical college. It's not Ivy League and never will be. The schools Vincent's brothers went to are."

"What are you saying?" Michelle wanted to know.

"Suppose you went to a lesser school than your brothers, and for some reason, you never graduated. In other words, what if Vincent never really earned his brass rat?"

Thaddeous said, "Couldn't he just finish up later on? Even in high school, they let you take classes over if you need to."

"He could have," I said, "but only if he told people about flunking. If you were in a really competitive family like his, would you admit flunking a class? Especially if you were the kind of person who puts on airs, like Vincent does?"

"I might not," Thaddeous said.

"If Vincent never graduated and Philip found out, that would have been one heck of a secret to hold over him. Not only would it have hurt Vincent's credibility at work, but he'd have been humiliated if his family found out. I don't know his wife, but it could have hurt his marriage, too."

"But you said Vincent graduated with you," Thaddeous pointed out.

I said, "Lots of people walk through the ceremony without actually getting a diploma. Sometimes they have a class or two to finish over the summer, but want to go through the formal ceremony. I knew several people who walked in June but didn't get their diplomas until later on."

"So how do we find out if he's really got a diploma?" Michelle asked.

"Well, he's got a diploma on his wall, and it looked okay to me, but I wasn't looking that closely. It could have been forged. And he has an MIT class ring, but anybody can buy one of those. Paw bought me mine months before graduation."

Thaddeous asked, "Is there any way we can get a good look at his diploma and find out if it's a fake?"

"I don't know about that, but we might can check his records at MIT." To Michelle, I said, "I think this is a job for you."

She looked surprised. "Me? *You're* the one who went to school there."

"But I was just one student at an awfully big university. And a university is like any business—it's the administrative people who really run things."

"Meaning that you want me to see what I can find out through the secretary's network."

"Exactly. Do you know anybody over there?"

"I might." She reached into her pocketbook and pulled out a small red address book. "Mind if I use your phone?"

"Not at all."

"It could take a while," she warned.

"Maybe I should call out for dinner first."

"No need for that," Thaddeous said. "I expect I can scrounge up something for dinner while you make your calls."

"It's a deal." She grinned up at my cousin. "Good looks, and he cooks, too. I must have died and gone to heaven."

Dinner wasn't exactly heavenly, but it was pretty good. Thaddeous made omelettes with some cheddar cheese I'd forgotten was in the refrigerator, and an enormous stack of buttered toast. And just like his mama, he denied it being anything special. "It's not much of a meal," he said, "but it's something to eat."

In the meantime, Michelle made I don't know how many phone calls. The preliminaries for each call were long enough to make a Southerner seem concise by comparison, but each time, she managed to get the conversation steered in the direction she wanted it to go.

Finally, just as Thaddeous finished fixing the last omelette, she wrote down a phone number and thanked the person on the other end of the line profusely before she hung up. "Pay dirt!"

"You found somebody?" I asked.

"It turns out a woman I know has an older sister who I've met a couple of times. This sister is working in the registrar's office at MIT. Which is where they keep the records on graduates. Plus, she's working tonight because it's the end of 'drop period,' whatever that means."

Thaddeous said, "Do you want to call her now or wait until after we eat?"

"Definitely eat first. My friend is going to talk to the sister and let her know I'll be calling, so I've got time."

Dinner was good, although we were crowded around my tiny kitchen table. Michelle was more than happy about the cooking. In fact, to hear her talk, you'd have thought he'd laid the eggs himself.

As soon as we were finished eating, Michelle went back to the phone while Thaddeous and I cleaned up the kitchen. The two of us didn't speak because we wanted to hear what Michelle was going to find out.

"Sarah? This is Michelle Nucci, your sister Teri's friend. How are you? . . . Good, glad to hear it . . . I'm fine . . . Your sister tells me she just got engaged. She says he's wonderful, but what do you think?" There was a long pause and I guessed that Sarah was telling Michelle everything about the bridegroom-to-be. Finally Michelle said, "Who me? Maybe." She looked over at Thaddeous, whose back was turned right then. "Too soon to tell. But it looks promising . . . Yes, he is." She giggled. "So how do you like it at MIT? . . . No kidding . . . I hope they're paying you for it . . . Good, good. Sarah, did your sister tell you why I'm calling? . . . That's right, I need a favor. It's a big one, too, and I want you to tell me if there's any chance at all that you could get into trouble." Michelle held up her hand and conspicuously crossed her fingers. "Okay, here's the story. Did I ever mention my cousin Carol to you? . . . She's a couple of years younger than me. Anyway, she's got this guy she's interested in. He's real good-looking and seems nice, but I don't know, Sarah. I just don't trust him. Neither does the rest of the family . . . I know she's a grown woman, Sarah, and normally I wouldn't interfere, but I've got a bad feeling about this guy. How would you feel if you didn't think your sister's fiancé was on the up-and-up? . . . That's what I thought. Well, Carol's like a sister to me and I want to make sure everything is okay for her. You see what I'm talking about?"

Michelle mimed drinking at me, and I took her a glass of water.

She took a swallow, then went on. "Okay, the reason I'm calling you is that this guy says he graduated from MIT, but I'm not sure I believe him . . . Yeah, I've seen his diploma, and it looks real, but what do I know? . . . What I'm hoping is that you can take a look at his records, and make sure he really graduated . . . You can? Oh, Sarah, I would owe you such a favor for this. Tell you what—are you giving your sister a wedding shower? Have you got a hall picked out? . . . Okay, when you get a date set, you call me. My uncle is a caterer. He's got connections with the best places in town, and I'll make sure he takes care of you . . . Hey, that's what friends are for. I know what a nice party costs these days . . . The guy's name is Vincent Noone. Or maybe Vinnie Noone, which he used to go by. Class of—"

I whispered, "Eighty-nine."

"Class of Eighty-nine . . . Sure, I'll wait."

It took a while, but finally Sarah gave an answer. Only I could tell from the look on Michelle's face that it wasn't the answer we wanted.

"He *did* graduate? What were his grades like? . . . That good, huh? You're sure it couldn't have been faked? This guy is a whiz with a computer. Couldn't he have gotten into your system and played around with the grades? . . . Yeah, that makes sense. As many computer jocks as you've got there, you must have a wicked good security system. What about bribes? Could he have paid off a professor? . . . No, I guess there's no way you could know about that. Well, thanks for looking . . . Of course I'm still going to get you a deal on the hall . . . I'd love to come. Just let me know where she's registered. 'Bye." She hung up the phone.

"Rats!" I said, which was all too appropriate. "I was so *sure.*"

"Hey, all it cost us was a few phone calls," Michelle said.

"And a deal on a hall and catering."

"So what? My uncle gives everybody a good deal. That's why he never makes any money. It drives my aunt crazy."

Thaddeous said, "It was worth a shot, Laurie Anne."

"I suppose," I said. "It's just that I'm running out of ideas real fast."

"You cut that out," Thaddeous said. "We're not out of this yet, not by a long shot."

"You tell her, Thaddeous!" Michelle added.

The both of them did their best to cheer me up, and I tried to act cheered, but I was glad when it was time to go to bed so I could quit acting. Philip had been dead over a week, and all we really knew so far was that we'd roused somebody's suspicions. I was going to have to go back to my real job in a week or so and Thaddeous was going to have to go back to Byerly soon. And I just couldn't stand the idea that I might never know the truth.

Chapter 29

I was hoping to wake up feeling inspired. I didn't, but I went to SSI anyway. While pretending to design screen formats, I kept thinking about that second straw poll, wondering who it was Philip had blackmailed into changing his or her vote. I mentally went through the board of directors.

Dee voted for Philip both times: once from loyalty and once because of blackmail. Dom voted for him the first time and against him the second. I was pretty sure that Jessie had voted for him both times because she was so loyal to the group that it was hard to imagine her voting to fire anybody. Murray had openly voted against Philip the first time, and I didn't think he'd changed his mind for the second.

That left Vincent and Inez. Both were publicly against Philip, but that didn't mean both had actually voted against him. If Philip blackmailed one of them into changing his or her vote, neither would have admitted it because that would mean exposing a weakness that the other one could use. That made Inez and Vincent the ones to focus on.

I went back over my reasoning. It was made up of guesses and assumptions that people had been telling me the truth, but it was something to go on. And I sure as heck didn't have anything better.

Next, I had to decide which one to go after first. Offhand, I couldn't think of any way to approach Vincent. The only lead I'd had was his brass rat, and that had turned out to be a waste of time.

Inez wasn't much more promising. She'd told me what it was Philip had used on her, so obviously it wasn't a secret worth killing to keep. Come to think of it, she had told me the story pretty quickly. At the time I'd been glad, but looking back, it seemed kind of funny. Inez and I had never been all that close, and certainly we weren't anymore. Why would she admit to an affair that was none of my business? With Philip dead, there was no other way I could have found out. Could she have lied in order to hide something else?

I drank down the last of my coffee to give myself an excuse to go by Inez's office. She was typing furiously at her keyboard.

"Hi, Inez," I said casually. "How's it going?"

She didn't look up. "Insane. Vinnie should have filed this paperwork last week, and the deadline is today. Which means that I have to get it done in the next hour and a half before I have to leave for a doctor's appointment, or we are screwed. So unless it's an emergency . . ."

"No, not at all. Is there anything wrong? For you to go to the doctor, I mean."

"Just a physical."

"Good. Talk to you later." I started back for my desk, but then I thought of something. If she was just going for a physical, why didn't she cancel and reschedule for a better time? I turned around and headed for Jessie's office.

She was working at her keyboard, too, though not so frantically.

"Hey there, Jessie."

"Hi, Laura. What's up?"

"Just stretching my legs," I said, and went in to sit at her guest chair. "How's it going with you?"

"Not bad. Just updating some records."

"Not with the same deadline as Inez, I hope."

She grimaced. "No, thank goodness."

"Jessie, is Inez all right?"

"What do you mean?"

"I thought she looked a little tired." That was a lie, but it was vague enough that I could get away with it. "And she mentioned that she had a doctor's appointment today."

"Really? She didn't mention a doctor's appointment to me. She didn't get an insurance form, either."

"Maybe she already has one."

Jessie shook her head. "The insurance company changed their forms, and we just got in the new batch last week. I didn't memo you because you didn't sign up for our plan. Anyway, the forms are right there and she hasn't asked for one." She pointed to a shrink-wrapped bundle on the shelf across from her desk. "Maybe I should go see if she needs one."

"I'm sure she'll come by if she does. And I might have misheard her, and she has a different kind of appointment." I steered the conversation to other matters for a few minutes before heading back for my desk to call Thaddeous.

"Fleming residence," he said.

"Thaddeous, this is Laura."

"Hey, Laurie Anne. What's going on?"

"I've got a job for you, if you're interested." I spoke quietly, this time mindful of the fact that my walls didn't reach all the way to the ceiling.

"You know I am."

I quickly explained why I had decided that Inez warranted another look, and why I thought she might be lying about having a doctor's appointment. "Do you feel up to following her to see where she ends up?"

"I could give it a try. But she's met me once, so I'll have to be careful."

"Wear your Walters Mill cap," I suggested. "You weren't wearing a hat when she met you."

"Good idea. When should I be there?"

"She said she had an hour and a half until time to leave. So if you could get here by eleven-thirty, that should be about right. I'd grab a taxi if I were you, just to be sure that you don't miss her."

"All right."

"I'll keep an eye out and see if she picks up an insurance form between now and then. There's a pay phone across the street, so call me from there and I'll tell you. That way you won't be going on a wild goose chase if she is heading for the doctor."

"I'll do it. 'Bye, now."

I had never drunk so much coffee in my life as I did in the next hour and a half. That and going to the bathroom were the only excuses I could come up with to keep going by Jessie's office to make sure that Inez hadn't unsealed that pack of insurance forms. When Thaddeous called, I was able to report that she hadn't.

The next two hours were painful. Even though I knew there was probably time for me to run out and get something to eat, I just couldn't bring myself to leave my phone. So I got Dee to pick me up a sandwich and ate at my desk. After that and all the coffee from the morning, I needed to go to the bathroom something fierce, but I resisted nature's call.

Finally, at about two-thirty, I saw Inez go by. A few minutes after that, Thaddeous called.

"Is Inez there?" he asked.

"She just got here."

"Good. I lost her on the way back, and I was afraid she might have made another stop."

"Where did she go?"

"She went to the doctor."

"You're kidding," I said, feeling let down. "But I'm sure she didn't get an insurance form. I guess she just forgot, after all."

"As a matter of fact, she paid cash."

"Really? Why would she do that if she's got insurance? Thaddeous, what are you not telling me?"

"She went to a doctor, all right, but I don't think it's her usual doctor. It was a clinic, one of those places that specializes in a certain kind of disease."

"Good Lord! Inez hasn't got—" I lowered my voice to a whisper. "She hasn't got AIDS, has she?"

"No, not that. As soon as I walked in the front door, a woman handed me a brochure telling me what kind of services they offer and how much they cost. It mentioned AIDS, but only to refer you to another clinic. What I think she's got is herpes."

"How can you be sure?"

"I'm not, but the money she paid when she was leaving was the same amount as for a follow-up visit for herpes. The only other thing that cost that amount was a check for cancer of the—for a disease she's not likely to have."

"You were there when she paid? She didn't see you, did she?"

"Not as far as I can tell. I was in a corner, behind a plant. I hung back, thinking I could catch up with her later, but I like to never have got out of that place. You see, I went in right after she did and read that brochure for the entire hour and a half she was there. I think the folks who work there thought I was scared to talk to them, because right after she left, the nurse came over to me and told me that I had nothing to be ashamed of and that nobody would have to know I'd been there, but it was real important that I get treatment for my problem. I tried to tell her that I didn't have a problem, that I was just picking up a brochure for a friend, but I could tell that she didn't believe me."

"I expect they hear that one a lot."

"I imagine they do, which is why I didn't want to be rude and run out on her. She was trying to help, but I was getting right embarrassed."

"What did you do?"

"I finally told her I had to get to work, but that I'd come back later. She still didn't believe me, but she said she hoped she'd see me again."

"Poor Thaddeous," I said, even though the situation struck my funny bone. But Inez's situation wasn't at all funny. "And poor Inez. I wonder how Philip found out?"

"Maybe he gave it to her."

"You mean she might have been telling me the truth when she said she'd slept with him? I didn't think of that. She'd have told him when she found out so he could get checked, too, in case she'd given it to him or he'd given it to her." Then, before he could ask, I added, "If Philip had herpes, he got it after we broke up. They checked for that when I got my blood test to get married."

"That's good to hear," he said mildly, which told me he had

been wondering about it. "I don't guess it really matters how he found out—from what you've told me about Philip, I bet he did."

"And used it to make Inez change her vote. That son of a bitch! Inez would have been pure out humiliated if people here had found out."

"Enough to kill him to keep them from finding out?"

"Maybe. What if her vote wasn't enough? What if he was trying to get money or something else out of her? She's strong enough, she's got a temper, and she lives fairly close to my place. Not conclusive, but a definite possibility. Thaddeous, you did good! You're wasted at Walters Mill."

"Well, I don't know that I'd say that," he said, but I could tell he was grinning.

Chapter 30

After I hung up, reality sank in. Okay, I was pretty sure that Inez had been the one to change votes. But even if Philip *had* been blackmailing her, it didn't mean that she'd killed him. Her motive was strong, but so was Dee's. Was humiliation worse than a ruined marriage? And I still had motives for Vincent, Murray, and Dom. So I shouldn't get cocky yet.

Still, I felt like we were making progress, so I decided to earn part of my SSI salary by spending some time with Neal hashing out product design issues. He had finally cleaned all the booby traps and such out of StatSys, meaning that we could get down to some heavy-duty planning.

Murray joined in, too. He was so glad to actually have a chance to make real changes to the product that he was almost giddy.

When I left Neal's office, I took a detour to the bathroom, and as I walked back to my desk, I saw Jessie sitting with Roberta, showing her something.

"Oh, Laura," Roberta said, "there was a call for you about an hour ago, but you weren't at your desk."

"I was in with Neal," I said. "Did they leave a message?"

"Somebody named Thaddeous wants you to call back."

"Was he at my place?"

"I don't know. He left a number." She picked up a yellow sticky note and read, "555-6789," then handed me the note.

Jessie said, "Isn't that your old work number?"

How on earth had she remembered that? "It sure is," I said, hoping she wouldn't ask any more questions. No such luck.

"Why would your cousin be at your old office?" Jessie asked.

I improvised. "You remember I told you he'd been dating somebody up here? It's the receptionist over there. I don't know if it's going to last after he goes back home, but they seem to be getting along pretty well."

Jessie nodded, satisfied by this, and turned back to Roberta's computer.

If I had had the sense God gave a milk cow, I'd have left it at that, but I had to keep talking. "It's a shame I wasn't working here when Thaddeous came up, Roberta, or maybe he'd be dating you instead of Michelle."

As soon as I said it, I knew it was a mistake. For once Roberta was paying attention to what I was saying.

She said, "Michelle? That's not Michelle Nucci, is it? She works at GBS."

I tried to look surprised. "Do you know her?"

"She's a friend of a friend of mine. I went out to lunch with her the other week. Just before you came to work here."

"No kidding," I said, trying to sound nonchalant. "It's a small world."

"Awfully small," Jessie said, looking vaguely suspicious.

"That Michelle sure was curious about SSI," Roberta said. "She asked a lot of questions."

I said, "Really? Well, Michelle is a bit of a busybody."
Now both of them were looking at me suspiciously. "I'd better get back to work. See y'all later."

I wasn't quite out of earshot when Jessie said, "What kind of questions did she ask?"

I was really starting to resent the fact that I didn't have real walls around my desk to provide the privacy I wanted. I called Thaddeous back, but kept my voice low. "What's up?"

"I just wanted to let you know that Vasti called."

"During daytime rates?"

"She called from my house—Mama told her you'd want to know right away."

"Know what?"

"Whoever it was who was asking questions about you and me ain't no reporter. He did talk to Hank Parker at the *Gazette*, but he said he was a historian and wanted to see back issues of the paper. It wasn't until he was gone that Hank noticed he was looking at awfully recent papers for a historian, papers that weren't but a couple of years old."

"Great, he knows all about us." There isn't a whole lot of news in Byerly, so Hank had written about our exploits in loving detail.

"The guy tried to get Junior to talk, too, but you know Junior. You have to get up pretty early in the morning to fool her."

"That's good, anyway."

"Anything going on up there?"

"Actually," I said, looking around to try to see if anybody was lurking, "it's not a good time for me to talk."

"Is there anything wrong?"

"I don't know yet."

"You're not in any kind of danger, are you?"

"Of course not."

"Because if you are—"

"I'm not," I said. "If I were, I swear I'd get the heck out of here."

"All right," he said doubtfully. "See you tonight."

I spent the next hour on tenterhooks, cursing myself for mentioning Michelle's name, but finally decided that I was home free. Then Jessie came by my desk. "Laura, have you got a minute?"

"Well . . ." I said, looking at my computer screen as if I really hated to tear myself away from what I was doing.

"It's important."

"Okay."

When I followed her back to her office, I was sure that my cover was completely blown and I wasn't at all reassured when she shut the door behind us. At least she sat down behind her desk, leaving me closer to the door, which meant that if I needed to, I could get to that door before she got to me.

"Laura," she said, "how committed are you to SSI?"

This wasn't the question I had expected. "I'm here, aren't I?"

"But *why* are you here?"

It sounded like she might be on to me, but I wasn't going to say too much this time. "What are you getting at, Jessie?"

"What I'm getting at is this: why have you been asking so many questions?" I was trying to think of how I could answer her when she went on. "It's quite a coincidence that the receptionist at GBS just happened to go to lunch with our receptionist right after you and I had lunch together. And it's quite a coincidence that you came to work here right after that, even though you'd never been interested in working here before. And since you've been here, you've asked me lots of questions, especially about how SSI is run. I checked around, and found out that you've been talking to other people, too. Now it turns out that your cousin is hanging around your old office. Why would your former boss allow that?"

She paused, and though I wondered if I should make a break for it, I decided that I'd wait until she made some kind of move. Unless she had a gun, I had a good chance of getting out of that room in a hurry, and as long as she didn't have a knife, I could probably fight her off.

"Do you know what the biggest coincidence of all is, Laura?" she said.

I shook my head.

"The biggest coincidence of all is that these questions started popping up after you talked to Philip and Colleen, and they told you things they shouldn't have."

She had me. The only question I had left was whether she was the murderer herself, or just wanted to protect the murderer.

Jessie leaned over her desk toward me, and I had to work hard not to flinch. "Tell me the truth, Laura. Is this about the public offering?"

The question came from so far out of left field that all I could do at first was stare at her. Finally I got out, "About the what?"

"I'm not naive. Knowing that a stock offering is coming could be worth a lot of money in the right places. GBS isn't a direct competitor, but it wouldn't surprise me to find out that they want to buy us out."

"Jessie, my being here has nothing to do with GBS."

"Then is it a personal thing? A get-rich-quick scheme? It's illegal to use insider information for trading."

"I'm not interested in stock offerings or insider trading or anything like that."

She looked me right in the eye. "I want to believe you, Laura."

I met her look straight on. "Then believe me. I'm telling you the truth."

"This offering means a lot to SSI. Maybe the difference between staying afloat and going under."

"I know it's important to you, Jessie."

"Not just to me. Look at Dee and Dom. They'll never be able to find a job working together like they do here. And Inez. She's the first in her family to go to college—if she loses this job, her family is going to tell her that she was crazy not to get a nice secretarial job in the first place. Vincent's trying to prove himself to his family, too. One of his brothers is a doctor, one's a lawyer, and one's in management at a big manufacturing company. Do you think Vincent wants to go work for his brother?"

I held up a hand to stop her. "Jessie, I know the offering is important to everybody at SSI, and I don't want to mess it up."

Jessie visibly relaxed and took a couple of deep breaths. "I'm sorry to doubt you, Laura. It's just that so many coincidences coming out . . . it sounded pretty bad."

"I don't blame you for thinking the worst," I said, but I wasn't about to start trying to explain away any of the so-called coincidences. "It did look bad when you put it together like that."

"And the questions you've been asking?"

"Hey, I've got a lot of years to catch up on. I'm curious." That wasn't exactly a lie, even if it wasn't exactly the truth.

I could tell she believed me, and now that I had her in a vulnerable position, maybe I could push a little. "But I have to admit that I've been hearing some funny things."

"Like what?"

"Like Philip trying to blackmail people into letting him stay at SSI."

She turned pale. "I don't know what you're talking about."

I decided to try and wait her out, the way Detective Salvatore had waited for me the night I'd called him.

After a minute of my looking at her, she said, "So he was trying to talk people into voting his way. That's hardly blackmail."

"It is if he threatened people."

"How could he threaten anybody?"

"He could threaten to tell secrets. Philip loved knowing secrets, didn't he?"

"What kind of secrets?"

I hesitated. Which of Philip's secrets would she be most likely to know about? I thought I knew Dee's and Inez's already, and I didn't think Murray or Dom had any. That left Vincent. Though Michelle's contact was sure Vincent really had graduated from MIT, there had to be *something* there. So I said, "Secrets about brass rats."

"Brass rats?" she stammered.

I nodded, again waiting for her to speak first.

She stared at me for the longest time. Finally she said, "He told you, didn't he?"

I still didn't say anything. I was afraid to—I didn't know who "he" was.

"Damn him to hell! I trusted him! He said he wouldn't tell anybody if I voted for him."

Okay, "he" had to be Philip, but how had he blackmailed

Jessie with Vincent's secret? "How did he find out?" I asked cautiously, hoping she wouldn't be able to tell how little I knew.

"I told him. Years ago, right before graduation. I was so upset about it that I cried on his shoulder. I knew I should have studied more, but so much was going on that last semester, what with me trying to get things started here at SSI. We were planning to open two weeks after graduation. I knew my grades were suffering, but I never thought I'd flunk two classes. One class would have been okay—I'd still have graduated. But not two."

Jessie was the one who'd flunked out? True, she had never been a great student, but she had always worked hard. Only from what she was saying, that last semester she'd worked hard at SSI, not at MIT.

"I didn't know what to do," she went on. "My parents never would have paid for another semester, not even just for the one course I needed. I was lucky they'd pay for the four years—they made that plain from the very start. But without a degree, I couldn't come work at SSI."

"Couldn't you have worked part-time and finished school?" I asked her.

"They needed somebody full-time. And if I didn't come then, I wouldn't have been on the board of directors. They'd have hired somebody else."

"Oh, Jessie! Don't you know how much you mean to everybody? The group would have fallen apart ages ago without you. They'd have waited for you. Or hired you without a degree."

But she was shaking her head. "What if they hadn't? I couldn't risk being left behind."

I remembered a boy I knew in elementary school. He was

a little shorter than the other boys, and not quite as good at sports. He lived in fear that they would leave him behind when they went out to play ball or wander through the woods or swim in the lake. I could picture him chasing after them, just as clear as day, calling, "Wait for me! Wait for me!" It was sad to see a child like that—to see a grown woman act that way was heartbreaking.

Jessie said, "It was Philip's idea not to tell anybody. He knew that the graduation program was printed up ahead of time, so my name was in it. And my parents hadn't planned on coming up anyway, so I had a perfect excuse not to attend graduation. Nobody ever knew that I never graduated."

"Except for Philip."

She nodded.

"And he threatened to tell people if you didn't vote for him."

She nodded again. "I voted for him the first time, but I wasn't sure what to do the second time. I had just spoken to Vincent in his office, and Vincent scared me into thinking that SSI was going to go bankrupt if we didn't fire Philip. Then he went to lunch. I was just sitting at his desk, trying to decide, when Philip came in, closed the door, and asked me how I was going to vote."

That explained why Roberta had thought it was Vincent's brass rat Philip was yelling about.

"I thought I should be honest, but when I told him I was still making up my mind, he started yelling at me. He said that he'd tell Inez and Vincent, and that they'd fire me. He was going to tell my parents, too. I couldn't believe he'd *do* that to me. I couldn't believe he'd *betray* me like that."

"What did you do?"

"What could I do? I voted for him. I'd have voted for him

forever. He was right—nobody else will hire me without a degree." She looked down at her hands like they didn't belong to her, and seemed surprised that they were tearing pieces off of her desk blotter. "When you called to tell me Philip was dead, my first thought was that I was safe. I was glad that he was dead." Fat tears rolled down her face.

"Jessie?" She didn't seem to hear me. I went over beside her chair, turned the chair to face me, and took her hands in mine. "Jessie, listen to me. Philip was a son of a bitch! He threatened to take away the thing that's most important to you. Of course you were glad he was dead, anybody would have been. Don't you dare spend one second being sorry!"

"But he was my friend."

"He didn't deserve a friend like you! I don't know that I do, either. If I had known what I was asking you about, I never would have said a word." I was starting to realize that there was a limit to what I'd do to find Philip's killer.

"I don't want to lose my job, Laura."

"You're not going to."

"You won't tell Vincent? Or Inez?"

"Of course not. But I don't think they'd care. You've done a terrific job for SSI, degree or no degree. If they were stupid enough to fire you, you'd get another job in a heartbeat." She started to say something, but I said, "But I'm not going to tell them. Okay?"

"You won't?"

"No, I won't. I promise."

The tears didn't stop at first, but then she threw her arms around me, holding onto me as if her boat had just sunk and I was a life preserver. I hugged back and patted her back and stroked her hair for I don't know how long. Like I told Thaddeous after I got home that night, if she had murdered Philip,

I don't know that I would have done anything about it after that. But I just couldn't believe that she had.

Michelle did point out that Jessie could have been lying about the whole thing, but I didn't believe it for a minute. A call from Michelle to her friend at MIT verified that Jessie had never graduated, and that was good enough for me. Thaddeous and Michelle might not have agreed, but they realized that my mind was made up and knew enough not to argue with me.

Chapter 31

After I finished telling them about Jessie, Michelle and Thaddeous wanted to get something to eat, but I wasn't in the mood to go out. In fact, I explained to them as politely as I could that I really wasn't in the mood for company. So I sent them off, promising them that I wasn't depressed or upset, just tired.

It wasn't true. I was a little depressed and a lot upset. And I did want company, just not Thaddeous's or Michelle's. What I wanted was to have Richard home, but since I couldn't have that, I was at least going to talk to him.

Richard must have finally been getting over his jet lag, because he was asleep when I called him, but he woke up quickly enough. As was becoming our pattern, first he made sure that nothing was wrong. Then he told me about the course and the plays he had been seeing. He was excited because he had seen the rarely-performed *King John*.

Then I caught him up on the investigation, telling him about the news from Vasti and my conversations with Dee, Murray, and Sheliah, and then describing today's discovery about Inez and my confrontation with Jessie. I concluded it with, "Richard, I felt so bad when Jessie finally calmed down. I made her go home early. Then I tried to get some work done, but all I could think about was what I had done to Jessie."

"You can't blame yourself for hurting Jessie. Philip did that, not you. And it would have come out someday. 'In the end, truth will out.' *The Merchant of Venice*, Act II, Scene 2."

"But she thought she was safe, and here I come sticking my nose in, asking about brass rats." I snorted. "What kind of rat does that make me?"

"Laura! Let's not forget that you're trying to find a murderer. If you'll allow me to return to the Merchant, 'To do a great right, do a little wrong.' Act IV, Scene 1."

"But I don't know that it is a little wrong. She crumpled when she thought I knew about her degree, Richard, just crumpled. How do I know how much I've hurt her?"

"From the way you've described her dependence on the group and on SSI, she's got psychological problems that you have nothing to do with. She's got a family that wouldn't pay for one extra class or come to her graduation. And she was convinced that her best friends wouldn't accept her without a degree. You didn't cause those hurts, Laura—they happened years ago, long before you even knew Jessie."

"What about Dee? I let her believe that I already knew her secret when I didn't have the first idea of what it was. At least Inez doesn't realize that I know about her herpes, but Dee knows that I know about her and Philip. I don't have any business knowing about either of them. Of course, I won't tell anybody other than you, Thaddeous, and Michelle, but can Dee be sure of that?"

"If she knows you, then she knows she can trust you," Richard said firmly. "So does Jessie."

"Great! I'm just the person they should be trusting. I

worm my way into their company just so I can find out my friends' deepest, darkest secrets."

"Let's not forget that one of these friends killed another one of your friends. Great right, little wrong—remember?"

"I'm not sure it's a great right, either. What difference does it make who killed Philip? After what he did to Dee and Inez and Jessie, and what he probably did to the others at SSI, maybe Philip deserved to die."

I shocked myself when I said that, and I guess I shocked Richard, too, because he didn't say anything for a long time.

Then he said, "Every time we've found a murderer, the murderer has said that the victim deserved to die. Do you think Slim Grady deserved to die? Or Small Bill Walters? Or Melanie Wilson? Did your grandfather deserve to die?"

"Don't you dare put Paw in the same company as Philip Dennis!"

"It's not the company Paw's keeping that worries me. It's the company you're putting yourself into that I'm concerned about."

"I'm not a murderer."

"No, but you seem willing to let a murderer go free."

"Since when is catching murderers my reason for living? Boston has a perfectly good police department—let them handle it."

"Do you think they're going to find out who killed Philip? Are they even looking?"

"That's not my problem."

He hesitated again. "I don't know how they taught things in your church, but in my church, I heard about sins of commission and sins of omission. Killing Philip was a sin of commission, but I think your not trying to catch the killer would be a sin of omission."

I had to count to ten in binary three times before I trusted myself to answer him. And even then, I came awfully damned close to slamming down the receiver before I spoke. The only reason I didn't is that I was afraid if I did, it would change things between us in ways I'd never be able to change back.

Finally, all I could say was, "It's not fair, Richard. I didn't kill Philip. And I don't betray people like he did. But I'm having to drag myself through the dirt like he did to find his murderer. It's just not fair." I wasn't crying, but I was as close to it as I could be and still be talking.

Softly he said, "I know it's not fair, Laura. I wish Philip had never shown up on our doorstep, or that I was there to do this for you. But he did show up, and I'm not there. And I don't think you can leave this thing alone. If you do, I'm afraid it'll hurt you worse than anything Philip did to the others."

"It was so much easier in Byerly," I said. "I was helping my family. I'm not helping anybody here—nobody really cares if Philip was killed. And why should I avenge his death? He doesn't deserve it."

"Do you remember *MacBeth*?"

"Of course I do."

"The night MacBeth and Lady MacBeth kill the king, all hell breaks lose. Thunder, lightning, hail. This was Shakespeare's way of showing us that nature itself was offended that MacBeth violated the rules of chivalry by killing his liege, and the rules of hospitality by killing a guest in his home.

"That's how I see murder, Laura: an offense against nature and an offense against man. When somebody kills a friend, there *should* be thunder and lightning. From what you've found out, Philip was with somebody he trusted, and that person returned his trust by hitting him over the head and leaving him to die in the snow. If I had a mad dog, I'd kill him myself before I'd let him die like that."

I remembered seeing Philip at my apartment. Then I remembered Detective Salvatore showing me Philip's body. Philip had done terrible things, but what his killer had done was even worse. Philip shouldn't have died like that. Had he lived, maybe he could have made up for what he had done. I didn't think it was likely, but it was possible. Now he'd never be able to, and the killer carried that on his conscience. I wasn't about to carry it on mine.

"Laura? Are you still there?"

"I'm here. Thank you, Richard."

"For what?"

"For being right."

He let loose a big breath, and I wondered if he had been holding it while waiting for me to answer. "I was just thinking that I must be insane for trying to talk you into doing this instead of trying to talk you out of it. If anything happens to you because I've convinced you to keep going—"

"It won't. And if it did, it'd be a whole lot better than what would happen to me if I did nothing."

"I wish I was there. Maybe I should cancel the trip."

"No," I said emphatically. "How long have you dreamed of a chance like this?"

"Not as long as I dreamed about having a wife like you."

I smiled in spite of myself. "Granted, but you've got me now, so you can pursue those other dreams. I'm being careful, and I've got Thaddeous and Michelle to look after me. If the two of them aren't enough to scare off one little murderer, then I don't know what is."

"Mad Dog Thaddeous?"

"Something like that."

"But you'll be careful? Not just physically—don't let what Philip did get to you."

"I'll try not to. Paw used to say that God never gives anybody a burden heavier than they can carry. I guess I just forgot that for a little while."

"I might add, 'With great power comes great responsibility.' "

"*Hamlet?*"

"*Spiderman.* But it's a great line."

"Good night, Richard. I do love you."

"I love you, too."

Chapter 32

I hung up and had just enough time to get something to drink before the phone rang. "Hello?"

"Laura? This is Jessie."

"What's the matter?" I knew that something was wrong because I could just barely recognize her voice.

"It's Murray. There's been an accident."

I felt that chill my Aunt Maggie claims comes from somebody walking across my grave. "Is he all right?"

"He's dead, Laura. He fell down the stairs at the office and broke his neck."

It took a while to get the whole story out of her because she wasn't very coherent. It turned out that the cleaning crew had found Murray's body and called the police. Then the police had called Murray's family and Jessie.

As far as the police could tell, there had been some snow or ice on the stairs, and Murray had slipped and lost his balance. His body was on the landing between the third and fourth floors, but his hat was on the sixth, meaning he must have fallen three flights.

"Jesus, Jessie," was all I could say. "I just can't believe it."

"First Philip, and now Murray. What is happening to us?"

I wanted to tell her that it was all just a horrible coinci-

dence, that the two deaths had nothing to do with one another, but I couldn't say it because I didn't believe it. As
Richard would have said, there was something rotten in the
state of Denmark.

Still, I comforted her as best I could. I tried to get her to
come over to my apartment so she wouldn't be alone, knowing that Thaddeous wouldn't mind being crowded, but she
didn't want to leave her cats. I settled for making her promise
to call if she needed me, and for promising to be at work early
the next day to help her do whatever it was that needed
doing.

Thaddeous and Michelle came in carrying a pizza box just
as I hung up the phone. Both of them knew me well enough
to see immediately that something bad had happened, and I
told them what Jessie had told me.

"Another one," Michelle said. "Tell me you don't think it's
connected with Philip."

I just shook my head, and Thaddeous said, "If this is a coincidence, then I'm a Yank—a beauty queen."

"All I can think of is how I wouldn't walk down the stairs
with him my first day back at SSI. If I'd gone with him today,
maybe this wouldn't have happened."

"And maybe you'd have a broken neck, too," Thaddeous
said. "Whoever it was ain't shy about killing, that's for damn
sure."

"You're right," I said, but I was having a hard time believing it. I just felt so bad about suspecting Murray after having known him all those years. The fact that the murderer was
likely somebody else I had known for years wasn't much comfort.

"You cut that out," Michelle said, shaking her finger at me.

"It wasn't your fault! Now, have some of this pizza we brought you. You need to eat."

"I'm not hungry," I said, but I followed them into the kitchen, and when Michelle heated up a piece in the microwave and put it in front of me, I did eat it. Of course, with the two of them watching me, I didn't have a whole lot of choice.

"How was your dinner?" I asked, wanting to talk about anything else.

Michelle looked at Thaddeous and smiled the cutest smile. "Very nice. You never told me Thaddeous knew so much about history."

"Didn't I?" Actually, I hadn't known that he did.

"The Civil War—I mean, the War between the States. And the World Wars, even Korea and Vietnam. He knows all kinds of interesting things."

"Michelle's just being polite," Thaddeous said. "I must have talked the whole time, and she was nice enough to listen."

He was looking at her, and she was looking at him, and it was time for me to go away. I finished the last of the pizza and said, "I'd better get some sleep. Jessie asked me to come in early to help make arrangements. I think it's more for moral support than for anything else, but I said I would."

"You're not going back to that death trap!" Michelle said. "Two people have already died there."

"Philip died here," I reminded her, "and I'm not moving out of my apartment. Besides, there's still a murderer on the loose. Now, more than ever, I have to find out what's going on." My conversation with Richard had convinced me of that even before I heard about Murray.

"Laura, are you crazy? Thaddeous, tell your cousin she's crazy."

But what Thaddeous said was, "Michelle, you're wasting your breath. If there's one thing I know about Laurie Anne, it's that she's going to do whatever she thinks is the right thing, no matter what anybody else says."

"You're both crazy!" she said.

Thaddeous just nodded. "You might be right. But if I can't stop her, and I know I can't, I'm going to see what I can do to help her."

She looked at him, then at me, then back at him. Then she said, "I guess I'm crazy, too. What do we do next?"

I said, "I thought I might sneak a look at Murray's desk, maybe find something there that will help. His being killed must mean he knew something, or had discovered something."

"That sounds like a winner," Thaddeous said. "Why don't you go on to bed, and Michelle and I will see if we can come up with any other ideas while I take her home on the subway."

"You don't have to do that," Michelle said.

"I'm not about to let you ride alone at this time of night. Not with strangers sniffing around and people dying."

I left the two of them arguing and went to bed. Maybe they'd finish fighting it out soon enough that they'd have time to neck a little.

Chapter 33

Never had I seen Jessie in the state she was in the next morning. Her eyes were so red and there were such dark circles under her eyes that I knew she hadn't gotten a wink of sleep. Murray's death coming so soon after Philip's had nearly done her in. And I was all too aware that our own confrontation the afternoon before hadn't helped her any.

I felt almost guilty that I had slept reasonably well, but then, Murray's death didn't really sink in for me until I saw his office with its ridiculous stack of papers and no Murray. The only reason I didn't start crying was that I knew Jessie needed my help.

As soon as the family called to tell us the time, we posted a memo to tell the rest of the SSI employees that the funeral would be the next day. Then we ordered flowers from the company. Next was a surprising amount of paperwork: insurance and tax information and I'm not sure what else. It probably could have waited, but Jessie was bound and determined to do it all right away. I figured that keeping busy was the best thing for her, and other than to bring her cups of coffee and doughnuts, I left her alone.

In the meantime, the rest of the SSI crew had started to arrive. Jessie had called Vincent the night before but hadn't tried anybody else. That meant that as anybody but Vincent arrived, I had to go through the whole story again. I couldn't help but watch each person's face, hoping to see some sign of guilty knowledge, but all I saw was shock.

The police showed up around ten. I wondered if Detective Salvatore was going to get involved, but then remembered that he was with the Boston Police. Since Murray had died in Cambridge, it was a different set of cops. This crew didn't seem to see anything odd about Murray's death. They did want to establish who had seen Murray last, but apparently it was just to fill out the paperwork.

It turned out that Inez had been the last one to see Murray, or at least, the last one to admit to seeing him. She'd spoken to him on her way out, but everybody else said his office door had been closed when they'd passed by. Everybody but Jessie and me, that is. Jessie had left early, of course. As for me, I couldn't remember if I'd seen Murray after the meeting with Neal or not. Some investigator I was.

Even after the cops left, nobody was doing much work. Instead, we all congregated in the break room, drinking coffee and talking listlessly about Murray. Time spent together like that can help, but I'm not sure that it did this time. We were too much in shock to get anything out of it. I finally suggested to Vincent that he close the office, and he agreed that it was the best thing.

Jessie said she wanted to stay a while to finish up something, and since I didn't want her there alone, I told her I'd stay, too. Besides, I still wanted to take a peek at Murray's desk.

I felt like an intruder when I went into Murray's office and sat down among all his papers and reports. The eeriest part was the smell. Not to sound rude, but most people have their own scent. With Richard out of town, I was particularly attuned to his and had found myself hugging his pillow as I went to sleep. I had never noticed Murray's scent before, but it was still strong in his office, a mixture of coffee and papers and the faintest trace of some aftershave I didn't recognize.

Even though I hadn't been that close to Murray or even liked him particularly, I felt terribly sad to be there when he was gone. I was mad, too. I could almost understand killing Philip—I couldn't understand anybody wanting to kill Murray, unless it was to protect himself or herself, and that just wasn't a good enough reason.

I had told Michelle and Thaddeous the night before that my guess was that Murray had found out something about Philip's death. This was part because of the timing of the death, and part because of who Murray was and where he had been killed. The question was, what had Murray found out? I was hoping there would be something in his office to tell me.

I started with the papers on his desk. The stuff on top was mostly printouts of code, and the first thing I checked for was the date they had been printed. It seemed likely that Murray must have found out whatever it was in just the past day or so. All of the printouts I saw were at least a week old, so I decided they weren't the answer.

The table where Murray kept his computer was also piled high with papers, as were two bookcases and a chair. There were even stacks on the floor behind Murray's desk and under the computer table. Some of these printouts were months old, and none of them looked terribly important. Certainly nothing looked like a motive for murder.

I opened the lap drawer on the desk, but found nothing except the usual assortment of office supplies, showing nothing more important than the fact that Murray liked red felt-tip pens. The second drawer was filled with diskettes, but they were marked as backups, so I didn't think I needed to mess with them. The file drawer made me laugh out loud. With all that paper everywhere, the file drawer was empty.

That was so like Murray that it brought tears to my eyes. I was wondering if he had kept a box of Kleenex among the stacks of paper when I realized somebody was watching me from the open office door.

"Neal?" I said. "I thought everybody but me and Jessie had gone home."

"I'm all that's left. What are you doing?"

"Just being morbid, I guess," I said. "It's hard to believe he's gone, isn't it?"

He nodded, but didn't step inside. "At least it was quick. The police said that they don't think he suffered at all."

I closed the file drawer. "Should we pack up his personal things?" There wasn't that much personal there. A coffee mug with a Far Side cartoon, a couple of photographs stuck on the bulletin board, and a paperweight were all I saw.

"Jessie said his family would be here tomorrow morning to do that," Neal said.

"Just as long as Jessie doesn't have to. She's in pretty bad shape." Noticing how pale he looked, I added, "It's been hard on everybody. Are you doing okay?"

"I'm all right," he said unconvincingly.

I didn't like the way he was standing there not meeting my eyes as he glanced around Murray's office.

"Come on," I said, getting up and firmly closing the door behind me. "Let's get Jessie out of here." Sometimes the best thing for an upset person to do is to focus on somebody else, and it seemed to work on Neal. He literally pulled Jessie away from her desk and put her coat on her. While I made sure that lights were off and doors were locked, he called a taxi and got into it with her, promising to make sure she got home all right.

With the two of them gone, I could have gone back for a more thorough search of Murray's office, but I couldn't bring myself to do it. As I told Thaddeous when I got back to my apartment, I didn't think it would be the safest place to be. Besides, the murderer had had plenty of time after killing Murray to take anything incriminating out of his office.

Thaddeous and I kicked around a few ideas that afternoon, but really didn't come up with anything. So he kept me company while I ran a few errands that had been piling up.

Michelle came over after work and caught me up on news from my real job. It was getting busy there and I was going to be pushing my luck if I stayed away much longer.

The three of us were discouraged that night and decided to eat out to try to cheer ourselves up. Unfortunately, I think the boisterous atmosphere at the Hard Rock Cafe did us more harm than good. Too many people were having a good time, and we weren't. After a while we quit trying to yell over the music, and just ate. That made me feel awful, because Thaddeous had been looking forward to eating at the Hard Rock, and now it was no fun at all.

Michelle took off for home straight from dinner, while Thaddeous and I walked back to my place. It was a long walk for a cold night, but I wanted the chance to clear my head.

We were about halfway home when I said, "I'm sorry I've spoiled your vacation, Thaddeous."

"You haven't spoiled a thing, Laurie Anne. I'm the one who talked you into getting involved in this—I should be apologizing to you."

"I should have known better. You didn't know what you'd be letting yourself in for."

"Well, that's true enough. It's not a bit like the Hardy Boys books I read."

"Not much like Nancy Drew, either. She always found nifty clues like secret passages and hidden compartments."

"Or codes—they were always decoding codes in them books."

"Well, we've got code, but it's not the kind you can decode."

"Not hardly," Thaddeous said.

Neither of us said anything for a while. I don't know why Thaddeous was quiet, but I was thinking about something. Maybe I couldn't decode the StatSys source code the way Nancy Drew would have, but I could do something a lot like that. I said, "Maybe we can decode something."

"I don't think I follow you."

"Philip liked to keep secrets and hide things. What if he hid information as comments in the code for StatSys?"

"What's that mean?"

"You know that a program is just a set of instructions telling a computer what to do, right?"

"Right."

"It's possible to stick all kinds of stuff in a program without actually affecting what the computer is doing. You can type in lines and mark them so the computer knows to ignore them." I tried to think of something similar. "Like in a script, there are stage directions or instructions that you don't read out when you're acting out the play. Stuff like, 'Exit stage left,' or 'Pick up book.'" The analogy would have been more appropriate for Richard than for Thaddeous, but he seemed to understand.

"So how does this help us?"

"Maybe Philip put something in the comments in Stat-Sys."

"Like what?"

"Like anything. The secrets about people he was using to blackmail them, or instructions for finding proof of something illegal—anything."

"He could have done that?"

"Absolutely. He'd have gotten a big kick out of it. And that would explain why he wouldn't let anybody at SSI look at his code." Then I stopped dead in my tracks. "Thaddeous, I just thought of something. Neal finally got all the booby traps out of StatSys yesterday, and Murray was real excited about having a chance to look at the code. He was probably looking at it just before he was killed. What if he found something in the code and confronted somebody about it, and that's why he was killed?"

"But Neal would have seen whatever it was first. Or do you think he was the killer?"

"Not necessarily. If he was, why would he have given Murray the code with the information in it? He could have just deleted the incriminating part."

"So you're saying that Neal didn't see it, but Murray did."

"Maybe it was hidden in such a way that Neal didn't understand it. Or maybe he just missed it—StatSys is a good-sized program, with hundreds and hundreds of lines. I don't know, but I do know that I want to look at that code."

"You better be careful," Thaddeous warned. "Looking at that code might just be what got Murray killed."

Chapter 34

With Thaddeous's warning fresh in my mind, I decided not to go through the StatSys files right there in the office. Instead, I figured the thing for me to do would be to copy the latest set of files from the network onto diskettes. So the first thing next morning, I stuck a diskette into my computer and accessed Murray's network directory. The only thing was, the directory was empty.

I tapped my fingers on my desk. At my real job, we keep all working files backed up on the network in case our individual hard drives crash. But I'd been told that the programmers at SSI tended not to keep much on the network because Philip had planted viruses in people's files as a joke, never caring how much work it took to clean things up afterward. Folks had gotten into the habit of only using the network to transfer files. When asked for the files, Neal would have copied them into Murray's directory, and then Murray would have copied them onto his hard drive, eventually intending to remove them from the directory.

Murray had been particular, but I wouldn't have expected him to delete the files from the network directory so quickly. He had gotten them from Neal Tuesday afternoon, and he died Tuesday evening. Why would he have been in such a rush? Or had it been Murray? Anybody could have trashed the files on the network. Did that mean somebody was trying to keep anybody else from looking at the code? With deadlines so tight, nobody else was likely to look anyway. Except me.

Unfortunately, now it was going to be harder for me to get the files. I was going to have to do one of two things: either check Murray's hard drive to see if the files were still there, or ask Neal for a copy of them. I didn't care for either idea. I sure didn't want to get caught in Murray's office again, and I didn't want Neal, or anybody else, to know I was that interested in the files.

Of course, I had the version of StatSys we were currently shipping to customers, and I could probably decompile it. But Neal had spent the better part of two weeks cleaning out the booby traps Philip had left in that code. I definitely didn't want to spend time duplicating his effort, and I wasn't even sure that I could. That kind of debugging isn't my specialty. What I wanted were nice, clean files, and I silently cussed out Philip for not keeping proper backups.

I spent a while weighing my choices, and when I made up my mind which to try, spent more time coming up with a cover story in case I got caught doing what I wanted to do. Then I waited until lunch, thinking that there wouldn't be many people around. I let myself into Murray's office and quietly closed the door behind me.

Murray's family must have come in already because the few personal items were gone now, and somehow it didn't seem as much like his office anymore. I booted the system and started looking through directories. I turned on the light, hoping nobody would see it through the crack at the bottom of the door, but no such luck. I had been in there for only five or ten minutes when the door opened.

"Laura?" Jessie said. "What are you doing?"

"Trying to find Murray's QA log," I said, as casually as I could. "He gave me a printout the other day, but I lost a couple of pages. Besides, it'll be easier to keep track of them online."

She looked mostly relieved, but not completely.

So I tried to sound embarrassed as I said, "He really wanted some issues taken care of for the next release. I thought this would be a way for me to say goodbye."

Darned if her eyes didn't tear up. "Oh, Murray would really appreciate that. Let me know if you need any help finding what you need."

"I will. Thanks."

She left, and I took a deep breath. The story had passed muster. Of course, Jessie was probably the easiest one to convince, but maybe nobody else would notice my being in there.

It took me another ten minutes to be fairly sure that there were no new StatSys files on Murray's hard drive. He could have worked from floppy disks, but that would have been slower because a floppy drive isn't as fast as a hard drive. It was more likely that somebody had erased the files, both from the network and from his hard disk.

The door opened again. This time it was Sheliah.

She blinked a few times. "I didn't expect anyone to be in here."

"Just getting a copy of the QA log," I said. "Stuff Murray wanted to be sure made it into this release."

She nodded, apparently satisfied. "Have you seen any

draft documentation in here? He was supposed to be reviewing some material for me, and I wasn't sure if he got to it before . . ." She didn't bother to finish the sentence.

"It could be in here, but I don't know where." I rolled the chair back from Murray's desk and said, "Maybe you should look for yourself."

She didn't seem to think it odd that I waited until she found what she wanted, and didn't even look to see what I was doing on the computer. Still, I was relieved when she left and I closed the door again.

Murray had the usual complement of utility programs installed, so I used one to find out if any files had been deleted in the past few days. I wasn't surprised to find out that a fair number of files had been, or that they were the StatSys files.

Normally, recovering a recently deleted file isn't that big a deal. Any reasonably knowledgeable user with a decent utility program can do it. That is, unless the files had been systematically destroyed, with every character erased. And that's what had been done to these files—I could access the file names, but I had more chance of bringing back the Old South than I did of getting those files back.

I checked the file modification dates and found out that the files had been deleted at seven-thirty Wednesday night, the day after Murray was killed. I had to be on the right track. The files had been there, and since somebody had gone to the trouble of deleting them, there had to be something interesting in them.

I was about to shut down the system when I remembered my cover story. Since I'd told both Jessie and Sheliah I was after the QA log, I really ought to get it. So I started it copying over to my directory on the network, and leaned back in Murray's chair while waiting for it to finish.

It was so ironic that Murray had been done in by being painfully thorough. Most QA people wouldn't have bothered to look at source files. They're only interested in the result, not the mechanism. But Murray was the kind of man who dotted every i and crossed every t, as my Aunt Maggie would have said.

I sat up sharply. Some programmers get lazy and only back up once a week, but as meticulous as Murray was in every other respect, surely he would have backed up his work every night. And didn't I remember seeing a set of backup disks in his desk?

I pulled open the middle drawer, where I thought they'd been, but it was empty now. So I tried the other drawers, but there weren't any diskettes in any of them. I was sure I'd seen them the day before! That meant that the killer had gone in behind me and cleaned up the last tracks. Damn, damn, damn! If only Neal hadn't caught me in there I could have grabbed the disks then. Or if I'd come back inside after Neal and Jessie left.

That got me thinking. Neal knew I'd been in Murray's office, and Jessie could have seen me come in or leave with Neal. Didn't that make it likely that one of them had been alarmed to see me in there, and therefore was the killer?

I shook my head. Though I was darned tempted to accept the idea just so I could eliminate some of the suspects, I couldn't. Anybody could have been waiting for the office to empty out to come back and delete those files and grab the diskettes. I messed up high, wide, and handsome, and I didn't know a bit more than I had before.

The QA log had just finished copying when the door opened one more time.

"Hi, Vincent," I said, deciding to beat him to the punch. "What are you doing in here?"

"I saw the light."

"It's just me. I'm copying the QA log to my directory."

"Good idea. I suppose somebody will have to maintain that until we replace Murray." I guess he realized that sounded cold, because he added, "Not that we can ever truly replace him, of course. But we will need somebody in this office."

"Absolutely," I said and looked down at the screen. "I'm done. Did you need this, or shall I shut it down?"

"Shut it down." He left without saying anything else, and I was more than happy to get out of there. I was so disgusted. Here I had meant to sneak in there to get those files, but I hadn't got a thing. And worse, now more people had seen me snooping in Murray's office. If they were innocent, maybe they believed my reason for being in there. But if either of them was the killer, I could be darned sure that he or she hadn't. I tried to tell myself that it didn't matter anyway, because the killer was already asking questions about me, but that wasn't very comforting.

Chapter 35

I went back to my desk, but goodness knows my heart wasn't in my work. I felt like I was being watched, but I didn't know if I was just being paranoid or if my subconscious was picking up something. So many people had seen me in Murray's office. Even if none of them was the murderer, they might have said something to the murderer. My best bet was to do nothing else even vaguely suspicious. So I sat at my desk and tried to look like I was working hard.

Thank goodness it was a short day. Vincent came around and told everybody to leave at one to make sure that we had time to get ready for Murray's funeral, and Inez came around after him to tell us to leave an hour earlier than that.

Thaddeous was waiting for me at home, and I told him about the deleted files and missing disks. Then he fixed grilled cheese sandwiches for our lunch while I changed clothes. Michelle had wanted to go with us to listen to the voices of the SSI crew to see if the man who'd called her was there, but we decided that that would be too suspicious. Roberta might show up, and we didn't want her seeing Michelle. So she settled for our promise to call her as soon as we got back.

Murray's funeral wasn't much like Philip's visitation. This

time I could tell that the folks there felt real grief, not just regret and awkwardness. There were lots of mourners, most of them related to Murray, and many tears.

There was one thing the services had in common. I felt the same nagging guilt about Murray that I had had about Philip. Rationally, I knew that neither death was my fault, but . . . In some ways, this time was even worse, because I couldn't help thinking that if I'd been a little quicker or a little smarter, I could have caught Philip's killer before Murray had died.

Thaddeous looked as ill at ease as I felt, so we left as soon as the services were over. Though Vincent had half-heartedly suggested that folks could go back to work after the funeral, I think he knew that nobody was going to take him up on it.

As soon as we got back to my apartment, we called Michelle at GBS, me on the phone in the bedroom and Thaddeous on the one in the living room.

"What happened?" she asked.

"A whole lot of nothing," Thaddeous said. Then realizing that didn't sound right, he added, "I mean, nothing to do with what we're doing. The service was very nice."

"Oh," Michelle said, sounding disappointed.

I said, "What did you expect? That the killer would confess in a fit of remorse? If he or she didn't break down at Philip's funeral, why do you think he would at Murray's?"

"I knew that," she said indignantly, but I had a hunch she'd been hoping for something dramatic. "What about the StatSys files? Have you had a chance to look at them?"

"I didn't get them," I said, and explained why not.

"Jeez! What are we going to do now?"

"I don't know," I said, feeling more than a little sorry for myself.

"Hey now, Laurie Anne, there ain't no call for that. You know where those files are. All we have to do is come up with a way of getting at them."

"I could ask Neal for a copy," I said.

"I don't think you should, Laurie Anne. We don't want anybody knowing you're interested in them. Can't we sneak into the office and get them?"

"That's an idea!" Michelle said. "We could wait until tonight."

I said, "We can't. There's an alarm system, and Jessie and Roberta are the only ones who know the code to turn it off."

"They didn't give you the code? That's nuts!" Michelle exclaimed.

"I know." Everybody at GBS has the security code so we can come in whenever we want—the last thing the boss wants to do is to discourage us from working extra hours. "But we don't have anybody like Philip. They all used to have the code, but then people started finding surprises when they got to work. Would you believe doggie doo in Murray's trash can, and a plastic spider in Jessie's coffee cup? Philip denied it, of course, but as soon as they changed the code and made sure only Jessie and Roberta knew it, the pranks stopped."

Thaddeous said, "That boy never grew up."

I agreed with him there. "Anyway, they bought everybody modems so folks could work at home if they really wanted to burn the midnight oil or work weekends." Then I stopped. "They work at home!"

"So?" Michelle said.

"Don't you get it? Philip worked at home, and I'll bet you

dollars to doughnuts that he had a copy of the source files on his hard disk at home."

"How do we know the killer hasn't gotten to them, too?" Thaddeous asked.

"We don't," I said, "but you can be darned sure that I'm going to find out."

Chapter 36

I'd told Thaddeous that I didn't know Colleen well enough to go see her. But I must have been thinking like a Northerner that day. Look at how Thaddeous had gone to talk to Dave and how much Dave had told him. Besides, I had the perfect excuse. She'd lost her husband, hadn't she? Friends are supposed to drop by at a time like that. Of course, friends don't usually check out your hard drive, but somehow I was going to have to come up with a way to look for those files.

Thaddeous and Michelle both wanted to come with me, but I talked them out of it. "I don't know Colleen well, but I do know her. She's more likely to talk to me if I'm alone."

Michelle said, "Are you sure that's a good idea? She's still a suspect, isn't she?"

"Not really," I said. "Maybe she could have killed Philip, but I don't think she'd have been able to get to Murray so easily. And how would she have known about Murray walking down the stairs every day? Or that he'd been looking at the StatSys code?" Neither Michelle nor Thaddeous said anything, meaning that they weren't convinced, so I added, "Besides, I'll be sure and mention that y'all know I'm visiting her. That should make her think twice about trying anything."

Of course, I couldn't go empty-handed. I spent the rest of the afternoon in the kitchen. By the time I got ready to go, found the listing for Philip and Colleen in the Cambridge phone book, and figured out how to get from the subway to her house, it was after six o'clock, so I was pretty sure she'd be home from work.

I looked up at the house after I rang the bell. It was an enormous white Victorian, with a tower and everything. It would have been glorious if half the shutters hadn't been missing and the paint hadn't been peeling. Knowing Philip, I suspected that he'd had big plans for the place when he bought it. But once again, reality hadn't cooperated with him.

Colleen opened the door, looking surprised to see me. "Laura?"

"Hi, Colleen. I brought you something," I said, holding out the pie I was carrying.

"Thank you," she said, and opened the door wide enough for me to come in. There were boxes stacked in the living room, and she led me past them and down a hall to the kitchen. "This is the only place where there's room left to sit," she said.

"I know most people bring food over right after a family misfortune," I said, using the excuse I had made up on the way over, "but my Aunt Nora always brings something a while later, when you've already eaten the other stuff." Though that was a out-and-out lie, it was the kind of idea that might occur to Aunt Nora.

"That's sweet. I didn't think people brought food for things like this anymore."

"My folks do," I said, looking around the kitchen. There was nothing on the counter, and an open cabinet door showed empty shelves. "Colleen, are you moving?"

She nodded. "This place is too big, and I can't really afford the payments on my own. And there are too many memories."

"I hadn't heard."

"I haven't told anybody. Nobody at SSI, anyway. Not that they'd care."

"Of course they'd care, Colleen. I know there was some awkwardness at Philip's visitation, but they're your friends."

"No, they were Philip's friends, not mine. They were nice enough to my face, but Philip used to tell me what they'd say about me behind my back."

This sounded an awful lot like what Dave had said. Once again, Philip had gone out of his way to cause problems between people.

Colleen went on. "I don't think they ever forgave me for not coming to SSI."

"I always wondered why you didn't work there."

"What kind of work did they have for me? Answering the phone? Running the mailroom? I'm a chemist, not a programmer. You know that crew. If you don't know computers, you don't know shit."

The SSI folks did have a heavy bias toward programming, which is probably why the business end of the company had suffered so. I wasn't immune from that bias myself—I had completely forgotten what Colleen's major had been. "I didn't realize."

"They just put up with me being around because of Philip. I haven't heard from any of them since the funeral."

"I'm sorry, Colleen, I didn't know." Then I thought of

something. "Oh, Lord, did somebody call you about Murray?"

"No, but I saw the obituary in the paper. I would have gone to the funeral, but I've missed a lot of work lately. Because of Philip, of course. And I wasn't all that close to Murray anyway."

"Still, somebody should have called. I apologize, Colleen. I was expecting Jessie to take care of it—I'm really embarrassed." Actually, I hadn't even thought about Colleen, which was even more embarrassing.

"It's all right. I don't expect you and me to be friendly. Not after Philip dumped you to date me."

That wasn't the way I remembered it, but I guess that's what Philip had told her. "It wasn't just that," I said. "When Philip and I broke up, the group cut me out pretty thoroughly. I always assumed that you took my place, both with Philip and with the others in the group."

I suddenly felt angry at the whole group, for cutting me out, and for cutting Colleen out, and maybe even for cutting Philip out. "What is it with groups of people, anyway?" I said, asking myself as much as I was asking her. "Who gets to decide who's 'in' and who's 'out'? It's like the group has a mind of its own. Everybody always fussed about it, worrying about how the rest of the group felt about something, and worrying about inviting one person out if you didn't invite everybody, and worrying about how it was running our lives, and worrying that it might break up. Nobody ran that group—it ran us."

At first Colleen looked taken aback by my vehemence, but then she started to nod. "You're right. Look at Inez and Vincent. No way should they be working together, but neither one dares to break away from that damned group. I don't think most of them even like each other anymore. It's like it's

got a stranglehold on them. There are families that don't hold
on to each other that tightly."

I nodded, feeling oddly relieved. For so long I had nursed
pain at having been dropped from the group, but now I was
just as glad I had been. "Maybe they did us a favor by cutting us out."

"Maybe they did. If it weren't for Philip, I'd never have
hung around any of them, anyway."

"Same here." I'd never thought of it that way before, but
she was right. "One thing you have to say about Philip: he had
great taste in women."

"Damned straight. Tell you what. I'll make some coffee,
and we'll cut into this pie of yours."

She rummaged around and found two mismatched mugs,
paper plates, plastic forks, and a half-empty jar of instant coffee. Then she filled the cups with water and put them in the
microwave.

While we waited, I asked, "Where are you moving to?"

"An apartment in Somerville."

"We'll have to get together sometime."

"I'd like that."

The microwave timer went off, so Colleen added coffee
crystals to the hot water and cut generous slices of pie for
both of us.

I let her take a bite first, and was pleased when she said,
"This is great."

"Thank you," I said. "It's my mother's recipe." I don't
cook much, but I make a good egg custard pie, if I do say so
myself. I wouldn't have felt right bringing something store-
bought on a bereavement call. Which reminded me that I was
there to do something other than work out old grievances and
eat pie.

"I know you're not a programmer," I said, hoping it sounded more casual to her than it did to me, "but I suppose you use computers a lot in the lab these days."

"Quite a bit," she said, "but I never got into them the way Philip did. When I get home, the last thing I want to do is to stare at a computer. I don't even play computer games. And now I've got all of Philip's equipment."

"What are you going to do with it?"

"Pack it up and store it, I guess. In fact, that's what I was about to pack when you got here."

"You know, I've been looking around for some decent used equipment," I said, again hoping that I sounded nonchalant. "Do you want to sell any of it?"

"I'd much rather sell it then store it," she said. "Have you got time to look at it now?"

"Why not? I've got a few minutes." In fact, I'd been hoping she'd say just that.

She took me to what had been intended as a large bedroom but instead was filled with unfinished pine bookcases, a old-style metal office desk, a couple of tables with woodgrain formica tops, and a ramshackle desk chair. The top of the desk and the tables were covered with a motley collection of computer equipment: monitors, CPUs, floppy drives, hard drives, and modems. I recognized some of it from when I was dating Philip, which meant it was long past its prime, but other pieces were newer. All were connected with an alarming array of wire and cords duct-taped to the walls and floor.

"Good Lord," I said. "What on earth did he do with all this stuff?" I was a computer nut myself, but I knew I'd have no use for that much.

"You got me. All I know is that he said he needed the big bedroom, and that I wasn't to move anything."

"I'm surprised it didn't short out your fusebox."

"It did—several times. Probably a fire hazard, too. Are you interested in any of it?"

I walked in and looked around. If the StatSys files were there, they were mostly likely stored on a hard drive. "I could really use more hard disk space. Mine is nigh onto full." That was true enough, though I hadn't considered buying more until just that minute.

"Just tell me what you want."

There were three hard drives of different vintage but all showing signs of wear. Any of them could have the StatSys files, so I resigned myself to buying all three. But first I had to make sure Colleen hadn't already deleted what I needed. "Are any of these empty?"

"No, they're all pretty full. Philip had been wanting something new so he'd have more room. A Zip drive or something. I tried to tell him that if he'd just clean out some of the files on one of these drives he'd have plenty of room, but he said I didn't know what I was talking about." She looked indignant. "I may not know computers, but I know he hadn't touched some of these files in years."

That was what I wanted to hear. "That's no problem, I can clean them off. How about all three of them? They're pretty small by today's standards, but put together, I think they'd be enough for me to back up my files." That last part wasn't just trying to drive the price down—they were pretty dinky. One could hold twenty megabytes of data, one fifty, and the third a hundred. These days, most people won't consider buying anything less than half a gigabyte.

"That would be fine."

"How much do you want for them?"

She shrugged. "You tell me what they're worth—I haven't got a clue."

"How about a hundred and twenty-five?" I thought that was what I could buy them for from an newspaper ad, and though my Aunt Maggie would have been appalled at my offering full market value, it just didn't seem right to bargain with a widow.

"Okay."

I wrote her a check, and we unraveled the trail of wires connecting the drives with the system. Then Colleen found a box big enough for me to carry my purchases in.

"What are you going to do with the rest of it?" I asked.

"I'm not sure. I hate to just throw it away, but it seems dumb to store it."

"There's a few places around that specialize in used equipment. You might could get a few bucks."

"Yeah? That would be great."

"Call me with your new address," I said, "and I'll send you a list."

"Thanks." Then she added, "I appreciate the pie and your taking the hard drives off my hands, and I hate to rush you off, but I've got a lot to do."

"Do you need help packing?" I felt like I had to offer, even though I was itching to get the hard drives home so I could look at them.

"No, thanks," she said. "Most of it's done. But I still need to sort some stuff and I've got a lot of Philip's things to send to his parents." She paused. "I wonder if I shouldn't give them Philip's piece of SSI after all."

Even though I knew from what Thaddeous had found out that Philip's family could use the money, I didn't want to push Colleen into anything she'd regret later. "That's a nice thought, but where would it leave you money-wise?"

"Not too well off," she admitted.

"Maybe you could compromise. If you and Philip had gone through with the divorce, you and he would have split things fifty-fifty, right?"

"Right."

"Why don't you give them half of that piece of SSI? He had a one-seventh share, so if SSI goes public, that would be a fair number of shares of stock for both of you."

"That's not a bad idea."

Then, to make sure that she knew what she was potentially giving away, I said, "I've got a hunch that this new release is really going to turn the company around. One-fourteenth could be a lot."

She shrugged. "If it is, then I'll be that much better off. If not, I haven't lost anything, and it might make them feel better."

"It would be a very generous thing for you to do."

"Like you said, if Philip had lived, it would have gone to him, so I'm not really out anything. Thanks for the idea."

"Don't thank me—it's your money."

"Yeah, but they should get something. I mean, he wasn't much of a son to them. Or much of a husband to me. You know, that's what makes me the sorriest."

"What?"

"That nobody's going to miss him. I've tried to cry for him. I've really tried. I just don't have it in me."

I knew a little of how she had to feel. My feelings about

Philip were pretty mixed, too. "Don't blame yourself, Colleen. Philip didn't make it easy to love him. He was easy to fall in love with, but not easy to stay in love with."

"Yeah, that was Philip." She held out her hand. "Thanks for coming by, Laura."

"I'm glad I did," I said, and meant it. Not just because of the hard drives, but because she had helped me clear up some of my own unfinished business. I didn't take her hand, though. Instead, I gave her a hug, Byerly-style. Philip was right about one thing: you can take the girl out of the country, but you can't take the country out of the girl.

Chapter 37

The box of hard drives was a little big for me to lug onto the subway, so I took a cab from Harvard Square to my place. Thaddeous and Michelle must have been watching for me, because they had the door opened before I could reach my keys.

"Did you get the files?" Michelle wanted to know.

"I don't know yet," I said. "Let me get my coat off and I'll tell you what happened." As I was talking, I was moving my portable PC to the coffee table. By the time I finished explaining how I'd ended up with the hard drives, I was ready to hook up the first of them. "Cross your fingers," I said.

Michelle and Thaddeous were sitting on either side of me, staring at the screen as I took a look at the directory.

"Are the files there?" Michelle asked. "Do they have any information?"

"Hold your horses," I said. "It's going to take me a little while to check." As it turned out, it took me quite some time because the hard drive was a virtual pigsty. Philip never had been very organized, and it showed in the way files were scattered hither and yon on that hard drive. Files that had nothing to do with one another were shoved into the same directory for no reason I could figure out. So instead of a quick look, it took me half an hour to be fairly sure that the Stat-Sys files weren't there.

"One down and two to go," I said, and unplugged the first drive to plug in the second.

Michelle said, "I can't stand just sitting here watching," and started pacing. "What if the files aren't there?"

"We'll cross that bridge when we come to it," Thaddeous said soothingly.

The second drive was just like the first. Well, the files themselves were different, but the condition they were in was just as bad. I spent another half an hour sorting through it all before shaking my head and saying, "Not in here, either."

"We're getting closer to that bridge, Thaddeous," Michelle said.

"But we ain't there yet," he said, as I plugged in the third drive.

I'd saved the twenty-megabyte drive for last. Since it was the smallest, the oldest, and the slowest, I didn't think Philip would have been as likely to use it for anything important. I was just hoping I was wrong, because like Michelle, I was worried about what we'd do if the files weren't there.

It didn't take me any time to see that the files on this drive were put together very differently. Files were much better organized—in fact, it was neater than I keep my own hard drive. It took me no more than five minutes to find a set of files labeled STATS, and maybe five more to be sure that they really were the StatSys files.

"They're here!" I said.

"Hooray!" Michelle said, and gave Thaddeous a big hug. He didn't seem to mind.

"And for once, Philip did the right thing and saved both the compiled and the decompiled files," I said.

"You've been talking about compiled files, and decompiled files, and source files, and I don't know what-all kinds of files. What's all that mean?" Thaddeous asked.

"You remember how I said that a computer program is a set of instructions? Well, the instructions have to be in a language the computer can understand. Computer languages are so wildly different from English that they're called code, which is why I talk about 'coding a program' or 'writing code.'"

"I'm with you so far, but it seems like it'd be right much easier if the computer could understand English."

"But then I'd be out of a job," I said with a smile. "Anyway, code has to be broken down into little bitty chunks. I couldn't just tell a computer to walk across the floor. I'd have to give it a list of instructions like (1) lift right foot two inches off the ground, (2) move foot six inches forward, (3) lower right foot to the ground, (4) lift left foot two inches off the ground, and so on."

"I thought computers were smart," Thaddeous said.

"Not really. They only do what you tell them to do. And even when I break instructions down into steps and write those steps in code, the computer still can't understand me. The steps have to be translated into what we call machine language."

Michelle said, "I'll take your word for it, Laura. You mind if I get something to drink?"

"Go ahead," I said, and continued explaining the process to Thaddeous. "We've also got to think about memory size and speed. Code takes up an awful lot of space in a computer's memory, and it takes a long time to read and follow the instructions. Just like it would be hard for you to remember umpteen steps to walk across the room, and it would take you a whole lot longer to do each little piece separately. Okay?"

"I'm still with you," he said, but he was starting to sound doubtful.

"A compiler program takes code and translates it into machine language. Moreover, machine language doesn't take up as much space as code, and the computer can read it faster. Translating code into machine language is what I mean by compiling a program. The code I started with is stored in source files—the translated files I end up with are compiled files."

"Then what's a decompiled file?"

"Once a program's been compiled, not even a programmer can read it—at least, I can't. But you can take a compiled file and decompile it to get the source files back out of it. That takes time, so if you've got any sense, you save copies of the source files until you're darned sure you won't need them."

"But Philip didn't do that?"

"He didn't do it at SSI, anyway. When Neal went looking for them, all he found was garbage. So he had to decompile. But we," I concluded triumphantly, "have the source files right here."

Michelle came back in with drinks for all of us and sat down next to Thaddeous. "Is the lesson over?"

"All done. Let's see what we've got here," I said, opening up the first program file. I don't know what Thaddeous expected from code, but I could tell from the look on his face that this wasn't it.

He said, "I can't make hide nor hair of this mess."

"Of course not," I said in mock indignation. "I spent four years in college learning how to read this mess."

"What do you do now?"

"I look to see what Philip hid in his comment lines, if you'll give me a minute." The minute stretched into several minutes, and into half an hour, and kept on stretching. The problem wasn't the code itself—it was some of the cleanest I'd ever seen. The problem was that there were so many comment lines. Most programmers, myself included, rely on memory to remember what a piece of code is doing and why it was set up that way. By rights, we should make comments about all kinds of stuff that we don't, either because we get busy or because we don't want to bother. Not in this code. Every step was thoroughly documented. The thing was, all the comments talked about was the program.

After a few minutes, Michelle and Thaddeous started talking in low voices while I worked. Then they moved over by the TV so they could watch it, keeping the sound down. An hour later, Michelle turned to me and said, "Well?"

I couldn't blame her for sounding impatient, but I had to say, "I can't find anything. No secrets, no instructions, no nothing. Unless Philip did something really sneaky, like the first letter of each comment line spelling out something. He tried to claim that tricks like that 'proved' Shakespeare was the Earl of Oxford, so I wouldn't be surprised if he tried it himself."

"Now you're talking," Thaddeous said.

I found a pad and pen, and I read out the first letters of a bunch of comments for Michelle to scribble down.

"Does it spell out anything?" I asked.

She looked at it, and shook her head. "Not in English, it doesn't. Not in Italian either."

I took a look, but she was right. It was gibberish.

"Rats!" I said. "I thought we were on to something."

Michelle looked disappointed, too, but Thaddeous said, "It didn't hurt to try."

"The answer has to be in here somewhere. Maybe if we took every third word . . ." I stopped. "No, Philip would never have done that much work. Besides, the comments are too well written. If he was forcing words in to make up a code, they wouldn't read so clearly. I don't think he could have done it."

"Maybe we should sleep on it," Thaddeous said, looking at his watch.

But something had just dawned on me. "You know, I don't think he could have done it."

"You said that already," Michelle said.

"I mean he couldn't have done any of this. This doesn't look like Philip's code."

"Are you looking at the wrong file?" she asked.

"It's StatSys, all right. I just don't think it's Philip's. I don't think he wrote this." I scrolled through more of the code. "I'm sure he didn't."

Thaddeous looked at it with me. "How can you tell?"

"Because programmers have different styles. I know you don't think of programming as creative, but it is if it's done right. No two programmers work the exact same way, any more than any two artists work the same way. Dee and Dom do serviceable, easy-to-understand code, but it's boring, with no flourishes. Philip's code was nothing but flourishes. Oh, it usually worked, but it was very idiosyncratic. Nobody could figure it out but Philip."

"What about your programs?" Michelle asked.

"Not as boring as Dee's and Dom's, but easier to deal with than Philip's." I didn't want to admit the next part, but it was true. "I'm not nearly as good as whoever it was who wrote this stuff."

Thaddeous didn't look convinced.

"It's hard to explain if you don't program, but trust me, this is very elegant code." I tried to come up with a way to show him what I meant. "Do you remember how Paw used to tell a story?"

"He was pretty straightforward. Just told you what he wanted you to know, and then went on."

"Right. How does Vasti tell a story?" I knew that our cousin had cornered him more than once, just like she had me.

He grinned. "She tells you all kinds of stuff that doesn't have anything to do with what she started talking about, but eventually she gets it all out."

"Well, Philip coded like Vasti tells stories. *This* code is what Paw would have done if he had been a programmer."

"Now I see what you're saying," he said.

"And there are all these comment lines. Philip almost never put in comments. He used to say that if a program was hard to write, it should be hard to understand. When we were in college, he always got points taken off because he didn't put comments in his projects. There's no way he'd have written as many as this program has—he'd have said that it was a waste of time. I'm telling you, Philip did *not* write this program."

"But if Philip didn't write it . . ." Michelle started to say.

"If Philip didn't write it," I said, "then he stole it."

Chapter 38

We didn't say anything for a minute, but then Thaddeous asked, "Laurie Anne, I know programmers make good money, but I don't know how much code is worth. Is it a lot?"

"Well, this core code is the basis for everything SSI has done over the past seven years. I don't know exactly how much money they've made, and of course, they've made enhancements. But even with marketing costs and company overhead, I'd guess that the profits would been in the hundreds of thousands of dollars. You could make a strong case that a good chunk of that money should have gone to the author of StatSys."

"It seems to me like even a hundred thousand dollars would make a right good motive for murder," he said.

"You bet it would," Michelle agreed.

"What I want to know is who wrote it, if it wasn't Philip," Thaddeous said.

"Not one of the MIT crowd, or they'd have said something years ago," I said. "They'd have recognized their own work, and I can't imagine any of them letting Philip take credit for their work."

Thaddeous said, "What about the way he was trying to

blackmail them into changing votes? Couldn't he have black-mailed somebody into this?"

I said, "Let's say Philip blackmailed somebody into letting him claim StatSys. And that person has kept quiet all these years. But then Vincent and Inez started trying to get Philip out of SSI, and Philip had to use that same threat to keep from getting fired. Only now the person being blackmailed is sick and tired of having whatever it is hanging over his or her head, so decides to get rid of him once and for all. That way his or her secret is safe, and SSI doesn't go bankrupt." It sounded more and more convoluted to me the longer I talked, but Thaddeous and Michelle were nodding.

"That might be it," Thaddeous said.

"But which one did Philip steal the code from?" Michelle asked.

"I don't know. Philip claimed to have developed StatSys during his last semester at MIT, and by that time I wasn't spending a lot of time with the group. I don't know who could have been working on a project that complicated. But Colleen might know."

Michelle handed me the phone. "So what are you waiting for? Call her!"

"I can't—it's almost midnight," I protested, putting the phone back. "I'll call her in the morning."

"Are you telling me that I'm going to have to wait until tomorrow? I'm going crazy here!"

"It seems to me like the best things are worth waiting for," Thaddeous said to her, and darned if he wasn't flirting when he said it. That distracted her enough that she agreed that I should call Colleen the next day. And when he announced that he was going to take her home in a taxi because it was so late, I think she forgot all about SSI.

Chapter 39

Colleen must have left for work pretty early the next day, because I missed her in the morning. And I guess she never checked her phone messages, because even though I left her a message every hour, she didn't return my call. After spending the entire day at SSI staring at my phone, waiting for it to ring and jumping every time it did, I was a nervous wreck. Only it was never Colleen—it was Thaddeous or Michelle checking up. I finally laid down the law and told them I'd call them just as soon as I heard from Colleen, but that only meant that the phone didn't ring at all.

I hated to leave the office because I didn't want to be away from a phone for the time it took me to take the subway to my apartment, but I needed the distraction. And I had been home just long enough to read the note from Thaddeous saying he was going souvenir shopping when the phone rang.

"Hello?"

"Laura, this is Colleen. I got your messages."

I almost said *finally*, but resisted. "Hi, Colleen. Thanks for getting back to me. I had a question about one of the hard drives."

"Is anything wrong with it? If there is, I'll give your money back."

"No, there's nothing wrong." The next part was going to be tricky. Despite having had all day to worry over it, I still didn't quite know just how I should ask her what I needed to know. Like a true Southerner, I decided to try to work my way around to it gradually. "I found some old StatSys files on the smallest drive and wondered if they were anything important."

"I don't think so," she said, sounding a little confused. "Unless SSI wants them. You'd know better than I do what's important."

I forced a laugh. "You're probably right. These are old files, probably from back when Philip first came up with Stat-Sys. I just didn't want to trash the files without making sure."

"Well, you don't have to worry about them," she said, and I could tell she was wondering why this was worth all the phone messages.

"You know, I was just looking at the code and it really is a remarkable piece of work. Even more remarkable when you think about Philip doing it all by himself."

"He always talked about it like it was good, but he said I didn't know enough about computers to really appreciate it."

That sounded like Philip. "I imagine it must have been pretty boring for you when the group talked about computers."

"I'll say. I got to the point where I'd just zone out when they got started. Especially Philip and Neal. If they weren't talking about computers, then they were talking about the statistics course they were taking. They'd go on for hours and hours. Until Neal left, of course. Philip was real broken up about that."

"He must have been, them being roommates and all," I said, but I was really just making conversation while I tried

to think of a way to ask more about StatSys. Which is why I
nearly missed what she said next.

"Yeah, he really threw himself into his work after that,
just spent hours on the computer. He said having the new
hard drive made it easier."

"Philip bought a new hard drive?" That didn't sound like
Philip. He was always broke and checked the trash behind the
computer lab every week to see if any usable floppy disks had
been thrown out.

"No, he scrounged it. It had been Neal's, but he left it
when he dropped out."

"Really?"

"He left his whole computer system behind, but parts of
it were broken. I think he'd gotten so frustrated because of
the virus that he'd thrown it across the room. And then kicked
it. There was glass all over the room from his screen, and the
CPU had been busted wide open."

"Bless his heart." I couldn't picture Neal doing it, but I
could understand it.

"Philip did salvage a keyboard and some other stuff. And
the hard drive."

"But Neal's hard drive had crashed. Did Philip reformat
it or what?"

"I don't know. He just started using it."

"And the virus never recurred?"

"Not that he ever mentioned."

Of course, Philip might have been able to get rid of the
virus that had so confounded Neal, but I was starting to think
that there might be another explanation. "Of course, I wasn't
around much then, so I don't know that I ever heard the
whole story." I was keeping my fingers crossed that Colleen
was too well brought up to ask why I wanted to know about

it now. Thank goodness her parents had done such a good job.

"There isn't that much to hear. He got a virus on his hard drive that messed it up right in the middle of working on his dissertation. When he couldn't get his data back, he left school. Philip and I were out of town when his hard drive crashed, so we didn't know anything about it until we got back."

"I always wondered how Neal picked up that virus," I said speculatively. "We didn't know as much about them as we do now, but he was always mighty particular about what diskettes he put into his system and who he'd let use his computer." I remembered an argument between him and Philip over that very thing. Philip had spilled Coke on Neal's keyboard once, and Neal had been furious and had absolutely refused to let Philip use his system ever again. Even though it was his own doing, Philip had been as mad as a wet hen.

Colleen said, "Philip would have given him a hard time about it if Neal hadn't left the way he did. Like I said, we were out of town, and when we got back to my place, Neal had left a note on my door. He was desperate to find Philip, said he'd tried everything and he just couldn't get the drive running again. I felt sorry for him, and Philip couldn't wait to get to their dorm room and prove how smart he was. He was so . . ."

"Full of himself?" I suggested.

"Exactly. But when we got there, Neal was gone. There was just a note and what was left of his computer. I didn't hear anything out of Neal for years, not until he showed up at SSI."

I should have talked to Colleen a little while longer to be polite, but I couldn't wait to get off the phone. I made an excuse about there being somebody at the door so I could hang up and try to put it all together.

The first piece was what folks at SSI had told me about Philip planting computer viruses and booby traps at the office. He'd played all kinds of practical jokes while we were dating, and while most of them had been ultimately harmless, they sure had been a pain in the rump.

The next piece was Neal being a much better programmer than Philip, and Philip hating to admit that anybody was better than him at anything. Plus, Neal had a better system than Philip that he wouldn't let Philip use.

The two pieces added up to a golden opportunity for Philip to play a nasty trick on Neal. Couldn't he have created a virus that would make it *look* as if Neal's hard drive had crashed irrevocably? And couldn't he have timed the virus so that it would go off while Philip was out of town so Neal wouldn't suspect him of being responsible? Couldn't he have messed up the backups, too? And wouldn't it have been just like Philip to show up his roommate by "fixing" the problem he'd caused in the first place?

If anybody else had done it and then found Neal gone, he'd have called Neal to get him to come back to school, but I couldn't see Philip doing that. I could see him getting rid of the booby trap so he could use the hard drive. And I could see him being nosy enough to look at Neal's files, and eventually finding StatSys and realizing what he could do with it. He used it to start SSI, and kept people away from the code all those years because he was afraid somebody would realize that it wasn't his.

Then Vincent and Inez started their campaign to get Philip away from SSI. And just when he was desperate to save his job, Neal came back. Maybe he was hoping Neal wouldn't get past the barrier of booby traps he placed or that he wouldn't recognize his own work. And maybe he had even worse viruses planned in case he did get fired. He must have been worried sick that Neal would recognize his own code. But he died before that could happen.

Hadn't he? Or had Neal finally found out what Philip had stolen from him and paid him back by hitting him and leaving him, just like he had his computer?

Chapter 40

I should have been happy. Neal being the real author of Stat-Sys had to be the key to both Philip's and Murray's deaths. It provided motive and explained the timing. But I didn't believe it.

I paced through the apartment, hoping Thaddeous would show up so I could talk to him, but he didn't. Then I called Michelle at GBS, but she'd left early and I guessed that she was on her way to meet me.

That left one person I could talk to, and that was Richard. It took him a couple of rings to answer the phone. "Hello?"

"Hey, there. Did I wake you up?"

He stifled a yawn. "Yes, but since I was dreaming of you, I don't mind."

"You do say the sweetest things. Even when you're not quoting."

"How goes the investigation? Have you solved it?"

"Maybe. I'm calling to bounce something off you."

"Bounce away."

I gave him a rundown of what Thaddeous, Michelle, and I had been up to since we'd last spoken, finishing up with my talk with Colleen. "That seems to clinch it. Philip stole Neal's code, and when Neal found out, he killed him."

"That's great!" Richard said. "You've got all the pieces."

"I guess I do."

"You don't sound thrilled."

"I'm not. This just doesn't make sense to me."

"It makes sense to me."

I didn't say anything for a while, trying to figure out exactly what it was that bothered me. "Richard, suppose you found out that somebody had stolen a copy of one of your papers and had it published in some journal under his own name. What would your reaction be?"

"Fury."

"What would be the first thing you'd want to do?"

"To get credit for writing the paper. Assuming it was a good one, of course."

"All your papers are brilliant. But my point is that you'd want to prove it was yours. You'd write a letter to the editor and tell him, maybe dig up old drafts, get people to swear that they'd seen you working on it, whatever it took."

"Is there something comparable Neal could have done?"

"I don't know, but I do know that if his goal was to prove StatSys was really his, killing Philip was the absolute worst thing he could do. His best chance was to get Philip to confess."

"Do you think Philip would have confessed?"

"Never in a million years," I had to admit.

"So maybe he confronted Philip, and Philip made it plain that he wouldn't confess. Then Neal killed him. What else could he have done?"

"He could have used the hard drive as proof."

"If he'd known it was still around."

"Okay, then the code itself could have been proof. If I

could tell that it wasn't Philip's code, then so could anybody else who had samples of his work."

"I believe you, but would those arguments be compelling enough to sway a jury? A jury that doesn't know a bit from a byte?"

I remembered how long it had taken me to explain the concepts to Thaddeous, and he wasn't a stupid man. "Maybe not, but if a lawyer could establish what kind of person Philip was and how he wouldn't let anybody look at the code, there would have been a chance."

"A small chance."

"A better chance than there is now. With Philip dead, for Neal to say that the code was his would just point to him as Philip's killer."

"But the police think it was an accident."

"Detective Salvatore doesn't. At least, he didn't act like he did at Philip's visitation. And you can bet that if a lot of money were involved, they'd take another look at the case."

"All right," he said, "I'll concede that Philip's death didn't do Neal any good financially. There's always revenge."

"I don't see Neal as the vengeful type."

"You said Philip was drunk the night he died. If Neal was with Philip, he probably was, too. 'One draught above heat makes him a fool, the second mads him, and a third drowns him.' *Twelfth Night*, Act I, Scene 5."

"But after all these years?"

"It happened a long time ago, but Neal only found out recently."

"True, but still ... You remember how I told you that Philip had fooled around on me?"

"I remember," he said softly.

"By the time I found out, I had been broken up with Philip

for over a year. I was upset, of course, but I wasn't nearly so upset as I would have been if I had found out as it was happening. It just didn't matter to me that much anymore." That was understating it, but only a little. "Mostly I was relieved to be away from Philip and his lies. Don't you think Neal would have reacted the same way?"

"Laura, you're a civilized person. Is Neal?"

"Yes."

"You're sure?"

"Yes. No. I don't know. Killing Philip for something he did so long ago just doesn't feel right."

"Revenge is a dish best served cold."

I waited for an attribution, but when he didn't give one, guessed, "*King Lear?*"

"*Star Trek: The Wrath of Khan.*"

"Richard!"

"Okay, how about, 'Vengeance is in my heart, death in my hand. Blood and revenge are hammering in my head.' *Titus Andronicus*, Act II, Scene 3."

"That's more like it," I said, but I was still amused, which was almost certainly what he had had in mind. How on earth could he read my moods so accurately from so far away? Then I said, "I have one other objection to Neal as murderer. Why would he kill Murray?"

"Because Murray figured out StatSys was stolen, just like you did."

"Then why kill him? Having somebody else find out would have been the best of all possible worlds. Neal could have acted innocent and said he never noticed. It would have been tough since he'd been working with the code, but I think he'd have been able to carry it off. Maybe he could use his nervous breakdown to claim amnesia."

"That's a little iffy."

"True, but Philip's death could have gone down as an accident without Murray's coming so soon after. So Neal would be in the clear. He'd get credit for his product, and that would be one more piece of revenge. What did Murray's death buy him? Nothing."

"But don't you think Philip's death coming so soon after Neal got back into town is too convenient to be a coincidence?"

"Coincidences do happen."

"I take it that this means you're going to keep looking for answers."

I thought about it. "It does."

"Then I'll remind you to be very, very careful. Don't forget MacBeth. The first murder was hard for him, but each time after that it got easier and easier. Your man or woman has killed twice already, and after checking up on you and Thaddeous, knows far more than I'm comfortable with."

"I'll be careful." I heard the front door opening and said, "Thaddeous is here, so I'd better go. Thanks for letting me ramble. I didn't even ask about what's been going on with you."

" 'How like a winter hath my absence been from thee.' *Sonnet 97.*"

"Richard, it is winter."

"Could Shakespeare call them or what?"

"Good night, Richard. I love you."

"I love you, too."

Chapter 41

Thaddeous arrived then with bags of gifts for the folks back home, but before he could show them to me, I told him what Colleen had told me. "I know it sounds like Neal is guilty," I said, "but I still feel like we're missing something."

"Are you sure you just don't want me to hang around Boston a while longer?"

"Thaddeous! Be serious."

"Seriously, then, maybe you don't want to believe an old friend would be a killer."

"Of course I don't want to believe it," I said, "but I went into this knowing that the killer was probably an old friend. I just don't think this sounds like the Neal I know."

"He might not be the man you used to know. Don't forget that nervous breakdown."

"Lots of people have nervous breakdowns and don't murder people afterward. In fact, if he's been under the care of a psychologist since then, he's probably as stable as anybody else at SSI."

"Well," he said, "you do have a fair to middling record of being able to judge people. So I'm willing to keep snooping around. What did you have in mind?"

The awful truth was that I didn't have anything else in

mind, and I wanted a way to avoid telling him. "Maybe Michelle has thought of something. I called the office a while ago and they said she'd left early, so she should be here soon."

We got something to drink, and then I admired the presents he'd bought. But after half an hour of looking at Red Sox hats and Celtics shirts and pub towels from the Cheers bar, I started to get nervous. It shouldn't have taken Michelle that long to get to my apartment.

"Maybe we should call GBS again," I said. "I might have misunderstood them."

Thaddeous dialed the number at GBS, waited a few minutes, then hung up. "It was a machine. She must be on the way."

I nodded but still felt uneasy. Somebody had been investigating me and Thaddeous since Monday. At least, that's how long it had taken whoever it was to get to our family in Byerly. How much could he have found out since then? He could have been following us, and I hadn't even thought to watch for a tail.

If we'd been followed, then he knew Michelle was involved because she'd been with us. By following her back to her house, the killer could have her address, and by following her the next morning, he could have found out that she worked at GBS. As for me, he'd know that I'd gone to Colleen's house and come back with something in a box. In short, it would have been pretty obvious that we were up to something.

I looked at the clock again. Michelle wasn't that late, not really. A delay on the subway could explain away that little bit of time. But the later it got, the harder it was for me to convince myself of that. As for Thaddeous, he looked as worried as I'd ever seen him. I wished I could come up with an excuse to reassure him, and me, too.

Chapter 42

The doorbell rang, and I said, "Finally," and buzzed Michelle up without saying anything over the intercom. But when I opened the door, it wasn't Michelle I saw coming up the stairs. It was Neal.

"Hi," I said, letting him inside and closing the door behind him. It probably wasn't the smartest thing to do with a murder suspect, but with Thaddeous there, I didn't hesitate. "We were expecting somebody else."

"Michelle?" he asked.

I looked at Thaddeous. "How did you know?"

"Michelle is the reason I'm here. If you two don't do exactly as I tell you, she's going to die."

"You son of a bitch!" Thaddeous roared. He threw himself at Neal and got both hands around his neck, then pounded his head against the door. At the second or third pound, Neal's eyes rolled up and he went limp.

"Thaddeous!" I said, trying to pull my cousin away. "If you kill him, we won't find out where Michelle is."

He let go, and Neal slid down onto the floor.

Obviously I'd been wrong, I decided. Neal was the murderer. "Do you think he's hurt bad?"

"There's no blood."

I wasn't real sure about how to wake an unconscious man, but I remembered the school nurse breaking an ammonia capsule under Vasti's nose when she faked a faint once. "Make sure that he hasn't got a gun," I said. "I'll be right back." I found a half-full bottle of ammonia under the kitchen sink.

"He's not armed," Thaddeous said, when I went back to the living room. "This is all I found." He pointed to a wallet, a bunch of keys, and some change.

"Let me see if I can wake him up."

"Then what?"

"Then we try to find out what he's done with Michelle."

"He's going to tell us, all right."

Later on, when I told Richard about all this, he wondered why I hadn't been more squeamish, but the fact is, I wasn't. I didn't even consider calling the police. I thought about Philip, and Murray, and Michelle, and my only concern was that Thaddeous not get himself into trouble. I opened the bottle of ammonia and waved it under Neal's nose.

He came to, coughing and sputtering. His eyes were watering so badly from the ammonia that I tossed a box of tissues into his lap and gave him a minute to pull himself together.

Then I said, "All right, where is she?"

He looked up at us looming over him, and I felt a little guilty at how scared he looked. But not guilty enough to back down.

"It's not what you think," he said. "I didn't grab her. It was Vincent."

"So the two of you are in this together," I said.

Neal shook his head, then looked as if he wished he hadn't. Wincing, he touched the back of his head.

"That headache is going to be the least of your troubles if

you don't tell us what's going on," Thaddeous said, in that quiet way that's far more threatening than a loud voice.

"We're not working together," Neal said. "I didn't want it to happen this way. I didn't mean for Philip to die."

I said, "So you just hit him and left him in an alley in the middle of winter because you wanted him to get some rest."

He started to shake his head again, then thought better of it. "Philip called me that day, the day he . . . the day you wouldn't let him stay. He said he had something he had to tell me. I thought he just wanted to mooch, and I didn't want him at my place, but I did feel sorry for him, so I was going to get him a hotel room or something. I drove over and picked him up. He wanted to go get a drink so we could talk. We went to a bar near my place, and I bought him a few beers and tried to get him to come to the point.

"He said he had a plan to bring SSI to its knees, to make Vincent beg him to stay. When I asked him how, he told me that SSI doesn't have legal title to the core code for StatSys, because it was *my* code, code I worked on in college."

I nodded.

"You knew?" Neal said.

"Not all along, just since today. I could tell it wasn't Philip's code."

Neal went on. "At first I didn't believe him, but he told me how he programmed my hard drive to crash while he was out of town so he could come back and 'rescue' me. He claimed it was just for a joke, but knowing Philip, he'd have done it and held it over my head for the next twenty years.

"Anyway, Philip just brushed that part off, like it wasn't important. What he said was important was for us to bring down SSI. He said that if I testified that the code was mine and he testified that he had stolen it, then I could get the title to the code and ruin Vincent's deal for taking SSI public. First he wanted to take over SSI and throw out Vincent, but then he had a better idea. He wanted us to start our own company, said you'd come in, too. He wanted to come talk to you so we could make plans."

"Are you sure you weren't just trying to frame Laurie Anne?" Thaddeous asked.

"No! Philip was the one who wanted to come over here, not me. I tried to tell him that Laura wasn't going to let us in any more than she had him, but he wouldn't listen. He really thought he was going to be able to talk her into it. He said she'd do anything for him." To me he added, "Laura, you know how Philip was."

Thaddeous looked at me, and I shrugged. It sure sounded like something Philip would have done. If Neal was lying, he was doing a good job of it.

"By that time, Philip was pretty drunk, so I let him keep talking while I got him back out to the car. I figured the best thing would be to go ahead and come see what you thought." He hesitated. "I guess I was buzzed, too, because Philip was starting to make sense. It was only on the way over that I started to think about what he'd said." He looked at me. "You know why I left MIT, don't you?"

I nodded. "The hard drive crashed while you were working on your dissertation." Then I realized what he was getting at. I had been so concerned about StatSys that I had forgotten all about Neal's doctoral dissertation.

Neal said, "When I couldn't fix my hard drive and I found out that my backup disks were corrupted, I thought my life was over. I guess I went a little crazy—I kicked my computer over, threw it across the room, really beat it up. I couldn't face MIT anymore, so I packed up and went back to California."

I said, "But the hard drive wasn't broken, and Philip found it when he got back."

"He fixed the crash right away, of course, since he had caused it in the first place. I don't know if he tried to call me or not—I wouldn't have been easy to find."

"I heard about your breakdown," I said.

He looked away for a second, then continued. "At some point, he must have looked at my files. I think I could have forgiven him for the StatSys code. I could have blown that project and still gotten my degree. But not without a dissertation."

"So you killed him because of your dissertation?" Thaddeous said, clearly not sure why any paper could be so important. I knew why. Richard and I had already been married while he was finishing his dissertation, and I remembered how crazy it had driven my normally calm husband. And his dissertation had gone relatively smoothly. How would Richard have reacted if he had had to start over?

Neal said, "I realized that he had kept me from getting my doctorate just as we pulled into the alley to park. I said something about it, but he said that we had more important things to worry about and got out of the car. It was dark and he told me to get a flashlight, ordering me around even after what he'd just told me. I got my flashlight out of the glove compartment, and I thought about how heavy it was. Then I walked up behind him, and . . . I don't remember hitting him, but I remember looking down and seeing him on the ground. Then I walked back to the car and drove away."

"You left him there to die," I said. Even allowing that ruining Neal's doctorate was a motive for violence, I couldn't excuse that.

"I didn't just leave him. As soon as I got home, my mind

started working again. I thought about calling the police, but I was afraid they'd arrest me. And I didn't have your phone number, Laura. I didn't even know your married name. So I called Vinnie and told him the whole story. He said he'd take care of it, that he'd go get Philip and make sure he was okay."

"But he didn't," I said.

"No, he didn't," he said. "The next day Jessie called to tell me that Philip was dead, and I called Vinnie again. He said that by the time he got there, Philip was already dead, and he thought that the best thing for all of us was just to leave him there."

"Did you believe him?" I said.

Neal looked down. "At first I did."

Thaddeous asked, "What about Murray?"

"That's when I quit believing Vinnie. The day after Murray died, I went to Vinnie's to talk to him. At first he denied everything, but he finally admitted that Murray had gotten into the code and realized that it wasn't Philip's. Vinnie told him to leave it alone, but Murray wasn't going to. So Vinnie pushed him down the stairs, then got the code out of his system so nobody else would see it. He said he did it to protect us, but I told him he was crazy, that I was going to tell the police. Then he said he'd tell the police about Philip."

"So you stayed quiet."

Again Neal looked ashamed. "Philip and Murray were dead, and I couldn't stand the thought of going to jail. Vinnie said if I kept quiet, everything would be all right. I didn't think anybody else was going to get hurt."

"Sounds to me like you didn't think much at all," Thaddeous said.

"How does Michelle figure into this?" I asked.

"I was worried. I heard you talking to Dom about the

vote, and Jessie told me that you had been asking her questions, too. Later on I saw you in Murray's office. Vinnie was already suspicious after the way you'd questioned him about Philip and the blackmail, and he heard you talking to Sheliah in the break room. So he hired a private detective to check up on you."

That explained the phone calls to Byerly and to GBS. "Then what?" I asked.

"This afternoon Vinnie called and said that the detective had found out you've been involved in stuff like this before and that you suspected us. It looked like you'd found out about the code, and the detective said that Thaddeous and the secretary from GBS were in on it, too. Vinnie wanted me to come get you so we could take care of all three of you."

"Finally going to get your hands dirty?" I asked.

"He said the detective would take care of . . . of that. Vinnie said he called the secretary and told her you'd been hurt, and got her to come to his place, so all I had to do was get you two over there. The detective would do everything else."

"You were planning to hand us over to a hit man?" Thaddeous said. "I ought to—"

"I never intended to go through with it. Why do you think I'm telling you all this?"

Thaddeous and I looked at each other, then Thaddeous shrugged, leaving it up to me. Paw had always told me to listen to my gut when it came to trusting people, but if my gut was wrong this time, Michelle could die.

What did I *know*? I knew that StatSys wasn't written by Philip, but that Neal could have written it. I knew Neal's story fit Philip's personality. And I knew that Vincent wanted that public offering to go through very badly, because of his family's expectations and because of his own ambition.

"What do you think we should do?" I asked Neal, stalling a little bit longer.

"Vinnie has the secretary—"

"Her name is Michelle," Thaddeous growled.

"Okay, Michelle. Vinnie has her in a storage building behind his house. What if I bring the two of you in, like I'm in charge, and then we make a break for it?"

It didn't sound like much of a plan to me. "What if we call the police," I said firmly.

Thaddeous looked like he wanted to argue with me, but he didn't say anything. I guess he figured out that it would be the safest thing for Michelle.

"Do we have to bring in the cops?" Neal said, almost wistfully.

"Neal, there's no way we can keep what happened to Philip and Murray quiet."

"You're right." He swallowed visibly. "Call them."

While Thaddeous relented enough to let Neal get up off of the floor, I found Salvatore's card and dialed the number. A voice I didn't recognize answered the phone.

"May I speak to Detective Salvatore, please?"

"He's not in the office right now. Can I take a message?"

"He's not there," I whispered to Thaddeous and Neal. Then, to the man on the phone, I said, "This is kind of an emergency. Is there any way I can reach him?"

"I'm afraid not. This is Detective Briggs. Can I help you?"

"This is kind of complicated—" I said, but Neal was shaking his head vigorously.

"There's no time," he whispered. "Vinnie said to have you at his place in Lexington by eight-thirty, and that if I couldn't, he'd have the detective take care of Michelle then and you two later."

I looked at my watch. It was eight.

"Miss?" Briggs said.

I thought furiously. Could I explain the story to Briggs fast enough for him to get the wheels moving in half an hour? Not to mention the fact that he'd have to get the Lexington police involved, too. This was Boston, not Byerly. It would take longer than we had. I said, "I'll call Detective Salvatore later," and hung up before he could ask any more questions.

"Neal's right," I said to Thaddeous. "His plan may not be good, but it's all we've got."

Thaddeous said, "Tell you what. I'll go in with him while you stay outside. We'll try to make a break for it, like he said, but if we don't make it, you can go for the police."

I didn't like my cousin going into danger while I stayed outside, but it made sense. Thaddeous was a whole lot bigger than I was, and a whole lot more likely to be able to handle Vincent. Plus I knew the area better, and as a local, I might be able to convince the police that there was something wrong more easily than he could. "All right."

"Do you have a gun?" Neal asked.

"Of course I don't have a gun." But there was one weapon in the house. I reached over the couch and pulled Richard's sword down from the wall.

I halfway expected Thaddeous to snicker, but instead he said, "I'd just as soon you had something to protect yourself with."

Chapter 43

The storage building where Vincent was waiting was as isolated as Neal had said it was on the drive over. The gravel road leading to it was accessed from the street behind the house, and with the trees and a small rise between them, I couldn't even see Vincent's house or any of the neighbor's houses. I had had no idea Vincent lived so high on the hog, and I remembered Inez complaining about his family helping him buy the place.

Neal stopped his car when we were just in sight of the storage building and turned out the dome light so I could slip out without being seen, sword in hand. I wanted to say something to Thaddeous, but there wasn't time. So I ducked into the woods on the side of the road and watched the car drive away.

I went a little deeper into the woods, then headed toward the storage building, its lights barely visible through the trees. It was cold and crisp, with enough light from the moon and stars to make me feel as if a spotlight were aimed at me. Every time I stepped on a branch or slid on leaves, I wished I had given the Girl Scouts one more try.

I heard the car stop, and then the light grew brighter for a second as the door to the building opened. There were voices, but none loud enough for me to make out the words. Then the light dimmed again as the door shut.

I kept making my way toward the building, hoping that they'd be too occupied inside to keep watch outside. Finally I reached the edge of the small clearing that surrounded the building. Did I dare go closer so I could peer inside the window? If not, how would I find out what was going on? As it was, they could already have killed Michelle and Thaddeous and I'd never know it.

I didn't feel safe looking in the front window, so I circled around to the side, hoping there was another window. Luck was with me. There was one, shadowed by an oak tree. As quietly as I could, I crept toward the house, sidling up to the window until I could look inside, every muscle tensed for someone to yell that he'd seen me.

Vincent's back was to me, almost close enough to hit with the sword, and it wasn't easy for me to restrain myself. Especially when I saw Michelle with her face tearstained and Thaddeous standing beside her, holding her hand. They looked very brave, despite the three armed strangers in there, presumably the hit men Vincent had hired. I started to sweat despite the cold. Neal hadn't said anything about there being so many—we had thought that there'd just be the one man.

Neal was talking to Vincent, and though I couldn't hear him, I guessed he was telling the story we'd concocted about my having gone out and his deciding it was best to bring Thaddeous along without me. Vincent turned his head enough for me to see that he was angry with Neal, but he seemed to believe him. He said something to the armed men, and it looked like they were going to take Michelle and Thaddeous away.

Thaddeous must have thought so, too, because suddenly he pushed Michelle behind him and grabbed the gun arm of the man closest to him. He brought the arm down hard across his knee, making the man drop his gun. A second man came from behind, but Thaddeous jerked his elbow into his side, making him double over. For a second, I thought it was going to work. He had two men momentarily incapacitated, and the other one was right next to Neal. All Neal had to do was grab that one's gun, and it would have been all over.

But Neal didn't move. He just stood there, his mouth wide open, while the third man brought his gun down on Thaddeous's head. Michelle screamed as my cousin hit the floor.

Chapter 44

I didn't need a second demonstration of the hit men's skills to tell me that Thaddeous was in over his head, especially with Neal freezing on us. I was just grateful that he hadn't told them about me, and reluctantly decided that I'd better get back to his car before he did. He'd given me his spare keys during the drive over.

I walked backward for a few steps, making sure that nobody inside the building heard me, then turned around. There was a dark shape standing in front of me.

I stifled a scream and brought the sword down flat on the head. I didn't get a whole lot of power into the blow, but he grunted loudly and fell down into the leaves. There was no reason to be quiet anymore, so I took off running for the car, not caring how much noise I made.

The only thing was, I went the wrong way. When I made it to the driveway, I was considerably closer to the storage building than I had meant to be. There were a good fifty yards between me and Neal's car.

People were coming out of the shed, and I saw Michelle silhouetted in the doorway as Vincent pushed her out in front of him. A second later, Thaddeous was shoved out after her. Everybody was yelling, but not so loudly that I didn't hear somebody moving in the bushes behind me. Either there was yet another hit man out there, or I hadn't hit mine hard enough.

I ran for the car, trying not to look behind me, but then I heard a gunshot. I didn't know if it was aimed at me or not, but I threw myself to the ground anyway, lifting my head just enough to see what was happening. One of the hit men was aiming in my direction, but he didn't seem to be able to see me clearly. I didn't have any idea that it would take him long to find me but luckily, it didn't matter.

While the one hit man was looking toward me, Thaddeous turned around and grabbed hold of the one behind him. He pulled the man's head down as he brought his knee up, then threw him down and jumped on top of him, arms flailing. That man's gun was knocked out of both of their reaches, and they grappled, each one trying to get to it while keeping the other away.

Vincent let go of Michelle long enough to grab for it, but as he bent over, she let him have it with a high heel to the groin. I had thought the tales about men making high-pitched squeals when that happened were jokes, but the noises Vinnie made weren't at all funny.

That still left one armed man, but finally Neal thawed out enough to remember which side he was supposed to be on. It was he who grabbed the gun and came up behind the other hit man to hold it against the back of his head and shakily say, "Drop it!"

I had forgotten the man I had surprised, but now he came out of the woods and tripped right over me. We rolled around, me trying to get the sword where I could use it, but he efficiently pinned me to the ground. There were voices and flashlights from further down the driveway, and I thought it was over.

Then one of the flashlight beams washed over the two of us, and I saw that the man holding me down was Detective Salvatore.

Chapter 45

It took a lot of explaining, but eventually we got it all straight. It turned out that Vincent had had no real concept of how to get a hit man. And hit men aren't all that easy to find, a fact I was glad to hear. What he had done was hire a somewhat shady private detective, but not so shady that he'd get involved in murder. When Vincent had broached the subject, the detective hadn't been sure if he was that stupid or just part of a particularly inept setup. Either way, he figured his best bet was to call the Boston police.

Word got back to Salvatore that Vincent wanted somebody dead, and he provided a team of cops posing as hit men to work with the private detective long enough to find out what the plan was. Unfortunately, Vincent was being cagy and wouldn't tell them in a way they could use as evidence. He wanted to bring the target to them, and so they arranged a setup.

"So Michelle was never in any danger?" I said to Salvatore. He, Thaddeous, Michelle, Neal, and I were drinking coffee at the Lexington police station.

"She was when she was alone with Vincent," he said, "but once our men showed up, she was safe."

"I'm just glad it was Vincent I kicked, instead of a cop," Michelle said with a grin.

All the men in the room nodded solemnly. Actually, Vincent had suffered no permanent damage, but he was going to be in pain for a few days.

"I feel so silly," I said. "Sticking my nose in where it wasn't needed."

"Don't be too hard on yourself," Salvatore said. "You did figure out the motive when we couldn't. And if you hadn't scared Vincent like you did, we might not have been able to bring him in. I suspected that both Philip Dennis and Murray Wexelbaum had been murdered, but didn't have anything concrete to go on. I didn't even have official sanction to check on Wexelbaum's death, because he died in Cambridge. It was only when Vincent tried to get professional help that we were able to get him."

"Just like him to hire somebody," Thaddeous said. "The man can't stand to get his hands dirty. He just let Philip die, and I'm surprised that he had the guts to push Murray down the stairs."

"He almost didn't," Neal said. "He told me he left chunks of snow on the steps and hoped that would work. Murray did slip, but was about to catch himself when Vincent pushed him the rest of the way."

"Anyway," Salvatore said, "I should have guessed that you'd get involved in all of this. Chief Norton warned me that you would, but I didn't take her seriously."

"You talked to Junior?" I said. "You *did* think I killed Philip."

"Not really, but when you called me and started asking questions, I started to wonder. And then I found out that you had started working at SSI just before Wexelbaum was killed, so I figured it was worth a phone call to check you out. Chief Norton was pretty sure you wouldn't kill anybody, but said that you have a way of getting yourself into trouble."

Thaddeous snickered.

"Laugh all you want," I said. "At least I didn't beat up a cop." The "hit man" Thaddeous had attacked had a cracked rib and lots of bruises. Fortunately, he didn't hold it against Thaddeous.

"He didn't use a sword on one, either," Salvatore said, rubbing his head. "Did you know that that blade is illegal in Massachusetts?"

I hadn't known, actually. "Are you going to impound it?"

Salvatore considered it. "I suppose that if you assured me that you won't hit any other police officers with it, I could change my report to read that you hit me with a board instead of a sword."

"I sure would appreciate that." Richard would have understood losing his prize in such a good cause, but he wouldn't have been happy about it.

"No problem. I wasn't looking forward to hearing the jokes when word got around the department that I was brought down by a sword."

It was long after midnight before we got back to my apartment, and instead of coming in with me, Thaddeous said he was going to escort Michelle home.

"Will you be coming back tonight?" I asked.

He turned bright red, but didn't say anything.

I grinned. "Then I'll see y'all tomorrow." As I let myself into my apartment, I couldn't help wondering how their relationship was going to stand the test of distance, but they were going to have to work that part out for themselves.

I was torn between wanting to call Richard immediately, and wanting to fall into bed just as immediately. Bed won, partly because I didn't want to wake him up and partly because I was bone tired.

I called him the first thing Saturday morning, this time not waiting for any Shakespeare reviews before launching into the story. I ended it with, "And I've already put your sword back."

"Laura, you didn't really think I'd be worried about a sword, did you?"

"No," I admitted, "but I didn't want to lose it if I could avoid it."

"You really hit a cop with it?"

"I didn't know he was a cop."

"Wait until Junior hears."

"If you think I'm going to tell Junior, you've got another think coming."

"You won't have to. Thaddeous will tell his mother, and she'll tell Aunt Daphine, and Aunt Daphine will tell Vasti—"

"And Vasti will tell everybody in the known universe. Maybe I should call Junior myself and get it over with."

"Now that I know the sword is safe, what about you? Are you okay?"

"A couple of scratches, and I bruised my knee, but otherwise, I'm fine."

"I don't mean scratches and bruises. I mean *you*. Are you okay?"

I took a minute to think about it and finally said, "I think I am. I didn't really owe Philip anything, but even if I had, all debts would be paid now. And I've been worried about betraying friends, but I don't feel at all guilty about getting Vincent put away."

"What now?"

"I guess I'll go to SSI on Monday and quit, then call the boss to let him know I'll be back at GBS on Tuesday."

"You're not going to SSI alone, are you?"

"I'll be fine. I need to do this."

"Call me afterward if you need to talk."

"Count on it."

Chapter 46

I spent most of the rest of the weekend by myself. Thaddeous and Michelle came by, but it didn't take a genius to figure out that they wanted to be alone. So I made a few excuses to let them off the hook. Thaddeous picked up some clean clothes and they were gone again.

Jessie called a couple of times, but I let the phone machine answer and didn't return her calls. I wasn't ready to talk to her or anybody else at SSI quite yet. I did call Vasti to tell her that Arthur wasn't going to be in a book, and then Junior to tell her about my swordplay. As expected, Vasti was disappointed and Junior was mighty amused.

Under the circumstances, I took my time getting to SSI Monday morning. I wanted to be sure everybody had heard all there was to hear before I got there. Even though it was nearly noon, Roberta wasn't at the front desk. I called out, "Hello?" and a few seconds later, Jessie walked in.

"I wasn't expecting you to come in today," she said.

" 'Twere well it were done quickly,' " I said, which I thought was an appropriate quote, even if I couldn't remember which play it had come from. "I take it that you've spoken to the police."

"And Neal," she said. "I tried to talk to Vincent, but all

he would say was that his brother the lawyer advised against his saying anything. I did talk to his wife."

"Muriel must be pretty upset." I hadn't even thought about her. How would it feel to find out that the father of your unborn child was a murderer?

"I guess so," Jessie said. "She seemed more concerned with finding out about the money from SSI, to tell the truth. Poor Vincent."

"I'm finding it hard to feel sorry for Vincent right now," I said.

She looked sheepish. "I can understand that." She paused for a minute. "I left messages for you."

"I'm sorry. I just wasn't up to talking."

She nodded.

"Where is everybody?"

"Well, Roberta quit. She said this wasn't a safe place to work. I suppose she's got a point. The rest of us have been trying to decide what to do next."

"Any conclusions?"

"Some ideas. Do you want to come join us?"

"I don't think so, Jessie. I was planning to clean out my desk and get out of here."

"I thought that's what you'd say. We'll be in the conference room if you need us."

"Thanks. Jessie, I'm really sorry about the way things turned out."

"I know you are," was all she said.

There wasn't a whole lot in my desk to clean out, which seemed odd. Though I had only been at SSI for a little over a week, it seemed longer. I was finishing up a note detailing the work I had done on StatSys when Inez came over.

"So you're leaving?"

I started to make excuses, but instead I nodded and said, "I talked to my old boss, and he wants me back." That was fudging a bit, but I didn't really want to admit that I had only come to SSI to find out about Philip's murder. Folks probably guessed as much.

"That may be for the best. SSI is on its way out anyway."

"I'm sorry, Inez. I know how much this company means to you."

She held up one hand to stop me. "Don't worry. We've got a plan. Jessie, Dee, and I are going to form a new company. A real one this time, not just a bunch of nerds playing business. We're going to buy StatSys from SSI, change the name, and start over. Having no reputation will be better than the one we've got after all this."

"What about Dom?"

"He and Dee decided it was about time they split up." Before I could say anything, she added, "Professionally, that is. They need some space. He'll get another job in no time. Besides, with all women running the show, we just might be able to swing a minority loan."

"Neal?"

"Well, first we've got to see what his legal position is. We found him a lawyer, and she's optimistic. Neal didn't mean to kill Philip, and he did help you guys at the end. Plus he says he'll testify against Vincent. If he stays out of jail, we'll hire him. He's one of the best."

"What about Sheliah?"

"We'll hire her, too."

"Inez, this is none of my business, but if I were you, I'd consider bringing Sheliah in as a full partner. She'll do better work for you that way, and y'all need new blood. It's been a long time since MIT."

"You've got a point. I'll see if I can talk Jessie and Dee into it." Then she smiled. "Not that I've got any worries about that. We're going to be great together."

"It does sound good."

"Sure I can't talk you into staying on? Full partner if you want it."

"It's tempting, but no thanks. I'm not one for taking chances with a new company."

"You'll chase after hit men with a sword, but you're not one for taking chances?"

I had to laugh at that. "I never said it made sense. Besides, y'all don't need me around, reminding you of other things."

"Maybe you're right. And I have a hunch that it wouldn't be easy to talk you into doing things my way."

"Damned straight it wouldn't be."

"Jesus, Laura, what happened to that quiet little Southern belle Philip brought by all those years ago?"

"She's long gone. And good riddance, too."

Chapter 47

My boss at GBS was glad I was coming back to work, and fortunately never found out about my undercover work at SSI because very little about Vincent or Philip made it into the newspaper. That was one advantage of living in a big town. The story would have filled up an entire issue of the *Byerly Gazette*.

Thaddeous and Michelle spent the next few days together, though they did include me some of the time. We tried to hit all of the tourist places we had missed, and as many good restaurants as we could stand. I did bow out when Michelle took Thaddeous to meet her family, but I was glad to find out that he'd passed inspection. He'd liked them, too.

Still, it was time for Thaddeous to think about going back home, and the next Sunday, Michelle and I escorted him to the airport. When we got to the end of the concourse, I gave my cousin a big hug and said, "Thaddeous, I'm so glad you came. You come back any time you want, you hear?"

"You know I will. Tell Richard I'm sorry I missed him."

Then I stepped back a few feet to let Thaddeous and Michelle have a little privacy, but not so far that I couldn't hear what they were saying.

"Michelle," Thaddeous said, looking down into her eyes,

"I've never met anybody else like you. You're beautiful, and brave, and smart, and . . ." Words failed him, so he finished up with a long, and from what I could see, passionate kiss.

After they both caught their breath, he went on. "I'm never going to forget you, not ever."

"You're damned straight you're not going to forget me."

"Of course I won't. If there was any way we could be together . . . Well, there's not and there's no point in wishing there was."

"Are you saying that this is it? That you're going to get on that plane and I'm never going to see you again?"

Thaddeous looked confused. Clearly this wasn't going according to his script. "Well, I'd like to come back up to visit, but I imagine you'll be with somebody else before too long, a woman like you."

"What do you mean 'a woman like me'? You think I won't wait for you?"

"I wouldn't expect—"

"Don't you tell me what you expect! Do you think you're going to get away from me that easily?"

For a minute he looked hopeful, but then he said, "Michelle, there's no way I could live up here. I like Boston and all, but it's not Byerly, and I just couldn't do it. No matter how much I care for you."

"Care for me? Is that all there is to it?"

"Well, no, that's not all."

"Then what?"

It like to have killed him, but he got it out. "I love you."

"That's what I wanted to hear. As it so happens, I love you, too."

"You do?"

"Would I say it if I didn't? Would I have kicked that man where I did if I hadn't been trying to help you? Of course I love you."

"But—"

"You don't want to live in Boston, we don't live in Boston. They've got apartments in Byerly, don't they? They've got jobs. I'll get Laura to teach me how to say y'all and I'll move down there."

"But—"

"But what? Thaddeous Crawford, you are the best thing that ever happened to me, and I'll be damned if I let go of you now." This time she pulled him down for a kiss, and this kiss made the other one look like a peck on the cheek.

When they came up for air, Thaddeous said, "Michelle, I . . . I can't wait for you to meet Mama." Which, funny though it might have sounded, was the biggest compliment that Thaddeous could have given her.

Fortunately, Michelle could tell. I guess Italian families aren't that different from Southern families. She said, "You tell your mama I'll be there just as soon as I can get there. And another thing—you so much as look at another woman until I get down there, I'll make a lasagne out of you."

"Why in the Sam Hill would I ever look at another woman?" he said. He reached for her and they kissed one more time, this time for so long that I got right jealous.

"All right, then," Michelle said, more than a little out of breath. "You'd better get on that plane."

I don't know that he needed the plane—from the expression on his face, I think he could have floated home.

Michelle watched him go down the corridor, then turned to me. "Do you think his mother will like me?"

"No," I said.

"No?"

"I think she's going to love you."

She grinned. "That's good to hear. And another thing. Who is this Sam Hill person you two keep talking about?"

Please turn the page for
an exciting sneak peek
of Toni L.P. Kelner's
newest Laura Fleming mystery
TIGHT AS A TICK
now on sale wherever
hardcover mysteries are sold!

Chapter 1

I wasn't there when they found Carney Alexander's body, but my great-aunt Maggie was, and like many Southerners, she has a gift for storytelling. Between her description and my getting a chance to see the place later, I had no problem imagining it.

The Tight as a Tick Flea Market was busy that Sunday, Aunt Maggie said. There were lots of people coming by her booth to look at Carnival glass plates, Fenton vases, and Occupied Japan figurines. But it wasn't too busy for Aunt Maggie to notice that Carney hadn't shown up at the booth where he sold collector knives. That wasn't like Carney. He usually got there at the crack of dawn, even earlier than Aunt Maggie.

Around ten-thirty, Bender Cawthorne came by to collect the day's rent, which he was supposed to do first thing in the morning. But Aunt Maggie said that Bender usually drank so much on Saturday night that ten-thirty was first thing in the morning for him. Aunt Maggie asked him where Rusty was. The half-chow, half-German shepherd was the only creature on earth who could stand to live with Bender. Bender explained that Rusty was at Dr. Josie's.

The people living near the flea market lot had been complaining that every puppy born for the past few years looked just like Rusty. Bender's brother Evan, who actually owned the lot, didn't like it when the neighbors complained, and he'd insisted that Bender get Rusty fixed. Bender had done what he was told, but he didn't see what the fuss was about. Rusty was an awful good dog, and those lady dogs could have done a lot worse.

Aunt Maggie told Bender he was probably right. Rusty was the smartest dog she'd ever seen, except for his taste in human companions, but she didn't tell Bender that. Anyway, after she paid her rent, Bender saw that Carney wasn't there.

He asked Aunt Maggie if she knew where he was, but when she told him that she didn't, he went to collect rent from the rest of the inside dealers. Aunt Maggie said he asked everybody near enough for her to hear if they'd talked to Carney, but neither China Upton, who sold country crafts, nor Obed the Donut Man had heard a word. Tattoo Bob said he'd been concentrating so hard on the dragon he was inking across a man's shoulder that he hadn't even noticed that Carney was missing.

In Aunt Maggie's opinion, if Bender had had a lick of sense, he'd have known something was wrong. Carney had been a dealer at the flea market for four years, almost as long as Aunt Maggie, and in all that time, he'd never missed a weekend. But then again, if Bender had a lick of sense, he'd have been doing something with his life other than running a flea market on his brother's property, and he'd be living someplace other than a beat-up house trailer in the back of the lot.

Bender didn't even think to check around Carney's booth to see if anything looked out of place, or to go get Carney's phone number and call him. He just scratched his head and went to collect rent in the other buildings.

Aunt Maggie admitted that maybe she should have done something herself, but she didn't even have a chance to take a bathroom break until nearly four o'clock. After that, there was a steady stream of business until Bender locked up at five. She didn't think about Carney again until the end of the day.

Once the customers were out of the building, Aunt Maggie straightened up her tables and set out fresh stock to fill the gaps from where things had sold during the day. China was doing the same thing while Bob cleaned his needles and Obed washed his pans and utensils. China finished before anybody else, and when she walked by on her way out, Aunt Maggie asked her if she knew anything about Carney.

She said she didn't, and when Bob and Obed joined them a minute or two later, they didn't either. It was Aunt Maggie who suggested that they look around his booth to see if everything looked all right, and though the others agreed, they acted like they felt funny about it. So they let Aunt Maggie go back behind Carney's table.

The sheet Carney used to cover up his display cases was still in place, and Aunt Maggie shook her head over its condition. Lots of dealers use old sheets to keep the dust off, but Carney's sheet went beyond being old. It was nothing more than a rag, and filthy dirty to boot. It was so nasty that Aunt Maggie didn't see the blood right away. There were dark brown stains along the edge touching the floor.

Aunt Maggie said that there was a smell, too, which she hadn't noticed before. Of course, with donuts and pork skins frying all day, she wouldn't have. Now that she did, she thought she knew what she was smelling. Anybody else would have left that sheet where it was, and called Bender or the police, but not Aunt Maggie. She just took a deep breath, grabbed hold of the sheet, and whipped it off. There was Carney, folded up under the table like a ventriloquist's dummy in a suitcase. Aunt Maggie didn't see the knife buried in his back, but she did see the blood. There was way too much of it for Carney to be alive.